LP

D0407272

THE SIGHT
OF
THE STARS

BOOKS BY BELVA PLAIN

HER FATHER'S HOUSE
LOOKING BACK
AFTER THE FIRE
FORTUNE'S HAND
LEGACY OF SILENCE
HOMECOMING
SECRECY
PROMISES
THE CAROUSEL
DAYBREAK
WHISPERS
TREASURES
HARVEST
BLESSINGS
TAPESTRY
THE GOLDEN CUP
CRESCENT CITY
EDEN BURNING
RANDOM WINDS
EVERGREEN

BELVA PLAIN

THE SIGHT OF THE STARS

DOUBLEDAY LARGE PRINT HOME LIBRARY EDITION

Delacorte Press

This Large Print Edition, prepared especially for Doubleday Large Print Home Library, contains the complete, unabridged text of the original Publisher's Edition.

THE SIGHT OF THE STARS
A Delacorte Book

Published by Bantam Dell
A Division of Random House, Inc.
New York, New York

Delacorte Press is a registered trademark of Random House, Inc., and the colophon is a trademark of Random House, Inc.

ISBN: 0-7394-4005-5

Manufactured in the United States of America

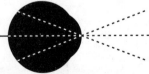

This Large Print Book carries the
Seal of Approval of N.A.V.H.

It is when we try to grapple with other men's intimate needs that we perceive how incomprehensible are the beings that share with us the sight of the stars and the warmth of the sun.

—Joseph Conrad

Prologue

He waited and watched while the elegant little car moved away, until the girl with the sea-green eyes was out of sight.

"If you're getting any ideas about her, you'd better forget them," they told him. "She goes to boarding school and she goes to Europe. They keep her safe as the gold in Fort Knox."

He understood. For he was nobody, and he had nothing.

Chapter 1

1900

He would always remember the weather that day. By nightfall, the rain that had started that morning was still whirling across the little town in New Jersey that lay on the brink of the Atlantic Ocean. You could imagine yourself, Adam thought, on a pirate ship with Long John Silver, sailing through high seas on the way to Treasure Island. Meanwhile, you were safe in the kitchen at the supper table next to the coal stove.

"Have some more stew, Adam. You must be tired after helping Pa in the store all afternoon."

That was Rachel, whom Pa had married after Adam's mother died. She was good to him, and he was fond of her, but he did wish that she wouldn't always be urging him to eat.

Pa laughed. "Such a typical Jewish

mother, stuffing the children with food. He's not tired. He's a strong man. In three days he'll be thirteen, a man of the new century. Nineteen hundred, Adam! How do you feel about that?"

Right now the only thing he felt was relief that the afternoon was over. He was finished with baskets and boxes and bags, loaded with just about everything a human being might ever want to put in his stomach: coffee, sugar, whiskey, and tea, carrots, potatoes, cookies and toffee candy; loaded too with the things men and women wear, the breeches, corsets, fichus, neckties, aprons, and galoshes. One thing was sure, though; one thing he knew. He was not going to follow his father and work in the store when he grew up. Maybe one of the other boys would be willing, but not he.

They were odd little brothers—half brothers—different from him, and so different from each other that Adam had to wonder what makes people who they are. What makes Jonathan, at four, so bright and happy that Adam really doesn't mind having to watch over him occasionally? What made Leo, at nine, such a nuisance, with his fresh mouth and temper tantrums that sometimes make you wish a stranger would come along and adopt him?

Still, you have to feel sorry for him, poor kid. With a face shaped like an egg, a long curve at the top where the forehead seems to bulge, and almost no chin at the bottom. He's too short and too fat. He always stands alone in the schoolyard. His only friend is Bobby Nishikawa, whose family owns the Japanese restaurant called Fugi on Main Street. Leo's too shy, too smart, and too clumsy. I've tried and tried to show him how to play ball, Adam thought, but I've given up. He only gets angry at me.

All of a sudden, Leo interrupted his thoughts. "Adam's a bastard! Did you all know Adam's a bastard?"

Rachel's and Pa's coffee cups clattered onto their saucers. "What?" Rachel exclaimed. "What in heaven's name are you saying, Leo?"

"Nasty," Pa scolded. "Decent people don't talk like that."

"Yes, they do. I heard them." Leo, now the center of attention, hurried along with his story. "They said it at the basketball game in the gym. Those two men behind me said it. When Adam put the ball in the basket and won the game, one said, 'It's too bad he's a bastard, a smart, good-looking boy like that.' I heard him, Pa."

"Ridiculous! He ought to be ashamed of himself, whoever he is."

Was I seven in second grade, or maybe only six in first grade, when a big fifth-grader told one of her friends that Adam Arnring was a bastard? The way the word was spoken and the laughing expression on her face told him that it was a shameful thing she was calling him—shameful like throwing up in the schoolyard, as he had done one day.

"I'm not!" he had protested.

"Yes, you are. Our neighbor told my mother. I heard her."

"Absolutely not," Pa had said. "That's nonsense. Don't even think about it."

So he had not thought about it. How was it, though, that he so clearly remembered it now?

"You're going to be punished," Rachel said sternly, "if you ever use that word again, Leo."

"I don't care."

"You'll listen to me, or you'll care very much. Now be a good boy and give these scraps to Arthur for his dinner."

Hearing his name, the old dog, a sturdy mixture of collie mother and unknown father, raised his head as if to ask a question with his mild brown eyes.

"I'll do it," Adam said promptly.

For no reason that he could explain, there came a rush of tenderness for this dependent creature who trusted them to care for him and never to hurt him. And setting the bowl of food before Arthur, Adam stroked his head.

As if nothing at all had happened at the supper table a moment before, Pa reminded him that it was Saturday. "I've put the washtub in the pantry, and I'm sure that kettle on the stove is already hot enough so you can have your bath, Adam."

"Not tonight, Pa. I'm more tired than I thought I was. I'm going up to bed."

Neither Rachel nor Pa said anything. Did they not wonder why he was going upstairs so early? Oh, they know there is something terribly wrong!

In the attic, where the peaked roof was so slanted that one could only stand upright in the center of the room, Adam took off his shirt and pants, lit the oil lamp, lay down with his book, and did not read. Rain drummed on the single window. The room was chilly, and covered as he was with his flannel underwear and the heavy quilt, he felt not merely cold, but naked, as if exposed to the world.

He had never thought much about his mother. She was dead, that was all. People died. She died in a diphtheria epidemic when he was three weeks old. Once in a while, a very long while, he looked at photographs of people he had never known and never would know: Pa's parents standing in front of a small wooden house in a country on the other side of the ocean; Pa and a young woman standing in front of a stone wall, she very small and slender beneath an enormous feathered hat.

Illegitimate. Bastard. Can those two people have done what he is now thinking about? When a person has reached thirteen, he is a man and he has learned a few things. A lot of his friends have older brothers who hire a buckboard on Saturday night to take them five miles out on the road to Gracie's house, Gracie being a fat old lady who lives with ten or twelve young ladies. And there the brothers "do things." You have to have some money when you go there. He understands.

But what husbands do with their wives is very different. They have babies because they are married. If they have babies without being married, it is like stealing. To have a bastard is a shameful thing, like walking out of Pa's store with a package hidden under your coat, without paying for it. You could never imagine Pa stealing anything. Pa wouldn't lie to him. Those girls in school and those men in the gym—they might lie, but Pa never would.

Here he was now coming up the stairs, his heavy tread making the old steps creak. When he walked in, he sat down at the foot of the bed, as if this was something he did every night instead of for the first time.

"Reading again, my Adam? What book is it now?"

"*The Last of the Mohicans*. It's about Indians."

"There still were a few Indians in Georgia when I first came to America. Most of them had long ago been chased out, poor people. Have I ever told you about them?"

Adam could have said that he knew the whole story almost by heart. He knew about the trip north because the South was so poor after the Civil War; he knew the tale of Whitey the horse and the wagon Pa had bought as soon as he had saved a few dollars; he knew about the arrival here in town and the opening of Simon Arnring's first little store. But he only nodded his head now, and waited.

"Nineteen hundred. Everything's going to be different. I don't know how, but it will be. That's what they say. After a while, I suppose I'll have to put in a telephone, won't I? They say that the price will be coming down pretty soon. If it doesn't, we'll just do without. Pennies make dollars. The world's been getting along pretty well all these years without this new stuff, autos and telephones and electric lights and whatnot. Yes, pennies make dollars."

Pa was frugal, but never stingy. Simon Arnring was known to be charitable beyond his means, and lenient with his poorest customers. Adam was aware of all that; he was also aware that Pa had not climbed upstairs to talk about either the Civil War in Georgia or the new century, so he nodded and waited again.

Pa had a way of talking in jerks. People

said he was a man of few words, which was true, except for the rare mood when words would suddenly start to roll from his tongue . . . and then, just as suddenly, stop.

"I think I hear Arthur struggling on the stairs. He can hardly pull himself up. At his age—"

Pa stared at the floor. There came a silence, vaguely sad and thick as a substance you might feel with your fingers. The silence lasted long enough for Arthur to come in, stretch out, and settle into his usual doze. Pa coughed and cleared his throat, began to speak, then stopped. Eventually he put on a bright expression and began afresh.

"I've never told you, never told you or anybody, that you wouldn't have been born if not for Arthur, have I?"

Adam thought: If he's come up here to amuse me with a dog story, I don't want to hear it. He should know better.

"It's a fairly long story. I can tell you if you want to hear it."

And hearing the scorn in his own voice, Adam repeated, "If it weren't for the dog, I wouldn't have been born? I don't understand. So I think I ought to hear it."

"Well, then. On the very last day before I

opened my store here, I had to deliver something at a farm. It was spring, and terribly hot for the season. The horse was tired, so I walked him slowly. That's how I came to see this terrible thing alongside the road, this dog that had just given birth. The pups, five or six of them, each hardly bigger than a mouse, were lying half dead beside the poor mother. She was too weak to move, panting there in the broiling sun, with her tongue hanging out. Some rotter who didn't deserve to live had dropped her off in the woods. God knows how long she had been there, all night maybe. So I picked her up and put her, with the pups, in the wagon, getting myself filthy, but I couldn't leave the poor creature like that. At the next farm I stopped and asked for water to cool them. And a young girl came out to help me. Eileen, she was. Eileen Murphy."

All this Adam already knew. Eileen was his mother. He knew about his birth in the room above the store, about the diphtheria epidemic. A sad story, too sad to tell again.

"I brought the pups and the mother back home with me and named her Queen. All the pups except Arthur died the next day. Queen, I think, must have been pretty old, because she only lived another year. At least she spent it in a good home."

Pa smiled, not out toward Adam, but inwardly, to himself. A secret smile, the kind people have when they are remembering something that nobody else knows.

"Eileen came to the store with a baby bottle of milk in case Queen might not have enough for Arthur. She's the one who gave him his name. Chester Alan Arthur was one of our presidents. She was patriotic." He stopped. "I have to collect my thoughts. It seems so long ago now. I had never met anyone like her. So delicate, so gentle, she was. She loved flowers, loved to arrange them. On the Fourth of July she put red, white, and blue bouquets in my windows. A gentle soul, too trusting . . . I don't know. Her father was a laborer on that farm where I found her. Worked hard, I guess, but not hard enough to keep him away from the saloons. He was tough, no good at all. I used to wonder how he ever had a daughter like her. I never found out, never knew much about her people, only that she was the youngest, the last one at home."

And again there came that secret smile, so sad and secret that Adam, for all his own confusion of anger, curiosity, and distress, still felt a kind of pity.

"We became friends. Sometimes when the store wasn't busy, we'd have a cup of coffee together. She had never been anywhere or read anything about other places. So I told her about where I came from in Europe, and about the tiny village where we all spoke German. She began to come more often. She used to tell her father that she would meet some friends at the soda fountain in the drugstore, while he was at the saloon, but instead she would come to my store. It was open most evenings and was probably a livelier place than the lone farm. What else besides the dog could the attraction be? I was a man almost thirty, and she was a girl of eighteen."

Something Adam feared to hear and yet needed to hear was coming. He waited.

"She seemed like such a child, not much older than you are now. Well, five years. But then, you have always been a whole lot older than your years."

Now it was coming, the thing Pa really wanted to tell him. At the same time, he seemed uncertain about whether he ought to tell it.

"One evening when she was there, her father came raging into the store. His rage was out of control. He called his daughter a dirty name. He threatened me with his fist. I tried to protect Eileen and managed fairly well, although he did land one blow on her cheek before I was able to shove him out onto the street and into his buggy.

"My heart ached for her. She was a proper young lady, and he had shamed her before all of the people in the store. Well, I did what anyone would do to comfort her. I washed her face and put some salve on the bruise. I gave her my bed upstairs and put a cot in the hall for myself. Her father came again the next day as I had suspected he would, but she stayed upstairs out of sight. I had a few friends in the police force, and I guess they had plenty to say to him, because after a few days he stopped coming. I heard that the farm where he worked had been sold, and he was no longer needed. So the next thing I heard was that he had left town and perhaps left the state, God knows where to . . ."

He's sorry he's told me this much, thought Adam. As in a puzzle, the pieces were beginning to join together in his head.

"We fell in love, Adam. It will happen to you, too, someday. Maybe when you least expect it, or even want it. It's nature, a beautiful thing."

"But you never got married, did you? And that's why I'm a bastard."

"Don't use that word! Whatever we did or didn't do has nothing to do with you. Remember that. You are as good as any human being in the whole, wide world, and better than most."

Still, that was no answer.

"You weren't married, and you lied to me, didn't you?"

"I did, and I'm sorry. It was wrong, but I wanted to protect you."

"Then why didn't you marry her? You married Rachel in the synagogue."

"It wasn't possible. I asked, but they wouldn't have Eileen."

"What about the church? The one on Main Street, or the one on Seaside Avenue."

"Neither. *They* didn't want *me*. Besides, her father had gone to all of them and told them terrible things about me." Pa looked down at the floor. "Well, some of it was true. She was his daughter, and I had done to her what I should not have done. In my heart, I have never stopped apologizing."

"Weren't there any other places where you could have gone?"

"To a justice of the peace somewhere, I guess. But we were confused. It's no excuse. . . . It just seemed as if we had been turned down everywhere, as if nobody wanted us. We weren't thinking. . . . I don't know."

Whenever his father said "I don't know," it meant that he had no more to say, or that he did not want to say any more. Still, there was one thing that Adam needed to ask.

"Are you ever sorry that I was born? You can tell me the truth, Pa. As you said, I'm thirteen. I'm a man."

"Sorry? My God, Adam, you're my right hand. You're my heart. If I could talk better English, I would say—" Pa's voice shook in his throat—"I would say everything I want for you. The whole world! Oh, people can be so stupid, so cruel. May nobody ever hurt you, Adam, as I did. But I have to tell you the truth now, before I die."

Pa went downstairs, silence swept across the space, and even the wind died down. Adam put out the lamp and lay still. Mixed feelings, he thought. The teacher had used the expression yesterday while reading aloud, and it was a good one: You could be terribly angry and terribly sad at the same time. He wondered how many boys had a story like this to think about. Of course he couldn't be the only one in the world, but he was sure he was the only one in his school, and probably the only one in this town. If there had been others, he would have heard about them just as Leo had heard about him.

So now he knew that he was *different*. His father had said that the world could be stupid and cruel, but so far he hadn't felt any cruelty. No doubt the time would come. It came back to him that Rachel had told him a few days before about her cousin who had not been allowed to go walking with a young man from a "bad family." What, then, he wondered, was Adam Arnring's family? Except for those people asleep downstairs, he had none. Who was he, then?

Oh, come on, Adam, he scolded himself.

You're at the head of the class. You're the best pitcher in the whole school.

And didn't Pa just call you his right hand?

On the floor between the bed and the window, Arthur, dreaming about a squirrel that had outrun him, whimpers in his sleep. Light from the white sky falls on his skinny old flanks. Fourteen, he is, and hasn't got much longer. He's ending, while I'm beginning. But we started out the same way, Arthur. Both of us were unwanted.

Chapter 2

The idea of leaving home is a long time coming. It might even have begun, Adam was to think much later, with some readings in a high school history class, when the word "west" first lured him with its "wide skies" and "high plains," along with its romantic Indian names: Nebraska, Dakota, and Idaho. Or it might have come on that night in the attic when he was thirteen.

Once it came, it stayed.

After his graduation from high school, Adam began to work full time in the store. Then it was that he began his evening walks alone out toward the ocean, where he would sit down on a rock or in the sand and gaze ahead to where the clouds and waves came together. It was the sense of space that he craved; his attic room, the store, and the town itself were all too small.

It was probably this same need that

brought him to the job as caddy in one of the new golf clubs that had been built on the farmlands not far from town. Every Sunday morning during the summer, a certain Mr. Herman Shipper would call for him, and they would ride together in Mr. Shipper's carriage and pair to the club.

On the drive back after a good game, for Mr. Shipper was a skillful player, the conversation was not the kind he heard at home. Mr. Shipper read a great deal, he had traveled abroad, and most of all, he seemed to enjoy conversing with Adam.

"You're a bright young man," he said. "I predict you'll go far in the world. I noticed a comment you made this morning about a house we were passing. You admired the columns. Like the Parthenon, you said. Not many young men would have noticed that."

"I've liked looking at houses ever since Mrs. May—she's a history teacher—showed me her books on architecture."

"Have you thought about studying architecture?"

"Not really."

One day Adam was invited to the Shipper house on Seaside Drive for lunch. High up it stood, with a magnificent view of the

Atlantic. The entrance hall was high and white. He had a hasty impression of chandeliers, a winding stairway, a vast room with sofas, a piano, and a patterned rug that felt like sponge underfoot before they passed through tall doors and came out onto a terrace.

Luncheon was already on a table under a striped umbrella. The noon sun glittered alike on the ocean and the collection of silver implements that lay alongside the food. Adam blinked, and sought something to say.

"Look there through the trees, Adam. You can just get a glimpse of that house. Can you name the style?"

Through the leafage one could see a pale tan wall crossed with beams of dark brown wood.

"It looks Elizabethan. Half-timbered oak."

"Right. I was pretty sure you'd know. Adam, you're meant to be an architect."

"Not possible. You have to go to college for that. And since that's out of the question—" Adam spoke simply, and stopped.

"Can't you manage with some loans?"

"No. Any loans we might be lucky enough to get must go to my brother."

"Why so?"

"Well, because Jonathan is very special. He's an unusual boy. Only eleven, nearly twelve, and he's doing high school science and math. They skipped him two years in those subjects. He wants to be a doctor, and there's not enough money to educate both of us."

"It's highly unusual for someone to sacrifice himself on behalf of his brother," said Mr. Shipper, shaking his head. "In fact, I'd call it heroic."

"I don't feel like a hero. It just seems to be common sense."

"And what about the other brother?"

"Just average, like me."

"Adam, you are not average. I know you pretty well by now. You have talent, and you also have a good head for business. And if you'll excuse me, you don't belong behind the counter of a little neighborhood store. You have a future, young man. You need to be thinking seriously."

"Well, I have been thinking. I thought that maybe if I could get some sort of job in a factory, I could earn more than my help at home in the store is worth—"

Mr. Shipper put up his hand and interrupted. "There's nothing worthwhile in this town. It's 1907, and we're in a bad state in this country. Three of the largest banks in New York have failed. You need to get out of this town. There's nothing here now, and there isn't going to be for a long time. Get out. Get out."

Good advice, but no job, Adam was thinking as he took his leave. Well, of course not. What would an investment banker do with me?

He looked back at the row of houses that fringed the shore. Surrounded as they were by hedges, lawns, and flowering shrubs, they were all, even the ugly ones, delightful. They were the homes of rich men. Were they the homes of the most intelligent, the most industrious, or merely the most lucky?

Whitecaps rolled in parallel lines and broke into froth upon the shore. Far out, he recognized the New York–bound steamer; now and then—oh, very now and then—he had ridden it to that city with just enough coins in his pocket to take him there and back: fifty cents one way, sixty for the round-trip, and a couple of dimes to spend while in the city. One day when I am old, he supposed, I will reminisce about those trips the way old people do. Some things you never forget. . . .

Coming up ahead lay the curve in the sandy bluff where he had lain one day with Rosie Beck, the prettiest girl in the senior class; she had a doll's face, and her waists were so tight that her breasts were outlined as if she were naked. Her body was hard in some places and soft in others; lying close, he used to imagine her with all her clothes off.

"I can't go with you to the prom," she had said that day.

"You can't? But you promised me!"

"I have to go with Jake instead. I have to."

"But that's crazy! Why do you?"

"He asked me, and my father says I have to accept."

"Your father says! I want to know why."

"Oh, Adam, I'm sorry, it's nasty, but they're saying I'm getting older and it's time to be with people I could someday marry. Families who—Jake's mother is—oh, Adam, I like you so much and I'm sorry."

To hell with her. He wouldn't want to marry her anyway.

After a while he turned and made his way inland to the heart of town. A Sunday quiet lay upon the streets that on the other six days were crowded with carriages and delivery wagons. Here was the "Shipper" side of the town. Storefronts were freshly painted. Window boxes were filled with flowers. Striped awnings protected the displays. The bank's brass door frames glistened like gold, as did the trim on the sign above the theater advertising vaudeville and movies.

At this last, Adam had to laugh. Pa was still warning him—at nineteen, almost twenty—about the lewd women in vaudeville who rouged their faces and kicked up their legs in pantalettes! Poor Pa had apparently never stopped to think that his son was a fairly steady visitor not so much to the theater as to Gracie's place, where he had seen and had enjoyed every kind of sex that had been written about for the last few thousand years.

Now, having passed the department

store's fine, carved stone entrance, he turned a corner and beheld a different scene. Here were the trolley car barn, the hospital, the blacksmith shop, and the livery stable. Then came the long streets filled on both sides with dull wooden houses, all with the same front porch behind a scrap of brown grass, and finally Arnrings' meager, neglected little house.

No sea breezes cooled the kitchen. It was hot. At the head of the table sat Pa, his eyes heavy after a Sunday afternoon's nap. He isn't old enough, Adam thought, to look so tired. He's in a rut and can't get out of it.

"I'm late. I'm sorry," he said, for they were already finishing the roast chicken that was standard on Sundays. "Mr. Shipper invited me to lunch, and after that I took the long way home."

"I suppose," Leo said, "you'll be moving over there, next thing."

"You're wrong. I'm not foolish enough to think I can ever live the way those people do."

"Oh, sure. That's all you think about."

He should save that tough sneer for

school, and maybe he wouldn't be the butt of other kids' sneers. But he can't help it, can he? Nature's played a mean joke on him. He's a born victim—born victim like the perfectly nice girl at the dance, the wall-flower whom nobody wants. It's wrong, it's mean, but I don't know when it's ever been any different. My God, can it be that his hair is already receding? Sixteen years old and going bald? No, it's the bulbous forehead that makes it look that way.

Calmly, Adam replied, "What did you do today? Out with Bobby?"

"I wasn't *out* with him. We were *in.* He has a Japanese newspaper, and I'm able to start reading it a little. Mrs. Nishikawa was aston-ished, she said."

"Well, it is astonishing," Rachel said.

"I have a gift for languages. I'm teaching Bobby to speak German."

"How much German do you think you know?" asked Pa, who could be terribly tactless.

"Plenty. I hear you and Ma, don't I?"

"That doesn't mean you can speak Ger-man. You know a few phrases, that's all. Don't go boasting about it in school. There are some new German immigrants in the neighborhood, and you'll make yourself look foolish." Pa, meaning well, continued to lecture. "People don't like boasters, Leo."

"I don't boast. I don't have to. I'm smarter than ninety-five percent of the people in that high school. They're a bunch of illiterates, and they know they are."

Nobody except Jon and me, Adam thought, would guess how smart Leo really is. But he's sixteen years old, and he talks so childishly. And why are his grades so poor? Why doesn't he take the trouble to do better?

"They all know it," Leo repeated, waiting for someone to argue with him.

Instead Rachel, ever the peacemaker, changed the subject. "Jonathan, you haven't told anybody you're marching in the Fourth of July parade. Of course, the whole class is marching, but I didn't know you were to carry the flag. Mrs. Ames told me yesterday."

"That's no big honor, Mom," Jonathan objected. "They draw lots for it. Anybody can get it."

That was not true, although Rachel wouldn't know it. It was only Jonathan being modest, and considerate of Leo's feelings.

A remarkable child. Jonathan has a rare mind and a rare spirit.

The guidance counselor had summoned Simon and Rachel, but they had lacked the confidence to go, and had sent Adam instead.

Every effort must be made to send him to college. It would be a tragic waste otherwise.

Pa and Rachel don't really understand the need to send Jonathan to college, Adam thought. They look at it as a luxury. But if Mr. Shipper is right about my head for business, then I will take care of Jonathan. And then perhaps take care of myself, too. I'll never be an architect, but I'll be something else.

On the porch in the evening, the rocking chairs creaked. Simon and Adam were watching Leo and Jon walk down the street. The eleven-year-old was taller than the sixteen-year-old, but no comment was made about that except for the father's long sigh. Then, after a while, he spoke.

"I try to be patient, but Leo's just—you can't depend on him. When he's in a good mood, he's all right, but you never know what mood he'll be in. Sometimes he's even unfriendly to customers. Fortunately, it's a neighborhood store and everybody around here knows him. They know him well."

"You can't expect him, at his age, to be tactful when he doesn't like working at the store."

"Why not? I had to do it when I was his age. You did it. You're still at it. He's old enough now to get used to the idea. He's lucky there's a business for him to go into. He'll never be unemployed."

That much was true. Bobby was already learning to help out in the Fugi restaurant. Mr. Shipper's son was also going into his father's business. Investment banking. Slightly different.

Dusk fell, and the rocking chairs still creaked; while a battle roared through Adam's head.

"Pa," he said suddenly, "I don't want to work in the store anymore."

Pa was surprisingly calm. "I've been thinking about that. Sort of expecting it for a pretty long time."

"I'm restless here. I've never been any- where. And I admit I want to see other places. But there's more to it. I have a feeling—maybe it's foolish, maybe it isn't—that I can do something big, that I can make money to help you all."

"A big heart you have. A good heart. But how do you see yourself doing it? Is it Mr. Shipper's house that's put this into your head?"

"Maybe a little. I don't know."

He's hurt, Adam thought, in spite of what he says.

"Well, I left home, too," Simon said, "so how can I object?" He swallowed hard. "Tell me one thing. Does this have anything to do with—with the business about your mother and me? Do you ever think about that anymore?"

"No, I put it aside years ago," Adam said gently.

He supposed it would always stay in the back of his mind, forgotten just as a significant book, once read and now neglected, rests on the topmost shelf.

Pa knocked the ashes from his pipe, his chair stopped creaking, and neither of them said any more. Then sorrow and tenderness moved Adam, and reaching across the little space between them, he laid his palm upon his father's hand.

Rachel made Adam's favorite pancakes for the last breakfast. Every time he looked up, he caught her worried, wistful gaze. Pa had put a "closed until noon" sign in the store's front window. The brothers, unsure about what to make of this break in the family circle or of how to behave, veered back and forth from curious glances to silly jokes to all kinds of questions that Adam was unable to answer.

Pa had provided him with a first-class, ten-dollar suit, railroad fare, and one hundred fifty dollars, which Adam had been loath to accept. Was he perhaps accepting these precious dollars only to waste them in the end? Would they not be better put toward future expenses?

Leo's eyes were wet when he left with Jonathan for school. Tears and a hug from Leo were rare, so rare that Adam could not at first remember when he had last seen them. Ah, yes, it must have been when Arthur died and was buried in the backyard. And he wondered now, as he watched him, what else might be hidden inside that prickly outside.

The day was vigorous and clear; the autumn air had a tang as he walked with Pa toward the ferry that would take him to that fabled westbound train, the Atchison, Topeka, and Santa Fe.

"For the first time I understand what my parents must have felt when I left them," Pa said.

"They knew they would never see you again. This is different."

When Pa's silence spoke, Adam countered it. "It may still sound ignorant to you in spite of all the times I've said it, but I'm determined that Jonathan's going to be a doctor, and you're not going to work so hard anymore, and Leo—well, I'm going to do something for him, too."

"You're a good boy, a good son, only—only don't do anything foolish."

They were late and Adam had to run for the boat. It was just as well. A prolonged good-bye embrace would have hurt too much.

"Adam, take care of yourself. I wish I could have done—" That was all he heard before the wind took the rest of the shouted words away.

Wish he could have done what? But he's done all he's able to do, so I will do the rest.

I will. I may be a fool, but right now, this minute, I feel I could conquer the world.

Under the morning sky, the old hometown gleamed white in its nest of reddening leaves. Three church steeples, the towering gas tank, the thick brown hulk that was the high school, the Ferris wheel in the amusement park, and the thread of fine houses that lined Seaside Drive all passed by. Then, in a burst of energy, the ferry gained speed and the town slid out of sight.

Chapter 3

On the third day, the train slowed and came to a screeching halt. A little bustle of talk broke out, remarks about a water stop and stretching one's legs on the platform. Sure enough, there stood the water tank and a place where people could look out into the level, blue-gray distance and see the narrow river that made a graceful curve around a town.

The conductor, standing beside Adam, remarked that it was a pretty sight, Chattahoochee. "There must be a powerful lot of money there. A lot of people get off this train at the capital and then take the Interurban back to Chattahoochee."

"Where does all the money come from? The place looks pretty small."

"Oh, ranches and farming."

"Since when do people get so rich from farming?"

"It's not what you're thinking of from back east. There's good black soil here, very rich, good for sheep, lumber, cotton—just about everything."

Farms. He knew nothing about them. Maybe he should have stayed with Pa. Maybe he could have helped him build up the store. But no, Pa was too set in his ways. It wouldn't have worked. Maybe he should try this town, do something, anything, to get some cash and then go on to California. Maybe the Indian name was a good omen. Chattahoochee!

After crossing the bridge over the river, which then looped and meandered away, the Interurban train went no farther. The heat was scorching, so the first thing Adam did was to stop at a bar for a cold beer.

The bartender had a predictable question. "Stranger in town?"

"Just arrived. It looks like a nice place," Adam replied, both because it was a friendly thing to say and because he meant it. Horses clip-clopped through the quiet street, and a small breeze rustled in the trees—cottonwoods, he thought, recalling a book he had once read.

Deciding to waste no time, he got to the point. "Any jobs in this town?"

"Offhand, I can't say. If you come around here at night, there's always a crowd, so you can ask and likely find something. Or take a walk around and maybe see a help-wanted sign."

So he walked and then walked on, turning corners and getting lost. He passed a dairy, cotton gins, blacksmiths, cattle dealers, a sawmill, a distillery, and a sign announcing that handmade furniture and coffins were available. But there were no jobs posted, and even if there were, he would not have the skills for them.

I don't know what I'm fit for, he thought, except to work in a store.

Then, abruptly, everything changed. On a central square not far from the Interurban station, so that he must have walked in a circle, was another world. Here were the neat buildings where doctors, lawyers, and assorted brokers had their offices; here was a high school like the one at home, a handsome Gothic church, the post office, the Chattahoochee National Bank, and a variety of expensive shops, among them a jeweler with an extravagant display of silverware in the window.

He stopped before an unexpectedly shabby store marked "Rothirsch's." "Red deer" it meant in German. Remembering that his two shirts had food stains, he decided to walk in and buy one or two more.

At the far end of a long, narrow room, a noisy argument between a large old woman and a large angry man was taking place. A very young girl was trying to intervene.

"Auntie! Auntie! Please don't!" she cried, pulling at the woman's sleeve. "You don't understand."

"No, she doesn't, Emma," the man said. "She has no heart. When Mr. R was alive, this was a good job. He was a human being, but she—she's—"

"Don't say it! Don't say anything you'll be sorry for, Reilly." And the woman shook her finger in the man's face. "The business is falling apart, and I'm tired of you."

The man roared back. "And you think I'm not tired of you? You're never fair!"

"I don't like your tone of voice, Reilly."

"Auntie," the girl said again, "don't. Please stop. I hate it."

All this was certainly no business of Adam's. Yet when people were wrought up as these were, there was no telling what might happen next. Alarmed and unsure, he stepped forward to make his presence known and to break the tension.

"I'd like to see some shirts," he said firmly.

The woman reacted at once. "I'll take care of this gentleman."

Her chubby face was flushed. He had an impression of silk and too much jewelry, as she rustled toward him and began to search on some shelves piled with a tumble of ruffled shirtwaists, corsets, and petticoats.

"Where—where on earth—this place is unbelievable, Reilly!"

"You're looking on the wrong side, Mrs. Rothirsch. This man isn't looking for a lace-trimmed shirtwaist."

"As if I don't know that! A person can hardly see here with all this stuff lying around. It's a mess."

"It's a mess because you were trying to straighten things out, Mrs. Rothirsch," Reilly said.

"Mind your tongue, Reilly, do you hear?"

"Yes, I'll mind my tongue. I'm quitting, Mrs. R. Nobody can work for you."

"They can't, can't they? What of this jumble over here?"

Here was indeed another jumble of unrelated objects: neckties, rugged boots, and Stetson hats. Somehow, from among all these, a white shirt was extracted. Adam handed over the dollar, and Reilly moved toward the door.

"Where do you think you're going, Reilly? Since when do we close at two o'clock?"

"I told you I'm leaving, Mrs. Rothirsch. I've had enough."

"What? Twelve years you've been here, and now you're walking away without any notice? It isn't even decent." The old lady's voice trembled and wailed. "I just don't know what I'm going to do. How am I going to find somebody at a moment's notice? I'm tired. I'm too old . . ."

"You're really not," the girl said. "You just get too excited, and it's bad for you."

It was then that Adam couldn't stop himself from speaking. The first words were hardly out of his mouth before he wanted to take them back.

"Perhaps I can help out."

"Help out? Who are you? What are you talking about?"

"I've worked in retail, and I could substitute for a couple of days."

From behind her glasses, Mrs. R.'s sharp eyes regarded him. "You're not making any sense. I don't even know your name."

Of course he was making no sense. That's what could happen when you had a brainstorm.

"My name is Adam Arnring. I'm new in town, so I have no reference. But if you accept me, and I should in any way misbehave, you can call the authorities."

Mrs. Rothirsch was so astonished that it was almost comical to witness. "Retail, you said? What kind?"

"A clothing store back east." So it was a white lie, not the worst thing in the world! "I could give you some good suggestions."

He had caught her attention, for now she challenged him. "Such as what?"

"Well, first you have to make up your mind whether you want menswear or women's. The place is too small to have both."

"Oh, really? Then how is it we used to be so successful if it's so small? Tell me that?"

"Auntie," the girl said, "you're forgetting that the whole back half of the place has burnt down and has not yet been rebuilt. He's right."

"You see? You listen to Emma, Mrs. R. She knows a thing or two."

"No, no," the girl protested. "I only meant to remind Auntie. She understands."

The girl was saving the old woman's pride. He sensed the undercurrents here as clearly as those at the supper table back home when Leo was in a bad mood.

Turning toward Emma, Adam was surprised to meet the direct gaze of her serious eyes. It seemed they were the only two people present who were in control of themselves—the only two people who understood each other.

Pulling his thoughts together, Adam resumed, "If you're going to stay in this space, you should decide which it's to be, a men's or a women's shop. I suggest women's."

"Oh, really?" The old lady was showing signs of scornful amusement. "Why so?"

"Because women spend more money on clothes than men do. That's simple."

An old wrinkled hand strayed to the triple pearl strands that lay among floral ruffles. She stared at Adam.

"How old are you?"

"Twenty-six."

"You don't look it."

"So they tell me."

"You're a college graduate, aren't you? You talk like one."

"Not exactly a graduate, but I have been studying a variety of subjects."

"You have an upper-class accent."

Mrs. Rothirsch had a foreign accent, from somewhere in eastern Europe, Adam thought. He had a suspicion that she was a kind of foolish snob. Suddenly reminded of the catsup stains on his shirt, he pulled his jacket close enough to conceal them, and with some amusement of his own, decided to use a vocabulary that would impress her.

"You have to get rid of all this superfluous merchandise. I am sufficiently experienced to say that some of the items on display here are definitely outmoded."

There was a long silence, during which the old lady simply stared outside through the dirty windows. Reilly shifted from one leg to the other and sighed.

Adam had always been an orderly person, certainly the most orderly even in a household that was always neat. His attic room had been the neatest, his bed without a wrinkle, his clothes hung properly in the makeshift closet, and his books arranged alphabetically on the shelves. And so, as he looked about him, he felt that it would almost be a pleasure to straighten out this place, while at the same time earning a few dollars to tide him over until he could find something better.

"All right. I see you're a very bright young man. Heaven knows, I can't expect anything new from Reilly. Maybe I'm crazy, but what have I got to lose? I'll pay you three dollars this time tomorrow if you clean it up. Is that all right?"

"Do you want a really first-rate job?"

"What do you think? Of course I do."

"Well, then, I'll need two days. And will you give me a free hand?"

In return for this question, Adam received a look of surprise. "What does that mean?"

"It means that I use my best judgment. I have been employed in some very fine shops, Mrs. Rothirsch. I know how to fix up this place. You'll see."

"Well, six dollars for two full days' work. I'm probably out of my mind, but I'll chance it. No funny business, though. I'm well

known in this town, I am, from the courthouse to the police department."

"Believe me, I understand."

"So. It's agreed. Here's the key. We open
at nine. And now I'm going home. Come,
Emma. I'm exhausted."

At the curb was a small electric car in
which ladies who could afford one traveled
soundlessly, at ten miles an hour, about their
errands. The sunlight, after the dimness indoors, burst upon its gleaming metal, on
Mrs. R.'s necklaces, on Emma's rosy dress,
her straw hat, and lastly, as she climbed in,
upon her face.

"Green eyes," Adam thought. "Amazing!"
Surely he must have seen green eyes on
other people. And yet these seemed like the
first he had ever seen.

"There's a Stanley Steamer in their garage,
too," Reilly said, as the car rolled soundlessly away. "She uses it when Rudy drives.
He and his wife Rea work in the house. The
old man paid close to a thousand dollars for
it, they say. You wouldn't think he could be
married to Sabine R. Like day and night. He
had a heart. He'd give to anybody—chari-
ties, churches, you name it. When he had
his stroke, there was no one to order new

stuff for the store, and business went way down. He lived four years without talking or walking. Then they had the fire. I don't know why she keeps me on because business is dead, but I'm glad she does, even when she gets mad. The wages are nothing much, but they keep the wolf from the door."

"So then you're not quitting?"

"Nah! We have these shouting matches every few months. Don't mean a thing." Reilly paused, and then, apparently feeling talkative, remarked about Emma, "That girl is a real peach, isn't she? Smart, too."

"She's a kid, isn't she? How old?"

Reilly shrugged. "Fifteen, maybe sixteen. You liked the red hair?"

"I didn't notice. I only noticed her eyes."

"Didn't notice that hair?"

"Can't say I did. Only the eyes. The face."

"Well, don't get any ideas if you stay here. She's kept safe. Summer camp in the East, boarding school and trips all over, even Europe. She plays the piano, I hear. The old lady locks her away like gold in Fort Knox. So don't bother."

"What would I want with a kid of fifteen?"

"You're a kid yourself, aren't you? How the hell old are you? Honest."

"Almost twenty."

"God Almighty, you've got some nerve. You think you can make sense out of this business?"

"Well, I'm going to try. Do me a favor. Tell me where I can get a place to sleep tonight."

"Go down Sixteenth and turn right at the corner where the highway is. The woman there keeps a boardinghouse for school-teachers. She might have a room. Nice and clean, too. Well, I'll be going along. I'll probably see you in the morning. Then I'll take the rest of the day off. You can have a nice time without me, cleaning up, though I don't know how the hell you're going to do it."

Dear Pa and Family,
I am writing this in a town called
Chattahoochee, at a decent
boardinghouse full of middle-aged
schoolteachers. So don't worry about
me. I'm going to stay here while I look
for some kind of job.

It's an interesting town. You have to
see it to believe it. I took a long walk
when I arrived and saw some unusual
things. One was a huge barn with a
sign that said "Jacks and Mules in Car

Lots." It seems that they sell mules wholesale for work on the farms. The grain fields reach from the edge of town for as far as I could see. There's a ranch, a couple of thousand acres' worth, right at the end of the main boulevard. Another odd thing I saw was a very old, circular house. It was built that way for defense against Indian attacks. All this history!

I'll write again the minute I have something to write about. Love to you all,

Adam

Early the next morning, Adam stood on the street outside Rothirsch's store and considered the scene. The old building had been well designed. Made of light-colored stone, probably limestone, it had fine proportions, with a classical pediment above the entrance and a narrow, carved frieze around the two large windows. It had the dignity of a bank and might well have been one in its time. But now, with the sun blazing on the drab display behind the dusty glass, it cried: Failure! Failure! Don't bother to come in.

But ideas had already begun to whirl through his head. First, turn the key and go inside. Next, sort out the menswear, the stuff that's still salable, but don't throw the rest away. Give it to anybody who needs or wants it. This will be great publicity. Then find the best-looking articles you can and arrange them in the windows with a notice: Sixty percent off.

When he had done all this, he went outside to study the scene again. By the day after tomorrow, she would pay him. But what if it were not enough to do what needed to be done? Suppose he were to use some of his own few dollars? It would be a gamble, but was his departure from home not a gamble?

There should be an awning, deep green. While he was at it, he'd have the windows painted to match; it would contrast to the pale stone. Flower boxes were important; at this time of year they should be filled with chrysanthemums, the bright yellow ones, not the dark ones.

It surprised him, as he scurried up and down the streets, searching for awnings, a painter, and a florist, to feel how much he was enjoying himself. This wasn't *architec-*

ture, but he was shaping something all the same. Perhaps he had not hated the idea of a store, of commerce, as much as he had simply hated his father's store.

Late in the afternoon, while he was helping the florist fill the planters, a man stopped by with a question. "What's going on? New ownership?"

"No, not at all. Just cleaning up," Adam said.

"And the sign? Do you mean that? You're really giving things away?"

"Why, yes. Go on in and help yourself. You can take whatever you like from that pile over there on the right. It's marked 'Free.' It's all old stuff, but usable if you don't care how old it is."

"Gee, just giving stuff away. I never saw that before."

"It's a fact. Help yourself."

"Well, I could use a pair of overalls for my yardwork. I'm a reporter, Jeff Horace is the name, from the *Chattahoochee Item.* Listen. I'm going to put this into tomorrow's paper. I'm always looking for interesting news. What's your name?"

It ought to be the old lady's name, not his.

Adam said hastily, "The store belongs to Mrs. Rothirsch."

"Everybody knows that. But I'd like your name for the article. I do sort of a human interest column."

"Adam Arnring. It's spelled the way it sounds."

"Say, aren't you new here? What happened to Reilly? He's a good friend of mine."

"He's here, only not today."

"This place was a landmark in the old man's time. I wonder why she hasn't kept it up, or even sold it."

"I've no idea."

"Well, it's nice to see the place being spruced up."

Adam was setting the last of the golden chrysanthemums into the earth when the reporter emerged, bearing two pairs of overalls and a compliment.

"You've really given it a cleaning. It's almost empty."

"I know. But it'll be filled again. All in good time."

At five o'clock, Reilly appeared. "What the hell is this?" he cried.

"Don't you like it?"

"What is there not to like? Flowers, fresh paint—but where'd you get the money?"

"I had a few dollars of my own. I figure I'll get them back when she pays me."

"Pays you!" Reilly laughed. "You'll be lucky she doesn't charge you for damages. No, I'm kidding. She'll pay you. That's one thing about her. I told you, she's honest. And look what you've done for her store—"

A few minutes later another man appeared.

"This is Ray Archer. He used to work here when we were busy. He couldn't wait to see what's going on."

"I heard about it at the barber's," Archer said. "Is it true that there's going to be something in the paper?"

Adam nodded. "Yes, and then there ought to be a big ad very soon, as soon as she buys more stuff to advertise. In the meantime, as you see, I put out the best things I could find. They don't look like much without mannequins, though."

"She'll never spend money like that."

"Well, it takes money to make more," Adam said seriously.

The men were giving him their own serious attention. Archer was half a head taller than

Reilly, and weighed half as much. Standing there so earnestly, they reminded him of two men in a comic strip. He did not know why they also made him feel sad.

The next day's traffic was surprising. People had read the "About Town" column, or had heard some talk and were now curious to see for themselves. Many bought, some praised, and a few were disappointed.

"There's nothing much here," they complained, "except leftover summer clothes."

"You're absolutely right," Adam told them. "We're in the midst of repairs in the shop, and so we're behind schedule." And he gave them a warm smile. "Please be a little patient with us, will you?"

From the remains of the menswear section he had taken a jacket and a new tie. Wearing these with a clean white shirt, he felt confident; they belonged with what Mrs. R. had called his "upper-class" accent.

Reilly apparently thought so, too, for after paying his compliments, he added, "I suppose if the old lady likes what you're doing, it's the end for Archer and me. What use are we in women's wear? In fancy women's wear? Twelve years in this place, and now— ta-ta. I guess that's it."

"Nine years for me," said Archer. "Part-time for the last two months. Three kids and a wife."

All of a sudden, Adam was seeing the unemployed customers in Pa's store. Then it was that he knew why yesterday Reilly and Archer had made him feel sad.

"She came in the afternoon, right after you had left," Reilly said on the third day. "We gave her your list. She wants to see you at the house."

"When?"

"Now."

"Was she pleased? Was she mad?"

"She wouldn't let anybody know if she was pleased. But she wasn't exactly mad, either. Or, maybe a little . . . You'd better go right away. She hates to be kept waiting. It's straight out Fourth Street, number seventeen, with an iron fence around it."

Vaguely, as he hurried, Adam remembered some quotation about "the die was cast." Well, his die could go three ways. He might get the promised pay and a simple good-bye, or the pay and a tirade over having spent so much, or perhaps the pay with a compliment.

The house, a fussy Victorian with a wrap-around porch of wooden lace, was the largest on the street. A pair of rounded turrets, crenellated like those on medieval castles, rose above the roof; the double doorway frowned like a surly mouth. The place was hideous. Costly and hideous.

Only once before, that time at Mr. Shipper's, had he been inside what you might call a mansion. This time, though, he was met with gloomy browns and tans; they covered the hall and the rooms beyond it, where in the distance a stained-glass window admitted a dreary purple light.

"You have some good ideas," Mrs. R. began. "Now about that extension in the rear. When it was damaged in the fire, I collected the insurance, but never used it, just put it in the bank. I'm a very frugal person, and I had lost all my interest in the business. But somehow—I guess it was this article in the paper, a very nice one I must say—I feel my interest coming back. Aaron built the business up from zero, you know, and I believe I owe something to his memory."

Yes, undoubtedly it was the *Chatta-*

hoochee Item that had revived the feel of past dignity, of the glory that had built this expensive house, bought the fine automobile and the bulky jewelry.

"I will give you fifteen dollars a week," she said. "It's more than I've been giving those two I have now. Neither Archer nor Reilly has one idea in his head. Actually, since it's to be all women's apparel, I don't even need them anymore."

She was moving too fast! Of course, it was her store, but still . . . He avoided looking at the sharp eyes behind the glasses. Were those two graying men to be tossed out because of him?

"Mr. Reilly said your husband liked him, him and Mr. Archer."

"Maybe he did, but what's that got to do with now?"

"Maybe he wouldn't get rid of them, if he were here."

"Oh, really? This bothers you?"

He nodded. "It does. It really does. I'm sorry."

Behind her head, there were shelves filled with gewgaws, porcelain cupids, and bead flowers in gaudy pots. Turning away from them in distaste, he rejected them, and the woman, too.

"For a man your age, you're mighty outspoken, mighty independent, Mr. Arnring."

"At my age, Mrs. Rothirsch, I can afford to be independent," he said quietly. "Mr. Reilly and Mr. Archer can't."

"Well, I never! I've met all kinds in my time, but I'm darned if I've ever met anybody like you. I suppose you think that because you're good-looking, young, and smart, you can get away with anything. The world's your oyster, isn't it?"

The world can be very cruel, Pa said that night. The wind was rattling the windows, and it was cold.

He stood up. "I'm sorry," he repeated. "I would have liked to stay. But I can't, if they have to go."

"No. No, wait!" Mrs. R. cried as Adam moved toward the door. She stretched out her arm. "You win. All right. There's no sense in my getting myself all upset. You win. Satisfied? I want your brains and your energy. I'll admit it, even though you are making me angry. So we might as well shake hands."

The rings cut into Adam's hand, but he smiled.

"We'll meet at the store tomorrow morning, Mr. Arnring. Ten o'clock sharp. I have to tell you I have no patience with people who are not on time."

"I'm like that, too, Mrs. R."

"Incidentally," she added as he opened the door, "I like the awnings and the flowers."

He had to stifle an impulse to whistle. If he had been wearing a hat, he would have tossed it up into the air. The old girl's bark was worse than her bite! Who would have imagined it? But of course, it was the good publicity that had most appealed to her. He ought to thank Jeff Horace, and he certainly would do so.

These were his thoughts as he leaped down the porch steps and almost stumbled over Emma, who was sitting on the last one. Somewhat flustered, he stepped back and apologized.

"That's all right," she said. "I'm not supposed to be sitting here on the steps, anyway. But it's nice to read here and watch the traffic, when there is any."

Aside from a horse and wagon that were disappearing around the corner, there was at the moment no traffic.

"Lonesome?" he asked.

He was not surprised when she nodded. "It's a very quiet house, and I'm used to all the people in my boarding school."

"So you're in a hurry to get back to school?"

"Yes, but I would never let my aunt see it. It would hurt her feelings too much. You know how it is with old people."

In the blue gingham dress, with the high-buttoned shoes crossed at the ankles and barely visible below the skirt, she looked demure. Yet he had already seen she was not demure.

One of her hands, with fingers curled, lay open on her lap. The nails were oval, glossy and delicate as the tiny shells that one sometimes found on the beach. The hand made him think of a painting or a sculpture, perhaps something he had seen in a book, or possibly something he only imagined.

"So you are going to stay," she said.

"For a while, anyway. How did you guess?"

"I didn't have to guess. It was obvious. The fresh paint, the flowers, and the newspaper. You did a lot in two days."

Standing above her as he leaned against

the stone wall, he read one of the titles on her books: *The Oregon Trail.*

He wanted to stay and talk, so he fastened on the books, a harmless enough subject.

"*The Oregon Trail.* You're a true westerner."

"One who spends almost all of her life in the East."

"Do you have to?"

"Yes. It's planned for me. In the summer I go to a music school and study piano. I'm supposed to spend the whole of next year in France studying more piano. Not that I mind. Who would mind a year in France? But my aunt thinks I'm some kind of genius, you see, and I'm not, not at all. I simply love to play the piano, and I'm pretty good at it, too, but so are plenty of other people. I'll be sorry for her when she finds out the truth." Emma laughed. "Sorry for myself, too."

"But why not tell her now and get it over with?"

"After what you saw the other day at the store, you can ask me that?"

Adam was silent. Don't interfere, he warned himself. Mind your own business. Don't say a word that might be quoted. Still, he was puzzled. The girl certainly didn't appear to be mistreated. And yet you never knew. Who was she, and why was she living with "Auntie"?

He was about to walk on, when from the porch above them, a sharp voice rang out. "What in the world are you doing, Emma? Aren't you supposed to finish those books during this vacation?"

"I'm almost half through the last one, Auntie, so don't worry."

"But then you have math to do." Mrs. R., as she descended three steps, was on a level with Adam. "You have to watch these adolescents every minute. They think they know everything. All about life, all about the world. They don't need their aunt to watch out for them anymore. Right, little Emma?"

"No, wrong."

"Well, I'll be on my way," Adam said quickly. "Tomorrow morning at the store, Mrs. R., and thank you for everything."

The message was clear: *This girl is out of bounds to you, Mr. Arnring.* She needn't have bothered. Girls—even girls with vivid green eyes—were the last subject on his mind right now.

His steps as he went down the street were jaunty. He couldn't wait to write home with the news. Pa would warn him as always not to take the job for granted. Never count chickens before they're hatched, he would say.

At the corner he turned and looked back. There, wrapped in sunlight, the girl was still sitting on the step. He had not really seen her hair until now. Probably that was because it had been pulled away from her face and caught in an almost childish bow at the back of her head. Why, it's russet, he thought. It's something you don't often see. Green eyes, and this extraordinary hair! Perhaps bronze is a more accurate word? No, bronze has more brown in it. Russet is better. Russet.

Dear Pa and Family,
I've waited a couple of weeks to write because I want to make sure of the facts. So here they are. You will never believe what has happened. I've got a steady job. Fifteen dollars a week. This very eccentric, cranky old widow owns a real clothing store that was almost going broke. I can't explain what got into me because I surely never knew or cared anything about ladies' dresses,

but all of a sudden it looked to me like a gold mine. All it needed was a pick and shovel. So I made a few improvements; Mrs. R. (I'll call her that because I can scarcely spell her name) liked the improvements, and so here I am. I'll wait another month or two. If she still wants to keep me, I'll rent two rooms for myself downtown near the store. I figure that I'll be able to save enough in the next few years to help you send Jonathan to college. More later. Love to you all.

Dear Pa,
This letter is for you alone. Did you know that Leo has already written to me? He is very bitter about his life, especially about helping you in the store. I know it is only for a few hours a week because you want him to study and improve his marks. Still, I am trying to think what else you and all of us could possibly do for him, but I haven't come up with any ideas. Nobody can make him popular and happy any more than they can turn him into a Jonathan. Now he seems to be thinking that I,

too, am having some kind of royal success, which is very much exaggerated. I have merely been lucky enough to find something that I like enough to stick with. So please don't talk about me to Leo. He's so—shall I say "sensitive"? I can't seem to think of the right word. But comparisons are very hard for him to take right now. Don't worry, because he'll straighten out when he's older.

I've sent him a few dollars so he can buy something for himself.

Love,
Adam

Chapter 4

Reilly was counting on his fingers. "Who needs a calendar? Ever since Adam took over two years ago, I can tell the month by his decorations. Pumpkins in October, then turkeys, Christmas holly, Lincoln's Birthday, Washington's portrait in a white wig, Valentine hearts, Easter bunnies, Flag Day, and the Fourth of July."

"You forgot Halloween," Archer said.

"I did not. What the deuce do you think we need pumpkins for?"

It was almost evening, the end of a long day, and having locked the doors, the three men were standing on the sidewalk in front of the windows. There were the handsome mannequins in quadruple silk flounces and cartwheel hats with roses and poppies on their brims, which had been bringing so many people into the store. Adam was thinking that it was time to be ordering for next spring. You had to be two seasons, close to three seasons, ahead.

"I heard," Archer reported, "that we've been taking a load of customers away from Cace Clothiers. They're losing a lot of business because of us."

"Well, why not? People can get the same stuff here without making the trip."

"Mrs. R. is sure raking it in," Reilly said, making a face.

"It's her store, her investment," Adam said. "Let's not begrudge her."

"Listen to him! He's a strange kid, isn't he?" Reilly said to Archer. "Even Mrs. R. is afraid of our Adam. She calls us 'Mr. Reilly' and 'Mr. Archer' because he told her to."

"You have to set a tone," Adam said. "With all these customers from the hill coming in, you have to act accordingly. It's what they expect."

No one answered. They were decent men, who could quite understandably resent him. So much younger than they, he had suddenly appeared on the scene and was now, though without any title, taking charge. It was he who ordered the merchandise and reported once a month to the accountant, Theo Brown, who in turn reported to Mrs. R.

And all this had come about almost from that first day when he had walked in to buy a shirt.

You have a good head for business, Mr. Shipper had told him.

Yes, he reflected, as the three men walked down the street. He, who had never given a second's thought to fashion, could just as easily have taught himself all there was to know about mules and jacks in car lots.

Sometimes he felt that he must guard against seeming too sure of himself, and especially when he was with Archer and Reilly. Was he perhaps a trifle arrogant?

But they didn't have his determination, nor did they look ahead beyond the week's wages and weekly expenses with a bit left over. Maybe they were more *human* than he? He hoped not.

"Mrs. R. came in yesterday with Emma," Reilly said. "She makes sure to come when she knows you'll be at Mr. Brown's, Adam," he added with his teasing grin.

"Jim, don't be ridiculous. That kid?"

"The kid's eighteen."

Reilly and Archer, the jesters, really could be ridiculous when they got started. All

Adam needed to ruin his situation was to get friendly with that girl.

"I heard the old lady's taking her to England next summer, or maybe the one after that. With Emma's looks and her nice pot of money, they'll probably come back with a banker or a duke or somebody."

"Emma should get ahold of you," said Archer. "You're a catch, Adam."

Everybody, including Adam, whose father had never told jokes, was used to these two men. Nevertheless, this kind of talk about Emma Rothirsch bothered him. He hardly ever saw her except at a distance when she came into the store accompanied by "Auntie." Why, he might not even recognize her on the street were he to see her there! She sits in sunlight with a book on her lap and her russet hair flowing down her back. That's all I see when I hear her name.

They had almost reached the place where Adam turned off to his street, and still the fun persisted.

"Get yourself a steady girl, Adam," Reilly said. "Quit running around the way you do. You've got half the girls in this town hoping."

"How do you know I haven't got a steady girl?"

"Because if you had, you would say something about her once in a while."

In the same tone, since they expected it, Adam joked back. "My problem is, I'm waiting till I can afford one of those fine rigs and a fine mare of my own, so I can take her out in style on a Sunday afternoon."

"I've a much better idea. Save your money and wait five years," Reilly said. "Then you'll be driving around here in an automobile, one of those Model T's that Ford's putting out."

"What makes you so sure I'll even be around here five years from now?"

Both men waved the question away. "You will be. You'll probably own the place."

Chapter 5

The mailbox was on the front porch, and it was Adam's first stop when he returned from work at the end of the day. Usually it was empty, but now and then there would be a letter from Jonathan or Pa. If, rarely, there was one from Leo, he could be sure it contained the usual litany of complaints.

Two flights of stairs led to his pleasant apartment on the top floor of a pleasant house owned by a pair of retired school-teachers. Even now in his third year here, he never entered this home of his without looking around and enjoying the change from his first two rooms in Chattahoochee. There was space here, space for books and for that marvel, the phonograph, which, when he wound it, brought him the voice of Caruso singing an aria from *Pagliacci*. This was the first place he had ever slept in that was not an attic where if he wasn't careful, he could bump his head against the sloping ceiling.

He went to the window. Below lay a great green yard that was filled with the family's hobbies: bird feeders and flowering shrubs. Everything is so large in the West, he thought, amazed as if he were seeing all of this for the first time.

When he had had enough of the scene, he opened the mail; there was only one letter, and it was in his father's familiar, foreign script.

Dear Adam,
I was so proud of the pictures, the ads and the newspaper clippings you finally sent to me. I knew you did not want to send them, and I guessed why. You are always afraid there will be some trouble with Leo. But I tell you that Leo is the way he is, and I am not going to hide things from him to keep him quiet, the way Rachel and Jonathan do. So I am proud they made you manager of a beautiful store. My own son, a manager! It was smart to hire a window dresser. Rachel loved the one with the mother in her beautiful dress with the

baby carriage, and the bigger sister walking next to her with matching dress. You are very, very clever, and I feel stupid. Thank you for sending the money. I feel bad and more stupid for taking it. I am only glad for Jonathan's sake. He is sixteen, but his head is sixty. With your help, he will do big things, I think. He acts like a doctor. He knows how to behave with Leo. Leo is never angry with him. Sometimes my heart beats so fast when Leo is in the store, I wish he would get a different job, but when he goes to ask for one, the people do not hire him, they look at him and do not like him, I think, and then I am sorry for him, but what can I do? Anyway, we miss you. Keep up the good work. Love from us all,

Pa, your Father

He laid down the letter, ate his light supper, and went to the desk where, after the usual period of careful thought, he began to write.

Dear Pa,
Please don't call yourself "stupid." I

know you say that because you are accepting money from your son. That is so wrong of you! You have always supported us; we have never gone in want of anything that we really needed. Even now, you surely do not need my money to get along with. It is just that we are both doing what we can and should do for Jonathan.

I know he has some strange feelings about it, too. Many times he has written to me that he will "take good care of all of us" when he is "grown up." I agree with you that he grew up years ago, even though he is only sixteen. Please tell him again that I am not "going without," as he once wrote, to help him. I am doing just fine.

I'm sorry to hear that Leo is so cranky. Of course that's nothing new and it's rather sad, but lately when I read about him in your letters, I get pretty impatient. If he can't find any job that he likes, he should be grateful for his job in the store.

I wish I could go home to see all of you, but it is a very long trip, and I don't think Mrs. R. would like me to take the

*time right now. She has just given me a
raise, and I don't want to ask her for a
favor so soon. But I will do it before
long, I promise. Love to you all,*

Adam

At the window again, he watched the first stars. Below their light more lights shone from houses that only a year ago had not yet been built. The town was expanding. In a few more years, he thought, cars will no doubt outnumber the horses; right now the college is turning gradually into a university. Someday the town will be a suburb of the capital.

All this means a new class of shoppers. We must keep them in mind and grow with the town. Already we could use twice the space that we have.

These thoughts pursued Adam when he pulled the shade and lay down for the night. They wandered between waking and sleep, then woke him again at the edge of sleep.

Those ads in the glossy fashion magazines. If I could go to New York and talk to some of the companies that import things. Should talk again to Theo Brown. Too soon, he says. Mrs. R. would never spend the money. But she is pleased with me, he says.

Young nobody walks in off the street. Imagine that!

You should study to be an accountant, Theo says. *You've the mind for it.* He reminds me of Mr. Shipper. We like each other. Funny, that first time we met at Francine's rich place. How could he have expected to find me there? Me? But I was there with Jeff Horace, the reporter. His boss owns the paper. All big names go there, respectable men, business, politics, lawyers, big names. Interesting talk you hear about what's going on in the great world. Francine's handsome parlors, her beautiful walled gardens. Otherwise, no different from Gracie's back home.

Reilly used to kid me about it because it's out of my league. So he thinks. He'd be surprised to know I've been there. More than once. I'm a little surprised, too. All those men like Theo Brown. Or Mr. Lawrence, Mrs. R.'s lawyer. All married. Why? Maybe I'm naive. Naive, like Pa.

Mrs. R. is pleased with me, Theo says. She'd never let me know. Wouldn't give me the satisfaction. Like ice down your back.

My God, how did a husband live all those

years with a creature like her? Came into the store one day last winter in her mink coat. Looked for a minute like a grizzly bear walking toward me. No wonder the poor man had a stroke. While she was yelling at him one day, he must have taken a good look at her and decided to die.

Adam's chuckle awoke him. *Be careful about marrying,* says Archer, who has a cranky wife. *But start looking.*

I do look. There's Fannie, only a short ride in on the Interurban, and never tired of having fun. Sees all the motion pictures, goes to all the dances, plays cards, has lively friends and a good nature. There's Geraldine. You go someplace with her and watch the men pretending not to be staring at her. There's Mabel, sweet and serious. Teaches kindergarten out near the boulevard. She would make a good wife. No question about that.

But I'm not ready to settle down for a lifetime. Will I ever be? Will I always be a bachelor, roaming around town and never marrying?

But I would like to feel *love,* and I never do. Something haunts me. Something is missing. I need to feel that I can't go on without the person, or I don't want her. What I mean is a kind of yearning, the kind that comes sometimes with music or grand poetry. Is that too much to ask?

Perhaps it was.

When he awoke in the morning it was already light. He remembered having had vaguely troubled thoughts before falling asleep. Then, alert, he remembered that a delivery of imported fabrics was expected today. He was hastily fastening his necktie, when there was a knock at the door. Mr. Buckley had come up with a telegram in hand.

"Western Union for you, Adam. I hope it's not any bad news."

As always, Pa was frugal. There were only six words: "Rachel died this evening. Heart attack."

Chapter 6

The train rumbled, was halted at watering stops, crossed the Mississippi, and neared the end of the journey. All through daylight and darkness there floated the kind face of Rachel, who surely had not expected to die so suddenly and so soon, the blue, distended veins at Pa's temples, Jonathan's eyes that missed nothing, and Leo's face in shadow . . .

Now and then Adam dozed in his seat, then he would wake, read a page in his book, and put it down to look out of the window.

"Mr. Arnring! What are you doing so far from Chattahoochee?"

Startled by the abrupt appearance of Emma Rothirsch, who must surely have come from a Pullman car, he stood and, in one brief sentence, gave the reason for this journey.

"I'm sorry," she said. "I wish I knew something better than that to say to you, but I can
never quite find the right words for death."

The train swayed, and they both caught
awkwardly at the seat back. Expecting her
to continue on her way, he waited for her
next words.

"Mr. Arnring, I was on my way to the dining
car. Would you like to join me?"

"Why, that would be very nice, Miss
Rothirsch."

Very nice, and very uncomfortable, too.
Some people, no matter whether one of
them may live in Brazil and the other in Aus-
tralia, no matter whether they have just met
five minutes ago, can still strike up a conversation with ease. But Adam did not fit so
well with the niece of Sabine Rothirsch, and
she ought to know it. Yet he could not very
well refuse the suggestion, and so he followed her into the dining car, where each
table was covered with white linen and held
a bowl of flowers. He recalled the fear that
had beset him the first time he sat in such a
place, fear of the unknown, and fear, too,
that he was using up his sparse dollars.

They sat down, and for once in his life, he
had nothing to say. Other than rare, formal

greetings on those few occasions when this young lady had come to the shop with her aunt, the only words that had ever passed between them were the remarks made some five years ago about *The Oregon Trail.*

The sun, a bright red ball in the sky, was glaring directly into her face. Seeing her reach for the window shade, Adam leaned forward over the table to do it for her, but she did not need him.

"I have long fingers," she said.

He thought of a response. "From playing the piano?"

She laughed. "They say it's usually the other way around. They find a child with long fingers like mine, and they say, 'Oh ho, let's buy her a piano.' "

"So they bought a piano for you?"

"Oh, yes, a marvelous one. It's a concert grand, and it takes up half of a room."

When Adam agreed that that was marvelous, he was contradicted.

"I appreciate it, but all the same, it's ridiculous."

He was becoming interested, and perhaps a little amused. "Why is it ridiculous?"

"Because. My aunt sees me going around the world giving recitals, having my name in the newspapers and being famous. I'll feel so sorry for her when she finally realizes that it will never happen."

"How can you be so sure it never will? 'Never' is a long time."

"If you ever heard me play, Mr. Arnring, you'd understand what I mean. That is, if you know very much about music."

"I love music, but I don't know anything about it, so I'm no judge."

Her glance flickered over him and then went to the menu. "I'm starved. They have fish soup, I see. I'd never expect to find it on a train. Do you like fish soup?"

"I don't believe I've ever had it."

"Try it. You won't be sorry. Or maybe you will be, and if you are, just say so."

He was beginning to feel more at ease with her. She was different, he thought. He couldn't have said just now what the difference was, but he knew it was there. Every so often while he ate, he glanced at her hands, at the narrow gold bracelet that lay below a sleeve of cream-colored silk. This simplicity was certainly not her aunt's taste. The green eyes within the pale oval of her face bore no resemblance, not the faintest, to the aunt, or to the uncle whose portrait hung above the mantel in the room where he had sat that one time and never once since. He had a picture in his head of that house with the fussy clutter and the mauve gloom of the stained-glass window; it seemed as if this young woman opposite did not fit at all into the picture. It seemed impossible that they could be related. On the other hand, people might say the same of Leo.

"I hope you like the soup," she said, "since I suggested it."

"I do. Very much."

"It needs wine. I make mine with plenty of good wine."

"Then you're a cook, too?"

"At college I live in an apartment with three other girls. And since the cafeteria food is horrible, we do a little cooking."

"The college is in New England, isn't it?"

"Yes, outside of Boston. I change trains in New York. My goodness, didn't you know where I go to college? Sometimes it seems to me that nobody in our whole town even knows I exist."

"It's not quite like that," Adam said gently, "but the fact is you're away almost all the time. You told me once that you never even went to grammar school in Chattahoochee, so how can people know anything about you?"

"You remember that conversation?"

"I certainly do. You were reading *The Oregon Trail.*"

"Yes, I was a bookworm when I was home. When I wasn't practicing at the piano, I was reading. That came of having no local friends."

The girl's locked away, Reilly had said, *like the gold in Fort Knox.*

He would have liked to know more, but did not ask. It was no business of his. Yet he could not resist one question.

"Do you like being away all the time?"

"Yes," she answered directly. "I do. I can take a cooking course if I want to, I can buy clothes according to my own tastes, I can march in a suffragette parade—"

"You did that?" he exclaimed.

"I did. Why? Are you shocked?"

"Not at all. Tell me about it."

"Well, I was in New York at a music school, when the suffragettes had a parade. Three thousand of them, I read the next day, marching down Fifth Avenue carrying banners and wearing sashes around their shoulders. I just walked up and joined, even without a sash, but a nice old lady gave me a little flag to carry. She smiled and winked at me, I remember. I thought the whole thing was great. And there were a lot of policemen riding horses. I wish I had a horse, but there's never enough time to ride, so it's just as well."

"So you think women should have the vote."

"Why not? The brain is an organ, like the heart or the kidneys, the same in a woman as in a man. It has nothing to do with the"— after a second's hesitation she finished— "the reproductive system."

Adam was fascinated. The young women he knew did not talk about "the reproductive system." At least to him, they didn't.

"Yes, it was an experience. They'll probably have pictures of it in the history books in a few years. There were photographers all over the place. Yes, it was great," she repeated. "I don't want to miss the next one if I can help it."

But if Mrs. R. hears about it, you'll miss it, Adam thought. It must be a challenge to rear a girl like her. When she's finished with college, it'll be time to find a husband. Who will be smart enough for her? Or smart enough to accept her independence? Who will be important enough to satisfy Mrs. R.?

He asked her whether she was still studying the piano.

"Yes, and I love it. Even though I'll never be a star. One has to know oneself, you see, and I do. I'm a realist," she said gravely.

When she had spoken about the suffragette parade, she had seemed very young, gleeful, and almost mischievous. Now he was hearing a much older voice. He calculated: She's at least nineteen. Did I know myself when I was nineteen? When I rode on this train in the opposite direction with no idea where I was going?

"What do you see outside that's so interesting?" she asked.

"Mostly trees. I was also thinking of my first trip, going the other way, and landing in Chattahoochee, a place I had never heard of."

She laughed. "Most people haven't. The day we met in the store was your first day there, I heard."

"First day, first hour—or nearly."

"It was horrible, wasn't it?"

Be careful, Adam warned himself. It was

no business of yours then, and it still isn't now. So, carefully, he replied.

"I was just—sorry. That's all."

"Sorry? For whom?"

"Just sorry about the—the disagreement. And for you."

"For me? You should have been more sorry for Aunt Sabine."

He must *not* become involved. He must not say anything that could be held against him. He had not come this far and gained so much to throw it away.

"I don't know about that," he said. "All I know is that everyone has treated me very well. I hear only good things about your family, your uncle, what a fine, kind man he was—"

"Fine? Kind? That shows you what people don't know. He was a monster! It's a wonder she has any sanity left. He despised her. He destroyed her. Sometimes, not often, he even struck her. It's probably an awful thing to say, but she's been gradually getting better ever since the day he died."

Imprisoned for the duration of dinner at his seat, Adam felt as though the chair were burning his back.

"Perhaps you shouldn't be telling me

these things," he said gently. "They're very personal, and you will probably be sorry tomorrow that you confided in me."

"I'm doing it because I'm so angry that I'm ready to burst. And I know you won't talk. I don't know you, but still I'm sure that you won't. I'm angry because of what people say about her. They say they can't stand her, and they laugh at her. And it's so cruel. I think of her alone in that awful old house, alone except for the times she visits me wherever I am, in college, or last summer at the music school in Paris. She only has one or two friends, lonely old women like herself who get dressed up and have tea together."

The train was passing through a tunnel of evergreens. Placid and cool they stood, while the flow of hot words continued.

"I don't know what you can be thinking, Mr. Arnring. I'm not being very 'ladylike,' am I? Not even very sensible! But I'll tell you. It's because of the things I overheard at the hairdresser's just yesterday. They were lies, so unjust that I had to get these things out of my system and tell them to somebody. And when you said that about my uncle—forgive me."

He looked at her and saw that there were tears in her eyes.

"It's all right," he said. "Say what you will."

"He never had a kind word for her," she resumed. "He wanted children, you see, and she couldn't have any. They had been fleeing the hate-filled years in Europe and she was pregnant. It was the worst time to be pregnant; they had no place to care for a baby, not even a place to give birth. So she went to a midwife and had an abortion. After that, she had no more children and he never forgave her.

"She got fat and homely. She didn't care. After he died, she had enough money to keep the store running properly, but she didn't care about that, either. I'm all she cares about, Mr. Arnring, although I must say she is very pleased with the things you've done in the store. And with the money that's coming in. She puts it all aside for me, although I don't need or want so much, I really don't. I plan to take care of myself. But that's another story. This story is about her. In her mind, you see, I'm taking the place of the woman she wanted to be. She wants me to have everything she read about, and heard about, and missed."

When she stopped, Adam was silent. Yet he did not disguise his frank examination of her face.

"Are you thinking that there is something wrong with me, Mr. Arnring? I can understand very well that you might think so."

Those vivid eyes were looking straight back into Adam's. Judge me, they said without fear.

"No," he said. "I don't think there is anything wrong with you. I am thinking that I should be honored to have your trust."

She smiled. He had a quick recollection of her on the step with her book. And of himself as he had walked away, thinking about the color of her hair. Red, he had thought then, and corrected himself. No, not red. It's russet. Yes, russet.

"Look," she said now, "factories. We're almost there. We'd better go back and collect our things. I know it will be hard for you at home, Mr. Arnring. But I hope it won't be too bad."

He went blank for an instant, and then he understood she meant Rachel's funeral. He thanked her for her sympathy.

Polite and proper now, she told him that she had enjoyed their dinner.

"We covered a lot of ground, didn't we? Besides my outburst, I mean. Pianos, women's suffrage—"

"And fish soup," he said.

They shook hands, and he watched her walk away, holding her black slender skirt just high enough to keep it from grazing the floor.

Pa was receiving people in the kitchen, where he had always been most comfortable. His first words to Adam were a lament.

"I wanted to wait for you, but they wouldn't let me. She thought the world of you, Adam. She would have wanted you to be here when she was laid in the ground."

No, she would not, Adam thought. Observant and pious, she had known that the dead must be buried on the second day, while Pa, in spite of his skullcap, was a freethinker. She was the mother I knew, Adam thought, as he saw her checked apron still hanging on the doorknob near the icebox. And as if she were still sitting there at her end of the table, he saw again her pale, anxious eyes and her soothing smile.

The house was full. Every chair was taken

and every flat surface covered with food. Neighbors were still coming up the front step with pies, roasts, and bowls of fruit. In the kitchen they spoke the usual comforting words to Pa, but he seemed hardly to hear them, and his replies were almost inaudible.

Then suddenly he bent, put his face in his hands, and cried, "She was my whole life, she was the only woman I ever loved!"

"Wait, wait," an old man murmured, "you will see her again."

But this is the second death, Adam was thinking. Can he have forgotten the first? And he stood there just looking at his father, not knowing what to say, until a woman came up to him and remarked how sorry she was for Leo and Jonathan.

"I feel so bad for them, losing their mother so young."

But he, too, had loved Rachel; did he not count?

Then he thought, No, it's true. The woman had spoken correctly. Rachel was their mother, not mine. So with a choking in his throat, he pushed his way out of the kitchen and through the crowded rooms, hoping to find his brothers.

Not finding them, he went outside. It was

Jonathan whom he saw first, standing in the front yard and looking up toward the room on the second floor where their parents slept. Was that where Rachel had died?

The two rushed together. For a few minutes, neither spoke, but held on to each other, while in Adam, a rush of emotions and memories collided and tangled: The years dropped away, and Jonathan, though now a young man, was still the brother he remembered.

"You look different," Jonathan said. "Is it that striped tie or the hat you're carrying?"

He was making up for his wet eyes with a joke, so Adam joked back.

"The hat is a boater. After Memorial Day a gentleman wears a boater. Don't you recognize a gentleman when you see one?"

"I'll learn. I'll take a special course when I'm in college."

Stepping back for a better view, Adam marveled. "College! Around the corner! I can't believe it. Let me look at you. When I left, you weren't shaving yet. And you were half a foot shorter."

"Just about. I'm six feet one."

"You beat me by an inch, little brother. Tell

me, where are you going? What college is it to be?"

"Someplace in New York, I hope, if I can make it. They say I probably will. I don't know, but I hope so, especially now. If I'm in the city, I'll at least be able to look in on them now and then. I'm thinking of how it will be when they're left alone together. It's not going to be easy without Mom."

Adam understood. Rachel had always tried to soothe tensions. She hadn't always succeeded, but God knows she had tried.

"Where is Leo? I didn't see him inside."

"He sort of fell apart yesterday after the service."

"So, where is he?"

"He went over to Bobby Nishikawa's house."

"And he's still there?"

"Yes. I went over last night to talk to him, but he wouldn't come back with me. He says this house will be unbearable without Mom. She was never cross with him, he says. And Pa—well, we know Pa—with all his good heart, used to correct him all the time. Well, you remember."

"Pa's tired out at the end of his day. What the devil is the matter with Leo, anyway?"

"Adam, I wish I knew. Maybe he's just made like that."

Bleak, Adam thought. The little brown house is bleak. When it rains, when the winter fogs creep in, everything turns gray. I can't do anything except send money. Jonathan's life, when he leaves here, wherever he may go, will be bright, while my own is bright enough and may, if I keep on working and if luck stays with me, be even brighter. But what on earth can I do for the two left here?

Another deep sigh rose out of his chest, and he was annoyed with himself for his anxious thoughts.

"Everyone's leaving. We'd better go in," he said.

They were at the front door when Leo came scurrying in—yes, that's the right expression, thought Adam, for this person who was moving swiftly with bent back in the hope of being unseen.

"Look at him," he said. "Is it because of me, because I've come home?"

"It could be. He's been hearing so much about you. It's too much for him."

"Pa still talks about me? In at least six letters, I have told him not to."

"He's proud of you. It's only natural, Adam."

"Of what? I've got a nice job at a fine shop, that's all. That's all I am. Why the pride? When you're in medical school, that will be reason for pride. Come."

Pa was still in the kitchen, sitting on the same chair. Near the window stood Leo. And there went Adam's quiver of nerves, for the picture of Leo that he had taken west with him was not what he was seeing now.

Poor fellow. No more than one inch above five feet, with his misshapen face fleshed out beneath that rapidly receding hairline. Barely into his twenties, and growing bald . . .

"How are you, Leo? It's good to see you," Adam said. He would have hugged him, but Leo had wedged himself into the corner behind Pa's chair, where he could not be reached. "I mean," he corrected himself, " 'good' isn't the word for seeing anybody on a day when we've lost our mother. What I meant was—"

"She wasn't your mother," Leo said quietly.

"Good God! Even today!" Pa shouted. "Even today. Leo, did you come in here to give us more grief than we already have? God, have you no pity? Your mother is dead, my wife is gone, my wife, the only woman I ever loved." Pa sobbed. "My God, my God."

Not my mother, too, who died and left you with an infant? Adam wanted to ask, but did not. And a silence like cold, still air filled the kitchen.

Jonathan was the first to take action. From the cluttered surfaces, the table and the counters, even from some of the chairs, he removed jars, platters, bowls, and pots of food, more food than this small family could consume in a month, opened the icebox, filled the shelves, discarded, and set straight.

"Come, Pa," he said when he was finished, "you've been sitting there all day. It's bad for your circulation. You have to get up and walk around. Are you hungry, Leo? There's enough food here for an army."

"I ate at Bobby's house. No, I'm going to bed."

"Pa and Adam and I will be out on the porch if you need us. Pa needs fresh air."

"You treat him like a baby," Pa grumbled when Leo had left the room.

"Sometimes that's what he wants. At

least, I think he does," Jonathan replied. "We haven't yet learned to read people's minds."

Outside it was still light enough for roller skates on the street. Two boys doing remarkable leaps and circles were delighted with Jonathan's applause from the porch.

"Do it again, will you, guys? Pirouettes! You're good enough for vaudeville. You're great."

"Pirouettes. That's what it's called?" A little smile broke over Pa's frozen face. "Fancy words my sons speak. Pirouettes. I'll bet those kids never heard the word."

Magic words, thought Adam. It's Jon who somehow or other always knows the magic words. And he looked at his father's sad old face, where a smile still lingered.

When the roller skaters had gone, an old couple came along walking together. As he watched them, Pa murmured something to himself. As full darkness arrived, the silence was broken only by the buzz and creak of rocking chairs.

After a while, Pa spoke. "The quiet, the quiet. All the good people today, all the talk. But I needed the quiet. And I have to say something now: I am so thankful for you both."

"And for Leo," Jonathan said. "He's angry that Mom died, angry at the world. But we can't know what the future will bring, can we?"

What future? Adam demanded in silence. Fifty years from now? Who has all that uncertain time to wait? I'm thinking of tomorrow morning, to say nothing of next year, when Jonathan would be away in college. What would happen to Pa and Leo? I don't have enough money to take Pa and Leo out west, to live with me.

"You must be tired after this long day," Pa said. "You had a long trip. Go on up to bed, Adam. I guess it will feel strange to be in it again after so long."

It felt so strange, so troubling, that he could not fall asleep. Yet he must have dozed for a few minutes now and then, because when he opened his eyes, he remembered shreds and pieces of disjointed, implausible dreams. He saw Rachel in the apron she had worn every day except Saturday, when she went to the synagogue in a silk dress and a necklace of amber beads. He saw himself taking his little brothers to the merry-go-round; Leo was excited, his homely face screwed into a laugh that touched him, Adam, with a sadness he had not then been able to explain, nor could he do it very well now. Mrs. R. was standing next to Leo, both of them in tears, Leo for reasons unknown, and she because her husband had hurt her. And Emma was trying to comfort them both.

Now he was wide awake. These senseless dreams came from being overtired. It is said by some that dreams are never really senseless, that if you take the disjointed sections apart and rearrange them properly, they will make sense.

His thoughts returned to Emma. You could see that Emma Rothirsch was a compassionate person. Her anger had burned not on behalf of herself, but on behalf of the old lady. He wondered whether the accusations were true. But of course they must be, for what sense or advantage would there be in making such things up? And that anger of Emma's had been genuine. There could be no mistaking it.

He had an idea that she was a very positive person. Women should have the vote. There should be wine in the soup. In the darkness he smiled to himself. She had a funny little laugh that curved her fine lips and her pretty teeth. She speaks perfect French, one of the saleswomen had said. And then there was that matter of the piano. Could Mrs. R. be right about her talent?

Oh, Adam, what do you know about her? You're only curious because of who she is. At heart she's no different from anybody else. She's no better than Fannie or Geraldine or anyone, except that she's better educated. So what is the fascination? It's nonsense.

A beam of light from the moon as it sailed through a cloud, or else from a new streetlamp on the corner, shot through the gloom and struck a wet spot on the ceiling. He had wondered about the bucket on the floor near the window. In the morning he'd have to talk to Pa about the price of a new roof.

When the beam of light shifted, it struck another spot on the floor where something lay, a shadow . . . It seemed to take on the shape of a sleeping dog. For there he was, that old friend Arthur, lying exactly how and where he had lain on another night years and years ago.

But the mind plays queer tricks, Jonathan says. I've been too long away from this house, anyway. It isn't home anymore. My thoughts are whirling. Let me go back to work. Let me get back to my home in Chattahoochee.

"You've been here for two days," Pa said, "so don't apologize for leaving. There's nothing you can do here anyway, Adam. You can't bring her back. And you mustn't risk your job."

As usual, they were all in the kitchen. And everyone looked toward Rachel's chair. Leo seemed even smaller than Adam remembered, bringing to his mind a child he had recently seen lost and bewildered in a crowd.

"She would want you all to go on with your lives and to learn to be happy again," Adam said, wanting to be tender, feeling tender, and yet in the next moment afraid he had been only pompous and trite.

Leo nodded, and Adam rushed on, if only to fill the painful silence. "You're a big help to Pa in the store, Leo. He tells me so all the time in his letters."

"The store!" Pa interrupted. "I'll give myself to the end of the week. Then it's got to be opened, or customers will get used to going someplace else. I'll have to pull myself together. I will."

He looks like a man in his seventies, Adam thought, and he's not yet sixty.

"Pa, take a rest. When have you ever had one? Let either Jon or Leo run the store for a few weeks. Jon can go after school, and Leo can manage the other hours."

Now Jonathan intervened. "I don't agree. It would be better for Pa to go right back to work. What else would he do with himself but sit here alone and think all day? Work is medicine, an anodyne."

Anodyne. Spoken like a doctor, Jon.

"Leo and I will help as always, Leo more than I do, as always," Jonathan said.

A faint smile touched Leo's woebegone face as he nodded, and Adam, seeing it, was moved to put his arms around his brother's shoulders, telling him that he *knew* he would be a help to Pa in this hard time.

"Mom would want you to help him, Leo.

She loved us all so much, and she wanted us to love one another."

Well, if I sound like a preacher, I can't help it, Adam thought. Sometimes the deepest truths can be embarrassing.

"When is your train? What time do you have to leave?" Pa asked.

"There's a lot of cold food here that needs to be eaten up. How about taking it outside and having a picnic before you go?" suggested Jonathan.

Clearly Jonathan was the one who would hold things together. But how, Adam worried, would it be after next year when he was gone?

Oh, sufficient unto the day . . . The morning is cool and bright. The green grass hasn't yet burned brown. In the icebox there's ice cream, made by Rachel. She would want us to eat it.

So they had their picnic. Neighbors, seeing them outside, came over to liven the little party. When it ended, they drove Adam to the ferry, which cut short the painful farewells.

Just as on the first time, he stood on the deck and watched the town slide away. He had had only one emotion then: a tremendous, overwhelming excitement. It had all been so *easy*! But now he had grown older—oh, a century older. And now there was the family here, the business there, and money to be earned, and Mrs. R. to satisfy, and Emma . . .

It wasn't easy anymore.

Chapter 7

Receipts and bills must be retained for three years, said Theo Brown, cautious accountant. Accordingly, one summer Sunday Adam opened a bottom drawer that was the only disorderly place in his orderly little room, and began to throw things away. It surprised him to find that among the pile of papers he had saved were a few personal letters, and curious now as to why he saved them, he opened the envelopes and began to read.

Dear Adam,
I found your check on my bed after you left. I only have to mention a thing and you take care of it, or did I mention the hole in the roof? I forget. Maybe you saw the buckets on the floor. Anyway, I thank you. Always, always, I thank you.

*It should be the other way around, God
knows.*

*We had a terrible two weeks, but now
in the third week I am pulling myself
together. Rachel talks to me. You have
to do your work and go on, she says.
It's God's will, she says. You mustn't
question it. She always knew all about
His will, but I don't know. Anyhow, I go
to the store every day. Leo helps, but
as soon as we close, he goes over to
the Nishikawas' house. So if he is
happy there, it's better for all of us.
Jonathan is the same. He and I fix our
supper together, and the neighbor
ladies help us so much. He is busy with
midterm examinations and will write
soon.*

Take care of yourself,

Pa

I saved this, I suppose, Adam thought, because I was moved by the sadness and the
courage. Yes, I remember.

There were two letters from Jonathan
dated only a few months ago, and not at all
sad.

Dear Adam,

I am squeezing this in between two exams, this morning's in biochemistry and tomorrow's in physics. It's tough stuff, but I am doing all right. I can't believe I am almost at the end of my first year in an Ivy League university. Here I am, poor in my own right, helpless without your help, in an Ivy League university! I know you don't like to have me thank you, but now and then I feel the need to, so don't be annoyed.

I get home every couple of weeks on a Sunday because it means so much to Pa. Leo and he, from what I can see, have made a kind of truce. When Leo is not with the Nishikawas for supper, he reads a book and Pa reads the paper, both of them together in the kitchen. Pa says they do have a blowup now and then, but it ends as it always did with Leo going up to his room. He seems to be studying something, Pa thinks, although maybe all of his books are for entertainment. He keeps them in a locked trunk, so I have no idea what they are. I feel so sorry for him, and I'm sure Pa does, too—when he's not angry.

All those rumors about the Cace Clothiers merger still floating around? I hope they aren't worrying you in any way.

I'm thinking of taking summer classes. If they can save me some time so that I could graduate sooner and go to medical school sooner, I would like to try it. But it's rather complicated, so I'll have to make sure.

I miss you so much, Adam. Friends are fine, and I have made some good ones, but there is nobody like a brother. Love,

Jon

And this I saved because "there is nothing like a brother"—a brother like Jon. What is it about him? He's serious, he's joyous, he's practical, and what else? Humane. Yes, that was Jon. Humane.

He had certainly not expected to find, at the bottom of the pile, a two-year-old letter postmarked in a small New England town, nor one written in a fine Spencerian hand on fine linen-woven paper and signed "Emma Rothirsch."

Dear Mr. Arnring,

I have been thinking about our conversation on the train last week, and am so distressed by some of the things I said about my aunt's life, that I feel I must write to you and try to explain myself. You probably know that it is often easier to talk freely to a stranger, or to a person who is almost a stranger, than to a person whom one sees every day. Still, it was very wrong of me to inflict such an emotional outburst upon you. But there was something about you that led me to confide in you things I have never told anyone, nor ever will again. It was not the way I usually behave. I am embarrassed by it, and I apologize to you.

I know that your time at home must have been very difficult for you and your family. They say that time does help to heal, so I hope this will be true for all of you. Sincerely,

Emma Rothirsch

Adam put the letter down, looked at it, wondered why he had kept it, then took it up and read it again. He recalled having written an acknowledgment, but had not heard from her or even seen her since then.

As he now threw it away, he felt a twinge of—something—he could not say exactly what.

This was a fine summer morning, though, and not a time for introspection. It was a time to get moving, and he did.

After he had bought the Ford Model T and learned to drive it, he had gotten in the habit of taking it out on the road with no destination in mind. Whizzing along at twenty miles an hour, he could feel the wind whip his cheeks, hear the thrum of the powerful engine, and recall the very different pleasure of listening to a horse's clip-clop. Now, whenever he stopped for gas, he remembered that other way when you stopped to water the horse, knock the flies off his back, and let him rest in the shade. He supposed you could make a good argument for either way.

Sassafras trees were thick along the roadside. From local children, he had learned the habit of chewing their fragrant twigs; in fact, he had a couple in his pocket right now. It was small acts like this that made him feel like a native; he had acquired a liking for certain local foods and had even become aware that his casual speech was dotted with local expressions. Already he had lived here long enough to note changes, for right now, on either side of the road where mules had striven through the fields, there were more tractors than mules. Every day there were more automobiles in the streets, and a few new houses were going up in the outskirts as the town spread toward the capital.

Here I stay. This is it for me. This is my place. And this is my day. No business, no worrying about Leo and Pa, or anything. Just live. Enjoy.

Near the river's edge, he stopped the car and took his things—lunch, blanket, and book—down the slope to his favorite spot, where he spread the blanket and leaned his back against a tree trunk.

Far down the river some boys were swimming, while in the other direction a man was casting a line for fish. If he had not felt a cold coming on, he would have been swimming, too, but a head cold was not an attractive thing to bring to work on Monday morning. He sneezed; the sound startled a pair of coots that were floating in shallow water close to the shore, and with a loud flap of wings, they skimmed away down the river.

The first time he'd ever seen a coot, he had been with Fannie, and called it a "duck," which she had corrected. It was a bird, she had insisted, and they had had a funny argument about that until he had looked up the subject and found that she was right.

As always, he had fun and laughter with Fannie. She had never wanted anything from him but fun, no hints by word or gesture about marriage, only a good time. Right! So settle down, Adam, eat, read your book. And at the end of this perfect day, go dancing with Fannie, or else go see Mary Pickford in her new movie.

Some hours later he was having a beer at the popular bar, the same one he had visited on his arrival in the town, when Jeff Horace hailed him.

"Where've you been all day? I've been looking everywhere for you."

"Loafing. Why? What's up?"

"What's up is that there's a war. The paper got a call through Associated Press. It's England, France, and Russia against Germany and Austria. Well, the Kaiser's been waiting for war for a long time, and now he's got it."

"All the young men who are going to die . . ." Adam said, shaking his head. "I wonder whether we'll get into it."

"Not a chance." Jeff gave an equivalent shake of the head. "What business is it of ours? No, Wilson will be neutral. Absolutely. He'll keep us out." Then, as he turned away, Jeff remembered something. "They tell me that the old lady has sent a cable. She and the niece are sailing for home tomorrow."

Chapter 8

Some ten days later, Adam received a plea from Rudy, the butler or houseman—he was not quite sure what the man's title might be—at the Rothirsch house. Rudy was supposed to meet the Missus and Miss Emma, who were arriving at the capital station that afternoon. The problem was that he, Rudy, had given himself a bad cut on his arm this morning, and it was so bandaged up that he wasn't able to drive the car. He had been trying to get somebody who could take his place and hadn't had any luck. Then his wife, Rea, had thought he might ask a favor of Adam. She had bought a couple of Christmas presents in the shop and thought Adam was very friendly. Besides, the new car was a Pierce-Arrow, and Mrs. R. wouldn't want just any unknown person to drive it.

"When I first saw you, you were driving a Stanley Steamer," Adam said.

"That's a long time ago. They're passé—if that's the right word. Anyway, that's what Mrs. R. says. Passé. The Pierce-Arrow is modern, a handmade car, very valuable."

Well, flattered though he might be, Adam was the owner of a Model T Ford and wasn't sure he knew how to drive a Pierce-Arrow. But he needn't worry. Rudy would explain; it was really quite simple.

Accordingly, Adam found himself later that afternoon at the wheel of a luxurious, gray town car, in which the passengers sat in comfort, while the chauffeur's seat was out-doors in the weather with, of course, a roof of rainproof cloth that could if needed be hastily attached. Mounds of luggage, along with Mrs. R. in duster and veil, occupied the rear seat, while beside him, to Mrs. R.'s con-sternation, sat Emma, also wearing a duster, but no hat or veil; her vivid hair, blown loose by the wind, streamed behind her.

"Your hair," screamed Mrs. R., who could barely be heard. "How does it look, riding in a car like this in the chauffeur's seat without even a proper hat on? I bought you one for motoring. What happened to it?"

Emma screamed back against the wind, "I lost it!" and then added, murmuring to herself, "Didn't look too hard to find it, either, the ugly thing."

"Emma! Your hair! Now, if you had had a permanent the way I wanted you to, but no—" The voice died.

"In case you're wondering," Emma explained, "she's talking about a machine that keeps hair in tight curls for a long time. They do it in France—somebody invented it there years ago. She thinks I would look better with curls."

Adam's sidelong glance caught her mischievous, soundless laughter. She's changed, he thought. No, not fundamentally changed, but there's a difference. Of course, she's two years older. A lot happens in two years. Even with his attention well fastened to the unfamiliar car, he was still able to take some more sidelong glances. Her long, supple fingers lay clasped on a purse and a book, obscuring the title, which seemed to begin with a *V.*

All of a sudden, she moved her hand, looked up at him, and exclaimed, "There. Now you can see. It's *Vanity Fair.*"

It's actually true, he thought, that you can

feel your own flush crawl up your neck. He could swear that never before had he felt quite so hot.

"You have X-ray eyes," he said.

"No. I only knew you love to read, so you'd be curious about the book. Have you ever read it? It's marvelous. I've met a lot of Becky Sharps."

"No, but now I'm going to read it."

In the very second when he looked toward her, she looked toward him. Then each turned away. If the old lady had not been in the seat behind them, would we have held the look? he wondered.

They had had one long-ago encounter in a dining car. She had aroused his curiosity then, and was doing it again now. Was she still devoted to the piano? Almost surely, she must attract many men. Still, she wore no engagement ring, no rings at all. He seemed to remember a gold bracelet. In each ear, a tiny diamond sparkled. When her coat parted, there was a narrow glimpse of a plain blue cotton shirt, bought perhaps in their own moderate-priced department? She puzzled him.

He was conscious of awkwardness. Any- one seeing them would assume that, despite the absence of a cap, he must be the chauffeur, which was fine with him; it was only because he was *not* the chauffeur that he felt awkward. Surely he should be finding something of interest to talk about.

Through the rearview mirror, he could see that the old lady, sitting correctly upright, was dozing. So he broke the silence.

"How was it in England? What's the spirit?"

"I suppose that depends on how much a person understands. A lot of the young men are raring to go to the great adventure. Others are quoting Lord Grey, who's supposed to have said that night, 'The lamps are going out all over Europe.' And something about how we'd never see them as bright again."

"Do you believe that? Do you believe we'll be in it? Most people I've talked to say we won't."

"Oh, I believe we'll have to. Germany is very powerful. I've been there twice, and for three months studying piano in Vienna. It seemed to me that they looked forward to war. It's a proud business. Manly. Noble. Losing both legs. Having your face shot away. Being a widow with the man's baby on the way. Ah, the poor souls, I'm crying for them already."

Adam was not thinking so much of what she said as of the fact she was saying it. The women he knew did not talk like this.

"What are you going to do, now that you're finished with college?" he asked.

"Going back for an M.A., a double in Music Education and Performing Arts."

"No conservatory?"

"I'm not good enough. I told you that, remember?"

"I remember that you were sorry about disappointing your aunt."

"I'm still sorry, or I will be when she finally understands the difference between the M.A. I want to earn and the worldwide fame she wants for me."

"Emma!" came the voice. "How can you expect the man to keep his eyes on the road when you keep chattering?"

"You'd better go back to your book," Adam said, and Emma sighed.

At the house Rudy came out with greetings and apologies. He had finally gotten hold of the gardener's helper, who would be able to unload the luggage in the morning.

Not at all, Adam objected. He would take care of it right now.

"There's a lot of heavy stuff," roared Mrs. R.

If they knew how many crates of potatoes and canned soup he had lifted in his day! And with a smile, he waved her away.

So, for only the second time since he had known Mrs. R., he entered her vast, gloomy house, piled luggage where directed, and accepted the welcome offer of a cold drink.

Emma suggested that they have it on the porch. "It's too hot and stuffy indoors."

Mrs. R. corrected her. "It's hot because it's summer. But it is not stuffy in this house. It never is."

She sat down on a wicker rocking chair and complained. "I certainly didn't think we'd have to cut our vacation short like this. War! There's no sense in it. I had a marvelous treat ready for Emma, too, a surprise, with music from some of the greatest stars in Wales. I can't remember their names right now, but they're world famous. Someday people will be going to festivals where Emma will be the star. I don't think anybody around here realizes it, but she has a brilliant talent. Even she doesn't realize it, but I do.

Yes. A brilliant talent, with a great career ahead."

Adam remarked with enthusiasm that he certainly hoped so. But it had apparently been the wrong thing to say, because the reply was every so slightly sharp.

"Hope so? I *know* so. Everyone who's heard her at the piano—people in the musical world—knows it, too."

"That's what I meant," he apologized.

"She must let nothing stand in her way. And I will let nothing stand in her way. She's my whole life."

Emma's hands were knotted together on her knees. It is taking all her control to keep quiet, Adam thought. And he wondered about the entangled relationships under this roof.

"If you want a true musical culture, you have to go to Europe," Mrs. R. continued. "We need to spend another summer abroad next year. We'll go to Salzburg, naturally, and—well, we'll miss nothing. This stupid war will be over by then, actually by Christmas, they say. Can we get you another cold glass, Mr. Arnring?"

"No. No, thank you."

He was thirsty and would have welcomed

one, but his need to get away was greater than his thirst. So as no one urged him to linger, he stood up, gave his thanks, and left.

Then from far down the street, where earlier in the day he had parked his car and was now cranking up the starter before jumping into the driver's seat, he saw Emma coming out of her house. She was standing in the doorway, looking right and left. Thinking that she might be looking for him, he pretended not to see her, turned, and drove away in the opposite direction. Entangled relationships! Did he not have enough of them with Leo and Pa?

Besides, he was almost late for his evening with Fannie.

Chapter 9

"It's been over a year, almost two maybe, isn't it, Adam, since I first mentioned Cace Clothiers to you?" asked Theo Brown.

"About that. But then, nothing ever seems to come of it."

On Brown's desk lay the usual manila folders with piles of the bills, receipts, and sundries that Adam brought in once a month to the company's accountant.

"Mrs. R. wasn't interested, you remember? Definitely not interested. The approach was only tentative anyway, nothing seriously official. But it looks now as if they're really ready for action."

"I'm not surprised. Every item we sell is one they used to sell."

"You're doing a great job, Adam. The windows, the seasonal displays, the advertising, all great. And every time Jeff Horace squeezes something into the newspaper, like that article about the Elks last week, where the singer was outfitted by Rothirsch's—well, it surely doesn't hurt. And I know you're pleased."

Adam was greatly pleased. "Jeff Horace is a great friend of mine. I'll tell you, I honestly believe he's responsible for my getting this job in the first place. It was that article in the paper that got it for me the very next day."

"Okay. But it's all your work since then that's kept the job for you. A doctor took a crippled child, put him back on his feet, and got him winning races. That's you."

Naturally Adam was touched by this praise. But he had always been comfortable in this office. His orderly nature took pleasure in Theo's precision, all those files in neat rows and the figures coming out just right every time, all these plus the fact that Theo obviously liked him.

He was a man about Pa's age, Adam estimated after a glance at the diplomas on the wall, but he looked twenty years younger than Pa. His expression, unlike Pa's which so plainly revealed fatigue and worry, was hearty and friendly.

"So to get back to the subject. Spencer

Lawrence, Mrs. R.'s lawyer—have you ever met him?"

Had Adam ever been introduced to Lawrence? No. How would a middle-level— very middle-level—employee in a local store ever get to meet a man like Lawrence, advisor to political figures and private fortunes?

But he had seen and heard him often enough at those evenings in Francine's place. A dapper gentleman, Lawrence was, correct and somewhat chilly; learned, too. He had drawn circles about himself to hear him speak about the war in Europe and the federal income tax, both of which he had predicted. More than once, Adam had stood unnoticed on the fringe of such a circle.

"No, I've never met him," he answered.

"Well, he's just asked me for the store's financial documents going back to Mr. R.'s time. Cace has been talking about moving your place next to theirs in the city and combining them, which would mean rebuilding, and a very expensive job. The reverse might be to buy that old building around the corner from yours, tear it down, and rebuild, also an expensive job. Which of them would cost more, I don't know, but you get the idea. Either way, it would cost plenty. The

result, though, would be the most important, prestigious store in the whole state."

"What does Mrs. R. say about it?"

"She can't seem to make up her mind. You
know how she is."

"Actually, I don't know. She and I never do
more than say hello when she walks through
the store."

"It comes down to money in the end.
She's old, and old folks are afraid to spend."

Pa, Adam thought. *A penny saved is a
penny got.*

"I suppose," Theo continued, "she doesn't
feel the need for earning anymore. There's
more than enough for their lifestyle, all the
tuitions and traveling . . . That's a beautiful
girl, don't you think?"

"She's unusual," Adam said briefly, not
wanting to talk about Emma Rothirsch.

"Nevertheless," continued Brown, returning to the subject, "with this new income
tax, you never can tell. Once a tax is levied,
it's bound to rise. So it only makes sense, it
seems to me, some sense and my obligation as an advisor, to encourage the
merger."

Adam was wondering how his own job

would be affected if it were to be done, when Theo went on.

"The reason I'm telling you is that if you should hear any more talk about the deal, about plans, I don't want you to worry. No-body's taking your job while I'm around. I was your age once, starting up the ladder and worried that somebody might push me off, so I know."

Adam was touched as on occasion a son may be touched by his father's concerns for him. "Thank you, Theo," he said simply. "Thank you more than I can say."

"Well, I've known you a long time, and I like you, Adam. If I had a son, I'd want him to be like you, smart, hardworking, and hon-orable," Theo responded as he stood and began to clear the desk. "On a lighter note, I hope the poor old lady won't wear herself out jaunting all over New England this sum-mer."

"Going to visit her niece, I suppose?" Adam asked.

"Who else? Emma's the only reason for all her trips."

"I haven't seen Emma since they came back from Europe last year."

"The time will come when you'll never see

her. Once she's got her M.A., she'll find somebody important to marry and settle herself in New York, London, or Paris, if the war's over. Far from here, anyway, you can bet on that. In fact, Mrs. R. did drop a little hint about a man in London. Well, I'm off to lunch. Take care."

Outdoors it was unmistakably May. Lilacs, tulips, and women's hats, along with small boys playing baseball in a schoolyard, proclaimed the season. It was a happy kind of day, and Adam felt happy as he walked the familiar streets, nodding and greeting and being greeted.

Tonight he was taking a new girl out for the evening. Maybelle Munoz, she was half Spanish, dark and exotic. Maybe she would want a Mexican dinner with plenty of hot pepper; on the other hand, since her mother was American, she might be as unused to spices as he was. They'd be driving to the capital; the old Interurban was no more, with its schedules and timetables. You were your own boss now.

That's what he was thinking when after stopping an instant to admire the striped tulips, imported from Holland, in the new window boxes, he stepped through the revolving doors into the Rothirsch store. There, pausing again to look around at the subdued color and glitter of expensive goods, he felt a rush of satisfaction.

There would be no need for many sales days this year. Merchandise at regular prices was flying out of the store.

"Hello, Mr. Arnring. We meet again," Emma Rothirsch said brightly. "Do you remember me?"

"I certainly do. Haven't you got somebody to wait on you?" he asked hastily, for she was carrying a pile of garments in her arms.

"Oh, I like to help myself."

He recognized her choices as she walked away. They were all from the budget side of the store, where a bicycle skirt cost three dollars, linen skirts cost four, and kid gloves were ninety-eight cents a pair. Strange, he thought, comparing her with her aunt, who bought twenty yards of imported satin for an afternoon dress to be made by her own dressmaker.

When Emma had paid for her purchases in cash and the pneumatic tube was sailing across the ceiling toward the cashier upstairs, he was surprised again: Mrs. R. had a charge account, as was only to be expected.

"I see you're looking at what I've bought," Emma said. "You won't make a lot of money from people like me, will you?"

"On the contrary. There are more people in the world who buy cheaper clothes than there are who buy designers' dresses."

"I think it's a great idea that you put in a low-price department. I used to feel conspicuous when I was younger and wore such elegant clothes in school. Nobody else did. So this really was your idea, I suppose?"

"Well, yes, since you ask, it was."

Her hair must have blown in the breeze, for a few waving strands hung loose around her neck. It seemed to him—perhaps because of their color?—that they would be warm to the touch. And with this thought, he felt immediately foolish.

"Have you had lunch? It would be nice to continue our interrupted conversations if you haven't."

My God, but she's bold, he thought, and thought again, as if to correct himself, she's not really bold, just inexperienced—or could one say naive?—not to see the difference between this place and the train and the chauffeur's seat on the Pierce-Arrow.

"I hear there's a very good new place behind the courthouse. All the lawyers eat there now."

He wavered. The last time he had seen her, she was at the front door of her house, apparently looking for him. And what had he done? He had turned his car around and fled away down the street. Why? Because he feared the old lady. Trembling in his boots, that's what he was doing. Had he no self-respect? And after the praise Theo Brown had given him half an hour ago? The girl was charming; he had been struck by her charm, as any man would be, from the very first time he had seen her. But, my God, he wasn't trying to seduce her! So what could be wrong with a lunch? All this went through his mind in a few seconds, while standing at the counter waiting for Emma's change to return on the pneumatic tube.

He looked at his watch. "It's twelve-thirty. I have one telephone call to make, so if you don't mind waiting five minutes—"

"Mr. Arnring," said Reilly, who had come up behind them, "you have an appointment at one with those shoe people. Oh, how are you, Miss Rothirsch? Back home for a while, are you? It's good to see you."

"You're wrong, Mr. Reilly. That appointment is for next week. Next Tuesday, not today."

Reilly smiled. "I'm afraid you're mistaken, Mr. Arnring. It really is for today, the seventh."

"You're sure? I have a pretty good memory."

"I'm sure, Mr. Arnring."

There was something in the steady fixation of Reilly's widened eyes that conveyed a message: *Listen to me.*

"Well," Adam said, "I guess that's it, Miss Rothirsch. No lunch today. I'm awfully sorry."

She smiled. "Another time."

She took her packages. Reilly leaped ahead to hold the revolving door for her, and returned.

"What the deuce is this?" demanded Adam. "That appointment's for next week, and you know it."

In the back of the shoe department among the shelves and stacks, Reilly spoke his piece.

"Adam, you can't play around with that girl. It's a good thing I happened to walk out there in time to hear you."

"Who's playing around? What the hell are you talking about?" Anger, such as he rarely felt, was hot in Adam.

"How can you even think of being seen with Mrs. R.'s girl? Seen in a place where anybody—that guy Lawrence, her lawyer, goes there. I read a piece in the paper last week in that gossip column about some meeting they had there, somebody from the governor's office or someplace. *'Oh, I saw Adam Arnring the other day having lunch with your Emma, Mrs. R.'*—can you imagine it? Geez, you might as well quit before she kicks you the hell out."

Now Adam's anger exploded. "You have no right to talk to me this way, Reilly. We've been good friends, but that doesn't give you the right to interfere in my private life and to scold me. Who do you think I am, your kid, or your neighbor's kid who spilled paint on your sidewalk or something? I'm still the manager here, remember?"

Reilly said calmly, "Yes, I remember, Mr. Arnring. I understand everything you're saying. I have not forgotten, I never forget, that you are the manager of this business. For now, you are. I know what dignity belongs here in this store, and I've never stepped out of my proper place. I'm doing this because you're only in your twenties, and I could be your father. I don't want to see you throw away everything you've earned on account of this girl."

"I have no intention of doing so," Adam said stiffly.

"People don't *intend* to fall in love. It happens. If you don't stop it before it happens, if you get my meaning. That girl likes you too much. It's plain as the nose on your face."

"That's nonsense. She hardly knows me."

"You don't have to *know* a person to fall for him. It can happen in ten minutes. That's the sad part of it. Look at the mess poor Archer got himself into with that wife he's got. You fall, and you can't pick yourself up again. Make believe for one minute that I'm your father and listen to me. If he was here, he'd say the same thing."

Maybe he would. Maybe that's what happened to him, and I'm the result of it.

"I haven't fallen for her. I have no plans to marry Miss Emma Rothirsch, only to have lunch with her."

"Adam, don't be stubborn. The old lady's got great plans for Emma. And you need money! You need to remember that there isn't a blasted soul on earth who can't be replaced. When McKinley was shot, we got another president in five minutes, didn't we?"

Adam was silent. He was beginning to feel a little ashamed. His pride had been affronted, and by whom? By Jim Reilly, who wouldn't be here if it weren't for him, Adam Arnring. But then . . . Perhaps he had been getting a trifle smug about his position? And looking back into the earnest face of this good man standing now between himself and a row of shoe boxes, this good man who had never reached and would never reach even as low a position as he, Adam, now held, he felt a wave of remorse.

"I'm sorry," he said. "I lost my temper, and it was stupid of me. I know you mean the best for me. You always have."

"You've meant the same for me, Adam."

"Yes. Yes, you're right. You were reminding me of my needs. There's my father . . . He's losing his health. There's my brother in college . . . And there's the other one, I've told you about him, so strange, poor guy . . . Yes, I do need money."

Reilly sighed. "Don't we all? But you've taken on very big responsibilities, Adam."

"How could I not take them on?"

"A lot of sons your age would know how not to. Well, that's it. I have customers waiting for shoes."

For a moment they stood looking out at the pleasant bustle of shoppers moving through the bright display. Then each went on his way.

Chapter 10

Looking back at the course of a journey, whether it is a cross-country trip or the map of a lifetime, it is easy to see the point at which, unrecognized by the travelers, a small event made an abrupt and drastic change in direction.

So it was for Adam Arnring in the autumn of 1915. At that time across the ocean, young men by the thousands were suffering and dying. But that was far away, and in the sunny, peaceful town of Chattahoochee, hard to envision.

One day when it was not sunny, he was walking home in a drizzle, thinking about the recent increase in his salary and about Doris Buckley, the girl with whom he had spent the last six months, which was the longest stretch of time he had ever devoted solely to any one woman. She was a lovely, quiet person, intelligent and pretty, a country girl who had come to town as a doctor's receptionist and to live where Adam lived, in the house that belonged to her grandparents.

Theirs had been an easy relationship from the beginning. The Buckleys had long been treating Adam not so much as a tenant but as a young friend, inviting him to share Sunday supper anytime when he "had nothing better to do," as Mrs. Buckley would say. So, when Doris appeared, all of this remained the same, only more so.

Now as he walked through the gathering rain, Adam reflected upon all those movie nights, the country rides in his "Tin Lizzie," the visits to the ice cream parlor, the hours spent "passing the time of day" with the old folks on the front porch. They would be wondering soon, if they had not already done so, when he was going to propose to Doris. It was only natural; she was twenty-three, almost twenty-four, and once a girl reached twenty-five without being married, she was over the hill.

When are you going to get married? Pa wrote. *You never even mention a steady girl. You're twenty-seven and a half. It's time to stop just running around. Jonathan's only halfway through college, and he has a won-*

derful girl, Blanche Berman, a beauty, a relative of Berman the tailor. I wouldn't be surprised if they got married someday. I'd be surprised if they didn't.

Well, maybe I will, Adam thought. I certainly miss Doris when she goes home to spend a few days. I've gotten so that I expect to see her when I come down the street. She'll be either weeding the flower patch in the front yard or else sitting on the porch with the newspaper or a book. Then I know she's not so much reading or weeding as waiting for me, although she would never show it because a woman isn't supposed to let a man know.

He smiled to himself, and reflected that she really was a sweet young woman. She liked what he liked; she took long country hikes and she read good books that they could talk about. Pa's right, he thought. What am I waiting for? She was probably wondering what was taking him so long. He decided to bring up the subject next week, maybe Sunday.

A gust of rain drenched Adam's head as he stepped off the curb. A horn blew, a car stopped, and a voice called, "Watch out, Mr. Arnring, I almost ran over you."

The little electric car was noiseless of course, but he had not been paying attention, and feeling foolish, he was prepared to apologize when the door opened and Emma Rothirsch summoned him inside.

"Please! This is a downpour. Get in."

At least it wasn't Mrs. R. at the tiller. He got in and remarked that he had not seen this car around the neighborhood in a long time.

"She's getting too old to drive it. Her sight's bad. Unless I get home now and then to use it, it stands in the garage. Where can I take you?"

"I was going home, out near the boulevard. But that's too far for you, Miss Rothirsch."

She smiled. It looked to Adam as though her whole face smiled, not only the lips, but the eyes and the rounding of the cheeks; all sparkled.

"Adam," she said, "you're making me laugh. Isn't it time that young people of our age should stop this 'Mr.' and 'Miss' business? You're Adam and I'm Emma."

He was very uncomfortable. This was behavior he could never have expected; he was sorry he had accepted the ride, and he did not answer.

"Tell me something. Is it my aunt and your job that you're worried about?" When he still did not answer, she continued, "Yes, it is. Well, I promise you that I would never let her know that we are Adam and Emma. Not that or anything else, although you may be surprised to know that her bite is nowhere nearly as dangerous as her bark."

Even on the ride back from the railroad station that time, he had not felt so uncomfortable.

"You turn left here," he said hurriedly, "then three blocks in."

"I'm not letting you out just yet in this deluge. Tell me, what are you afraid of? We've met a few times, four to be exact, counting the times when I was still in high school. And each time I've had the feeling that we could be friends. I've wanted to talk to you, and I knew you wanted to talk to me."

"How could you possibly have known that?"

"Simply by the way you looked at me. That time I suggested lunch at the restaurant in back of the courthouse, you were ready to go until Mr. Reilly stopped you with his fib about another appointment. I knew that he was afraid for you, but I couldn't get too annoyed with him. I've known him since I was in kindergarten. He always had a chocolate lollipop for me."

I feel, Adam thought, like a—like somebody on a speeding sled who's trying to stop it before it crashes into a tree.

"You did want to go that day, didn't you? If I'm mistaken, please tell me. If you think it was 'forward' of me to invite you, please say so." Having stopped the car, she was able to turn, look at him, and draw an answer from him.

"Well, not exactly forward, but—"

"But unwise. Tactless. I guess it was. But listen to me. If you had been the son of the owner and I a saleswoman, you would think differently about it. Probably you might not have made the invitation as public as I did, but that's the only difference. It's the man's way versus the woman's. Perhaps that will change someday, I don't know, but it won't for a long time, if it ever does. It will be long after I'm around, I'm sure."

Adam smiled. He could see the justice—and the humor—in her remarks.

"Well, isn't it true that I shouldn't be talking like this because women are not allowed to be as free as I'm being? Now tell me, isn't it?"

Unwillingly, he replied that he supposed so.

"Oh, Adam. I don't want anything from you! This is totally, totally innocent. If you think I'm dying for a man, you're all wrong. I have more invitations, decent invitations, with nice men, than I can use. Most of them, I don't accept. I've wanted only to be your friend. I've felt that way about you from the start."

"But how could you feel that way, or any way, when you don't know a thing about me?"

She threw up her hands. On one arm he recognized the gold bracelet. She was telling him about fish soup. She was walking away with her hand on the edge of her narrow skirt. And he was standing there until she had gone out of sight.

"You go into a room full of people you've never seen before, and there among the crowd you find the ones, or the one, whom you want to know. That's true, isn't it?"

A fierce burst of rain hammered the roof of the car and laid a gray sheet over the windows. It would be senseless for him to step out into such a storm. So they sat, close enough for him to become aware of perfume, one of those fragrances that were advertised with discreet references to the goddess Aphrodisia.

It was his turn to speak, and he decided to take a chance.

"What do you do on Sundays, Emma?"

"I'm free next Sunday if you're interested. After that I go back east. So where shall it be?"

For a second he had a mental glimpse of that riverbank, the deep shade, the blue water, and the coots.

"How about the new little park across from the school?"

"Perfect. Let's say three o'clock. Aunt Sabine takes a nap after midday dinner, so I won't have to answer any questions about where I'm going."

As abruptly as the cloudburst had arrived, it now passed. In front of his house Adam got out of the car, thanked Emma, and went inside with a strange sense of excitement beating in his chest. Rare she was, as special and unusual as Jonathan in her way.

He was halfway up the stairs when Doris

called to him from below. "However did you manage to keep dry in that rain?"

"Somebody gave me a lift."

It was awkward to stand on the stairs that way, so he came back down. She wore such a broad, expectant smile that he couldn't help smiling back.

"You look as happy as Christmas morning," he said.

"No, no. It's my dress. I bought it at your place. Do you like it?"

Blue cotton with a white frill around the neck, it matched her eyes, and he told her so, which always pleased her.

"I thought you'd like it. I'm going to take it off now and keep it for next Sunday, but I wanted you to see it first."

"Doris, you don't have to please me or anybody," he said gently. "You must wear what you like."

"I *want* to please you. When a girl goes someplace with a man, she wants him to approve of the way she looks. It's only common sense."

Common nonsense, he thought. Or maybe it isn't. I don't know. Standing there with a faintly hurt look on her pretty face and two little lines between her eyebrows, Doris made him feel sorry for her.

"You look lovely. You always do," he said. Then a thought suddenly wrinkled his own forehead, and he exclaimed, "Sunday? Did you say Sunday?"

"Of course. My cousins Bob and Lucy, their anniversary party. Don't tell me you've forgotten."

Real distress struck him then as the palm of his hand struck his forehead, and he had to make his apology.

"Oh, my God, forgive me! I did forget. My boss has asked to see me on Sunday, and I can't refuse. There's no possible way I can refuse. You do see that, don't you?"

"Well, if you did, you did. It can happen to anybody," she said, looking woebegone. "Lucy and Bob will be disappointed. They like you so much."

So Lucy and Bob and all the rest of the relatives had been discussing him. There were few things more boring than a party with Doris's relatives. All the same, he didn't like doing this to her. But he didn't want to cancel his meeting with Emma, either. He *wanted* to meet her in the park. He wished he didn't feel so guilty about it.

"What would you like to do this evening?" he asked brightly.

"Anything you want," she answered just as brightly.

"No, you choose."

"The movies maybe?"

"Fine. The new one at the Colony downtown. I heard it's very good, but I don't really know."

Doris smiled. "Sometimes I think you know everything, Adam."

He was amused. Somebody had told her, or perhaps she had read someplace, that a woman must say such things if she wants to hold a man's interest.

"We'll go early so we can park and eat," he said.

Back in his room, he went to the window and looked down at one of his favorite sights, the birds clustered around the feeder and drinking at the bath. The Buckleys had a collie, a beautiful creature marked in brown and white; there it lay on the wet grass chewing away at a soup bone. Prince, he was named. Prince had nothing to worry him. Adam Arnring hadn't had much to worry him of late, either. But right now, although he couldn't say exactly why, he felt uneasy.

Down below, Doris was pouring clean water into the birdbath. She had changed from the new dress, wanting to save it for the anniversary party. Lightly and quickly she moved, whether there in the yard or in the kitchen; often she sang. An unexplainable pity touched his heart as he watched her now. Was it because he had lied to her about next Sunday? Was it because he feared that he might lie to her again?

But no. This encounter with Emma was as meaningless as the minor adventure of a man who stares at the star on the screen or in the great cities waits at the stage door for a sight of the prima ballerina.

He would put aside his strange mood, change his shirt, put on a good tie, go downstairs, and take Doris out for the evening.

Sunday was surprisingly hot for the season. Not surprisingly, the little park, usually crowded on a Sunday afternoon, was almost empty. Adam, arriving early, found a bench under a tree and waited. Every few minutes, he drew out his pocket watch, both wanting her to arrive and feeling apprehensive about it.

At five minutes to three, she came down the grassy walk. Her white skirt barely brushed the ground, her straw hat bore one heavy rose on the brim, and he thought instantly that he had seen such a picture before. Was it some Impressionist painting in one of the art books in that bookstore downtown? He stood, brushed off the seat with his handkerchief, and sat beside Emma on the bench. For a few moments they looked at each other in silence. Then each began to laugh.

"Isn't this ridiculous, Adam? Wanting to meet, then meeting, then having nothing to say?"

"Yes," he said, "it's not like me. I usually have a lot to say, too much sometimes, and now I can't think of anything except that you look beautiful. Like a painting."

"Thank you, but in your business, you must know I'm completely wrong for the season. One isn't supposed to wear white or a straw hat after the first of September."

"Don't worry, I won't tell anybody. By the

way, how did you get here? You didn't walk all the way?"

"Of course I did. If I had been seen in the car, I'd have had to answer too many questions. Even Rudy and Rea still keep track of me. I was two years old when they came, and they think I'm still two. But they're sweet, and I don't mind."

"How about getting into my car and going for a drive? It's parked over there at the gate."

"I'd love it. We could go out to the river. I love it there, and I never get to go. Would you like to?"

"It's my favorite spot, at the bend near the swimming hole. I go whenever I can. I take a sandwich and a book."

"Well, I can't take my clothes off and dive into the swimming hole, but I could sit on the grass and take my shoes off. They're new, and they hurt like the dickens."

The car hummed through the town onto the boulevard, then onto a dirt road, where the cottonwoods met each other overhead. Emma had put her hat on the floor, so that the wind ruffled the loose ends of her hair, as it had done that day in the store. Her russet hair, he thought.

"Since you're looking at me, let me look at you," she said. "Tell me what a man who reads good books is doing in Rothirsch's store."

"What has the one got to do with the other?" he asked.

"Commerce doesn't seem to go with reading your kind of books. I don't think my uncle ever read a book in his life outside of a ledger or a stock report."

"Well, I'm me, and he was he."

"Yes, my dear man, and it's a good thing for you that you aren't he."

"Ah, let him rest in peace," Adam retorted, as Pa would have done.

He was enjoying this girl's talk. It was spirited and yet with an underlying softness.

"Tell me, Adam, are you really interested in that store? Really?"

"I'm interested in the business. It provides a service, since people need clothing. And also, why shouldn't people make a good living out of providing the clothing?"

"But all the beautiful trinkets that cost a fortune?"

"If you can afford to buy some beauty and you're not hurting anybody, why shouldn't you do it?"

"Well, I guess so. Tell me, were you ever very poor, Adam?"

"Not starving poor. My father had—still has—a small grocery store, and we had a good home. He's an immigrant, a hard worker."

The car was bumping down the dirt road; it slowed and stopped at the spot where he always parked it, and they got out. There was nobody in sight. The afternoon was asleep, and he did not want to discuss the grocery store or anything gloomy.

"I guess you can't understand poverty very well," he said. "It's hard to describe, anyway."

"Oh, you're wrong. I was very poor when my aunt and uncle took me in. I had nothing. But you're right, we'll change the subject. First let me take off these shoes."

When she bent to do so, Adam saw her legs as high up as the knees. Whether she knew he must be seeing them, he could not tell, although she most likely did not, for there was nothing at all suggestive in her manner.

As they reclined on the grass, Emma sighed, "Ah, bliss! All that's lacking is some wonderful music."

"Piano? Your concert grand?"

"Oh, anything, even a solitary flute. But of course I love the piano best. I actually miss mine when I'm away. Universities don't provide pianos like that. It's funny, I was so annoyed when Aunt Sabine bought it."

White clouds, so gauzy that the sunlight pierced them, floated over the river; a pair of coots floated down the river; the planet floated through the blue.

For a moment they looked, and were silent. Then Emma said, "There's nothing here that's man-made except your car. It's all nature. Have you ever heard that poem: 'Nature I loved; and after Nature, Art—'?"

Into Adam's head there popped a poem that he could not have heard or read since his high school days. And he interrupted her.

" 'I warmed both hands before the fire of life—' "

" 'It sinks, and I am ready to depart,' " she finished.

Adam laughed. "You're surely not ready to depart?"

"No, not for a long time. There's too much I want to see and do."

"Such as?"

"Well, children. Most of all, I do want children. And of course, I want to make music, too."

"After you have your M.A."

"It's not long till then, only another year." And with a glance at her watch, Emma added, "We'd better start home, or they'll be worried."

On the ride back, it seemed as if the zest had gone out of the afternoon. Neither one of them said very much until they reached Emma's street, and she directed him.

"Go around to the back door, please."

He did not mind. No doubt it was better so. But he could not resist a question. "Are you so afraid of your aunt?"

"I'm not afraid of her at all, Adam. I just don't want to upset her. Anyhow, I want to go to the kitchen and get some water for that poor dog," Emma said, pointing to a small white dog that lay panting on the sidewalk. "Poor Tony. He lies on the stone to cool off. He belongs next door, and I can't stand the way they treat him. He's outdoors in this heat, and in the middle of winter, he lies outdoors freezing. I'm going to take him into the kitchen and hide him for a while."

"Why do you have to hide him?"

"Aunt Sabine won't have a dog in the house. She's afraid he'll damage something." And then came the delightful, mischievous laugh that made Adam laugh, too. "A little damage could only be an improvement, if you ask me."

"So you're leaving tomorrow?"

"Yes, bright and early. It was a lovely afternoon, Adam. Thanks so much. I'd ask you to stay awhile, but—"

"I know," he said.

But he could not let her go without one more question. "Is your aunt going to decide whom you marry, Emma?"

With a glance that could only be called indignant, she threw up her hands and replied, "What on earth can you be thinking of me? Marriage is *love*, Adam. I marry for *love*, Adam, and for nothing else. Nothing."

She's something like Jonathan, he thought again as he climbed the stairs to his rooms. She's one of those people you want to be with. For no specific reason, you feel lighter and happier afterward.

But no, he thought as he opened the door, why should I feel happier? There's no reason for it. It's ridiculous. What is Emma to me? We've spent some pleasant hours together. She comes and she goes. Once she has her degree, she'll never come back to stay. And if she ever did stay, what difference would it make? You already have a fine girl waiting for you, Adam.

At the window, propping his elbows on the sill, he looked out into the yard. There were no sounds from below, for they had all gone to the cousins' party and would not be home until late. Relieved, because he did not feel like being sociable, he let his thoughts roam at random.

I have a good life, so why should I be in any hurry to change it in any big way, such as getting married? All in due time . . .

In the meanwhile, he would go to bed. It had been a late night Saturday, a long Sunday, and tomorrow was a workday.

He lay down, slept and woke, slept and woke, disturbed each time by foolish dreams. Emma was there, bare-legged far above the knees, with a rose on her hat. Theo Brown was talking about the million-dollar merger. And Mrs. R. was laughing with pleasure over Emma's engagement to "a very distinguished young man." Doris stood next to Sabine, crying because there were stains on her new blue dress, and it wasn't nice enough for a wedding, anyway.

He woke late, dressed in an anxious hurry, and left without breakfast.

Some days later, a letter arrived. It even looked like Emma, smooth and elegant, with the name embossed in a dark blue script that, Adam saw, was a copy of her own firm, graceful writing. He read:

Here I am hard at work, loving it as always, and yet for the first time, feeling a trifle homesick. That Sunday afternoon was so beautiful! I had never realized just how lovely that spot by the river really is. As I think I mentioned, I had gone there before, but somehow this time it was different. Perhaps the next time, we could rent a canoe. What do you think?

His eyes raced over the two pages that, after mentioning the chilly New England weather and the quartet in which she was to be the pianist next week, ended with *Best wishes, Emma.*

Adam then began an analysis: *This time it was different.* Why was it different? Then there was the canoe, which clearly showed that she did expect another meeting. But the signature, "Best wishes," was certainly formal. Still, what should he expect? "With love"? All in all, it seemed to be a warm letter unless he was reading too much into it.

At this point he turned to an analysis of himself. Had he not made a surprising decision yesterday? After his recent, well-thought-out decision to propose marriage to Doris, he had made an abrupt, not at all well-thought-out decision not to propose it. Why had he had that light sense of happiness as he came up the stairs? And why had last night been so troubled by dreams?

There came a knock at the door. By the soft sound of it, he knew it was Doris. Most likely she was coming to listen to the phonograph, her grandfather having obviously decided that he, Adam, was trustworthy enough for her to be alone with him in his apartment.

"Oh, am I disturbing you?" She looked hesitant when he opened the door and let her in. "Am I too early? You said six o'clock, didn't you, before we go downstairs for supper? Gran's got a roast, and it isn't ready yet, anyway."

He had forgotten. . . . "No, no, it's fine. Go ahead. Wind it up and choose a record while I go over my mail. I've got letters from home, and I have to write an answer."

Dear Emma, I know what you mean. It really was a wonderful day for me, and I'm glad you thought so, too. We certainly can rent a canoe and maybe go for a hike, too, farther west along the river, if you would like to.

The pen paused. Mustn't be too eager, scare her away, you hardly know her. On the other hand, don't act too cool, that's insulting, but you could say something about "happy to start a friendship"—no, that sounds like a business letter from a new manufacturer. Damn, why is it so hard to write a letter? Oh, just say what you're thinking, short and sweet:

I am looking forward to seeing you when you come here for Thanksgiving

vacation. I assume that you will be
coming. I hope that you will.

Now for the ending. Can't make up my
mind. Maybe just sign my name.

Caruso's voice began to die away as the
phonograph wheezed, and Doris jumped up
to wind it.

"Gramps says he'll buy one soon, since I
love it so much," she said. "I'll be glad because I'm afraid I bother you coming up
here to listen."

She was waiting for him to protest that she
did not bother him, and so he did.

The truth was that usually he was glad to
share the phonograph with Doris, but right
now she annoyed him; he wished she would
go away and he wished he didn't have to go
downstairs for supper.

Surely it couldn't be on account of Emma?
That made no sense. After those few hours
with her, what could he know about her? It
made no sense.

"Adam," remarked Mr. Buckley at supper
downstairs, "you look as if you have something on your mind."

"I admit I have. Thanksgiving and Christmas are coming up, our busiest season."

"Well, I can understand that, but don't forget to enjoy yourself, too. You're only young once. I tell Doris that all the time, don't I, hon?"

It was not hard to imagine what else he was telling her. And Adam, eating their dinner with these decent, kindly people, felt suddenly like a thief, or at least an interloper, here under false pretenses. Until last week, they had not been false, but now as he looked across the table at Doris's bland, pretty face, he knew they were.

"Everybody missed you at the anniversary party," Mr. Buckley said. "You've made a hit with the family. They all asked for you."

Ineptly, Adam had to reply that he was sorry he hadn't been able to get there. And all through the rest of the meal, his thoughts raced; even while he joined in the general conversation, he was wondering whether he ought to move to a place where he wouldn't be seeing them all every day as he came and went, to a place where, gradually, the relationship would die a natural death. Then, when he looked across the table at Doris, he could not believe what was happening to him.

"You're getting absentminded," Reilly told

him the next day. "You forgot to call New York about those evening slippers I ordered, and you forgot to put in an order for the French Christmas chocolates. Cace Clothiers has them every year, you know."

Because the vacation was too short to warrant the long trip, Emma was not coming home for Thanksgiving, and Sabine would be going to her instead. They would have a nice few days in Boston, where Emma had friends and Aunt Sabine could shop on Newbury Street.

Friends, Adam thought. So then there must be a man there, or Mrs. R. would not be going; she wants to meet the man and look him over—although perhaps she already knows him, and they are making arrangements.

What is happening to me? I can't stop thinking about her. And the memories went flickering through his mind: the delight in her laugh, her grace as she crossed the grass, and even the way she had picked up and carried that little white dog.

Haste and uncertainty were in the air. Time rushed by. There was too much happening, or on the verge of happening, for the nation and for Adam Arnring as well. The *Lusitania* had been sunk last spring; the President was campaigning on the slogan "He Kept Us Out of War," while many citizens were predicting that the war would soon be our war, too. And Adam's private life was just as confused.

Friendly letters from Emma kept arriving, and he kept answering them. She wrote about her musical education classes, sometimes quite seriously and sometimes comically, about a cute little boy who was all thumbs. Adam replied that he personally wasn't even good enough to move his thumbs. She wrote about the very interesting newspaper article that Aunt Sabine had sent, and was it true that the deal between Cace Clothiers and "our store" was really going to happen? Theo Brown was very optimistic. Adam answered that Theo Brown had been saying the same to him, and that you could depend upon Theo as you depend upon the rising sun.

But what do these letters back and forth have to do with us? he asked himself, while at the same instant rebuking himself for being an utter fool. She was little more than an *acquaintance!* So why couldn't he get her out of his mind? Was he obsessed?

"You seem so nervous," Doris said. "Is it because of that stuff in the paper about a merger with Cace Clothiers?"

"Well, if there's a chance I might lose my job, that's something to be a little nervous about. Cace has its own people they'll want to keep, so one never can tell what will happen."

Although there was no chance at all of his dismissal, according to Theo Brown, who ought to know, it was not a bad idea to let Doris think there was, and so start looking for a more dependable man.

But she was confident, and very kind. "If it should happen, which I doubt, you'll get another job. Easily, Adam."

So here was another worry, loaded with guilt, even though he had never told her that he loved her or wanted to spend the rest of his life with her. That didn't seem to make a difference to women and their relatives.

Then there were the letters from home. In

one delivery there was a batch of bad news, good news, and very good news.

Very good was news from Jonathan.

. . . and, Adam, you cannot believe how lovely Blanche is. There's so much I could tell you about her if I had any talent with words. It's easy enough to describe, as I have done, a piquant face—isn't that a great word?—and short, dark curls, but how to describe a spirit? You will have to see for yourself and then you'll understand what I mean. She speaks so well that nobody would guess she's such a recent immigrant. She's much too talented to be working for Berman the tailor. She could be a really great dressmaker, I think. She makes her own clothes and looks so perfect that even Pa makes comments about it. We are so in love! What else can I say? I've been taking a few short weekends as often as possible so I can find a little time to be with her. We plan to be married when I graduate from here. She will get a better job wherever I may end up in medical school. I'll work in the lab

some nights, and with the help that you so generously give and for which I am so thankful, we'll do all right.

I wish you could come home sometime soon. But I know the trip is terribly expensive, and your job is very demanding. When we have our wedding, though, you'll have to come.

Bad was a long postscript in an otherwise loving note from Pa.

The doctor tells me my heart is not beating right. I have to take it easier, he says. But you know that's hard to do in my business. Anyway, I don't want to do it. What else would I do with my life? I like being in the store, where I know all the customers. I grow old with them. I want to die with my shoes on. Not yet, though. I'm fifty-eight, that's pretty old, but I have cousins in the old country older than that. They don't write often, but they're still around working. Leo works all right, but hardly ever talks to me unless he's feeling nasty. He goes upstairs and reads his books. He never did much in school,

*you remember, so I don't understand
why he reads now. But it's none of my
business. Let him read. I would like so
much to see you soon. Maybe you will
visit. But I know you are busy.*

Love, Pa

Bad again was another letter from
Jonathan.

*I hate to put sad words on paper. I
imagine your face and the gloom you
will feel, but still I think you should
know that Leo is giving Pa an awfully
hard time right now.*
*Did you know that for years he has
had an ongoing crush on Bobby
Nishikawa's sister? I never knew, and
neither did Pa. But now it seems that
he has gotten very serious, and that
she doesn't want him. They had a
terrible argument, and he was a wreck
when he came home with Bobby, who
was trying to soothe him. Leo swears
he will never again go near the
Nishikawas' house, won't even walk on
that street. You know how he is. One
nice thing is that Bobby says he will still*

be Leo's friend—the only friend Leo's ever had. It seems that the girl's family didn't want her to get too involved with Leo. But then, Pa didn't like the idea, either. Of course, it's the racial thing on both sides, but in Leo's case, it's more. They wouldn't want him even if he were Japanese, and he knows it. The poor fellow has never had a girl, any girl, to love or be loved by. I feel so terribly sorry for him, as I know you do. He is so frustrated. People don't give him a chance. They retreat from him, they pass him by as you ignore a stranger who keeps smiling at you on a streetcar. You feel that there's something wrong, and you shrink away. I must admit that if I were not Leo's brother, I might do the same. And yet I grow awfully impatient sometimes. I feel like shaking him when he's sarcastic, especially with Pa, who is growing old too fast and, though he tries not to show it, is still in mourning.

Such letters cast a pall over Adam's spirits. Fortunately in Adam's case, this last letter was shortly afterward followed by a cheering word from Theo Brown that the merger, at Mrs. R.'s request, was now in the hands of Spencer Lawrence, who had started negotiations with Cace's lawyers. It looked, Brown said, like a settled agreement. Mrs. R. had become quite enthusiastic about it and, he had added, she would be "richer than Croesus." He had added that of course Adam need have no worry at all about his job.

On the very same day, there was a package in Adam's mailbox, containing a book of poems by Robert Frost, along with a note.

Dear Adam,
I bought this book for myself and loved it. Then I bought another copy for you because I believe you would agree with me. If you already have it, you can give this away to somebody like yourself who'll understand how smart and sad and funny and wise and loving these poems are. Best wishes,

Emma

P.S. I will be home for three weeks on midwinter vacation through New Year's.

Chapter 11

"You're mighty hungry, aren't you?" Rea said. "There's enough here for two." Rea winked.

Emma wore a bicycle skirt and a new puffed-sleeve blouse printed with red poppies. In the basket were chicken sandwiches, homemade doughnuts, and a thermos full of coffee.

Sabine poked her head into the kitchen. "Five days in a row!" she exclaimed. "I don't know that it's so smart to go pedaling by yourself way out on those lonely roads."

"Oh, Aunt, you're such a worrier! I go straight through Three Corners village, and I've already made a friend who rides her bicycle with me. She teaches school, and we ride together. It's fun. She's a lovely person."

"Well, all right, but do be careful."

"I will."

On the next street over, almost hidden beneath a spreading sycamore, Adam waited with his bicycle. He was too far off for Emma to see his face, but she did not need to see it; she knew it as well as she knew his tenderness and his strength, as well as she knew his words, his touch, and his kiss. Even his silences spoke to her.

People would say that we do not know each other well enough, she thought. But I remember that time we came back from Europe, when I wanted, oh, I wanted so much to see him again! I was not yet in love, but I knew that someday I would be. I knew, and I know now. How can I put this into words? Even the most sublime writers have not been able to do it.

Now, catching sight of her, he rode to meet her, leaned across the two sets of wheels, and kissed her on the lips.

"Last day," he said. "Back to work tomorrow morning."

"That's horrible. I have a whole week more. When do you get another vacation?"

"A week next summer. Two weeks a year."

"That's horrible, too. How will it be for you if this merger goes through?"

"That depends on the position I get. The higher you climb, the more free time you get. Also, the farther you fall, as they say."

"Stop joking. Do you think the deal will go through?"

"It looks that way, according to the lawyers and accountants. But tell me what's doing with your friend 'Susan' today."

"At the present moment, Susan and I are riding through the prairie out as far as the ridge, where it gets too steep to ride. Then we'll go back fifteen miles, turn toward the river, rest on logs, and eat. Rea made doughnuts. She's a darling." Emma laughed. "She knows all about 'Susan.' "

"I worry," Adam said. "I don't like these lies."

"But what else can we do? Anyway, let's not talk about it now. The day is too beautiful."

So it was. The warmth, unusual in late December, seemed to be releasing into the air the fragrance of pine. Riding beneath peaceful white clouds, they passed fallow fields, winter rye, grazing cattle, and dense groves of trees that stood like islands on the level land.

Adam broke a silence. "We've had one full week, plus ten evenings pretending you were at the movies, either alone or with that

Susan you've invented. And now you're leaving."

"There's the telephone. There are letters and thoughts, always thoughts. We'll still be together. You worry too much."

"I know. I can't help it."

"Yes, you can. Come on. Let's race these bikes for a couple of miles, shall we? Then back to the river."

On the blanket that Adam had brought, they lay in the sun. Even through the thicknesses of layered clothing, she felt his heartbeat, as his lips pressed hers. More, she thought, there needs to be more. Not only more time, a thousand nights of it, but deeper.

"I can't," he said, and moved away, letting her go. "There's only so much a man can stand."

"I won't say no to anything you want," she murmured.

"No, no, I won't do that to you."

"Why? Who would ever find out?"

"Emma! You *are* innocent after all, aren't you? What if you—if you were to have a child, and—"

"We would get married. Isn't that what usually happens?"

Then as she heard herself flirting and teasing, but actually trying to divine his intentions while not fooling him for a second, she was ashamed, and changed her tone.

"Since I have no idea whether marriage is in your plans, and really don't care, I'll promise to divorce you after the child is born."

He joked back. "That's no way to get married, a pregnant bride in a white veil—"

When he stopped, she was moved by the sudden sadness that came upon him. Then, remembering what he had told her about himself, she laid her hand upon his and spoke softly.

"You're thinking about your mother. I understand. Do you think of her often?"

"Not often."

"You must have pictures of her."

"Only one, a snapshot, and not a very good one."

Now something was leading her to tell him things about herself that nobody except Sabine could know.

"That's more than I have," she said. "You see . . . you ought to know . . . I'm not Sabine's niece. I'm adopted."

For a moment, while his kind eyes examined hers, he did not speak. Then he said, "Try to remember that your mother loved you enough to see that you went to people who would care for you."

The hard knot that sometimes rose—oh, very rarely, because she would not allow it to—now constricted Emma's throat. And the voice that came out of her throat did not sound very much like her own.

"I don't think my mother could have loved me very much. I was a foundling, dumped on the steps of a church in New York, without a name, without a note, without anything."

Now it was Adam who reached for her hand. And she continued, "You are the only person I've ever told this to. What's the use? It's only food for gossip, a good story for people to pass around. Who was my mother? A terrified girl from a strict family, or a prostitute? Who was my father? God knows. I used to walk on strange streets, see faces, and wonder: Is she the one? Is he? Especially if the person had hair the color of mine. I have felt so sorry for myself, you can't imagine. But long ago I decided that this was sick, not worthy of myself. I am *me,* and it doesn't matter at all who *they* were.

"So you see why I owe so much to Sabine. She read about the abandoned baby, and she took me in. She treats me like a princess. It's absurd. The more she can buy for me, the better she feels about herself. Money is everything to her because she can't forget the time when she had none. So she wants me to marry somebody rich and distinguished, somebody powerful, who will never lose his way."

"Have you ever met any man like that?"

"Yes. There are families you meet in college, the kind who donate a building that has their name on it. Yes, I have met them."

When he did not speak, she understood his thoughts: that as far as Sabine was concerned, he was nobody, and he had nothing. Nothing, she thought, except that he loves me. And he also has a tremendous powerful pride that will never bend.

The mood of the day had changed, and it was time to leave. As the sun moved westward, the light dimmed with it, and by the time they were again back in the town, it was chilled with a deep, gray dusk.

✳

There was a pain in his heart, although hearts are not supposed to hurt. Every day they go about their steady beat, and people don't think about them . . . until one day you feel a pain there. Standing before the mirror, Adam gazed at himself.

I feel weak, as if my legs don't want to move. I have never felt weak like this in all my life. Emma fills me and drives me.

He walked to the window and looked into the night, as if there in the rising wind he might find an answer. Old Mrs. R. had all the common sense on her side. What had he to give to Emma, she with her beauty and talent, her degrees and her future success? To say nothing of the Rothirsch money, which he would never, so help him, never accept?

For a long time he stood there, while a surge of emotions heated his face: feelings of pride, of anger, and also of shame. Hiding himself on the street behind that house so that Mrs. Rothirsch would not see him skulking like a common thief! And worst of all, lying, lying to that fierce old woman as if he were afraid of her!

Then suddenly he knew what he must do. Out of his closet, he took his best suit, put on a white shirt and a fine striped tie. He would present himself as a gentleman, "upper class," as Mrs. Rothirsch would say. There was no time to get the Tin Lizzie out of the garage down the street, so he walked and, energized now, walked faster and faster toward the boulevard, up the hill to the great, grim place that looked like the witch's house in the fairy tale. He rang the doorbell.

"They've just finished dinner," Rudy told him, looking surprised. "Does the missus expect you?"

"No." Then it seemed to him as he followed Rudy that he had not even decided what he was going to say. Emotions, all kinds of emotions, had simply overwhelmed him, and here he was, confronting both Mrs. R. and Emma, who, having heard voices, had come to see what was happening.

Mrs. R.'s frown darkened her broad face as her voice boomed.

"What is it? What happened? Is the store on fire?"

"Nothing's happened. No troubles. I only—it's only that there are some things I wanted to talk about," he faltered, looking not at her, but at Emma's great, startled eyes.

"Talk about, Mr. Arnring? You couldn't have waited until tomorrow during the business day, instead of intruding on the privacy of my home?"

"It's not about business, Mrs. Rothirsch. It's personal. A personal matter."

Emma said, "Not now, Adam. Oh, please."

"What's this about?" demanded her aunt. In the brief silence that followed, she whirled to look at Emma, whirled to look at Adam, and then burst out with what seemed to Adam was like the roar of a wounded beast: "Don't tell me that there is something between you two! Is that what I'm seeing on your faces? Is it?"

"You see—" Adam began, but was interrupted.

"Yes, I do see. I suspected something, out every afternoon on her bicycle since she's been home, this girl here, out to the movies in the evening, out to dinner with some unknown friend driving through on the way to California, somebody she could certainly have invited to dinner here—oh, yes, I suspected there was someone else. I told myself I was wrong, but still I was wracking my brains trying to figure out who the man could be. How could I have dreamed it was a thing like this, a crazy thing like this—"

"Sabine. Aunt Sabine," Emma cried. "This is not crazy. *Not crazy,* I tell you. You don't know anything about us, and you have no right to call us crazy!"

Adam moved, put his hand on Emma's shaking shoulder, and soothed her. "It's all right. It's all right. Leave this to me. Let me do the talking."

And Adam, seeing how Mrs. Rothirsch's face was turning as red as a wound, knew that it was his possessive hand upon Emma's shoulder that had infuriated her.

"We can be angry without being frantic," he said quietly. "You and I had some words once before this, if you remember, Mrs. Rothirsch. But that was a long time ago, and a lot of water has flowed peacefully under the bridge since then."

"That has nothing to do with this, young man. You are still the employee, and I'm still Mrs. Rothirsch."

"I'm well aware of that, and always have been. So may we sit down and talk to each other? Emma is trembling."

"Emma, trembling? That's not like her. She

can be pretty defiant when she wants to be. I should be used to it."

"Dear Auntie," Emma said, "don't be angry with me. Come, sit down on the sofa here and let us explain—or let Adam explain. That's why he came."

"Oh, so you knew he was coming?"

"I didn't. It's a good thing I didn't because I would have talked him out of it, and now I'm glad he's here."

The old lady, as if she had felt a sudden weakness, sat down on a side chair so much too fragile for her weight that it creaked. Her suspicious stare traveled from Emma to Adam and back.

"Have you come here, for God's sake, to tell me that you've run off and gotten married?"

"No," Adam said, "I guess I've come here to say that we'd like to do it someday."

"Well, that's a relief. A person would think, the way you're holding on to her, that you already were married."

"He loves me, Aunt Sabine, and I love him."

These words, which had never been spoken between them, now rang out as a single note of music might ring through a silence.

"Well! Well, I've seen a lot of crazy things in my lifetime, but this is one of the craziest. You're a bold, ambitious young man, Mr. Arnring, too ambitious for your own good. You don't let anything get in your way, do you?"

Maybe I don't, Adam thought. I am the one who pulled your dying business out of a hole and set it on its feet, after all. And standing tall above the two women, he answered proudly, "Yes, when it's right and just to do so, I don't let anything get in my way. Not anything or anyone."

Mrs. R. threw up her hands and cried out, "You! Who do you think you are, to go after this marvelous, talented, beautiful girl? And she's rich, too, isn't she, Mr. Arnring? Of course, that hasn't ever entered your mind, has it? Of course not, you'll tell me."

"You're quite, quite wrong, Mrs. Rothirsch. It's been on my mind all the time. If Emma had nothing, there'd be no problem. We'd manage, as most people in this world do."

"Talk sense, will you? If you can."

At the far end of the dismal room hung the portrait of this woman's husband, his face glowering, his thick fists resting on a table-top. *He wrecked her life. He even struck her now and then.*

"You're being horribly mean, Aunt Sabine," Emma said now. "You ought to know better. You've been through enough in your life to understand why a person wants to keep his pride. It's why—why he hasn't yet asked me to marry him. I know that, even though he hasn't said so. It's because he has nothing—"

"What do you mean, 'nothing'? Complaining about his salary? That handsome salary? Let's see, for the last five years, let me calculate—why, he must have a nice few thousand in the bank—"

Emma interrupted. "He takes care of his family! A father with a heart condition, a brother who's next to useless, and another brother in college preparing for medical school—"

This was all too personal, making some sort of virtuous hero out of him, and Adam broke in. "It's nothing extraordinary. You take care of your family when they need it, that's all. It's elementary, nothing to be proud about."

There was a long silence. The clock, a chunk of marble between two naked marble nymphs, struck eight. Adam sat down on the sofa and took Emma's hand, while Sabine Rothirsch stared at the floor.

When a few minutes had passed, she looked up and said quietly, "Pride. I suppose there's nothing wrong with it, unless it's false pride."

Adam had had his full share of all that: Leo's gibes, when he was really angry, about bastardy, or that girl who had broken her promise about the senior prom. Strange how such unimportant blows to one's pride can still occupy a tiny slot in one's memory.

Sabine was never accepted by the people whom she most respected. They laughed at her house, her clothes, and very probably her husband. Was that false pride? He thought it probably was.

"If you're not ready to marry my niece, why are you here?"

"I guess it's mainly that I wanted to make my position clear so Emma wouldn't have to sneak out of the house to see me, and so I wouldn't have to do any sneaking myself."

"We've been writing to each other all year," Emma said. "We're adults, and you can't stop us from doing whatever we want to do. But Adam's right. It's better and only decent that you should know everything."

"Oh, I suspected something, Emma. That day you sat in the chauffeur's seat with you both talking and laughing, and he the good-looking man he is, too good-looking. My mother always told me never to bother with handsome men because they can't be trusted. And I listened to her, and—"

Sabine's eyes were staring straight at the fierce-looking husband in the portrait. When she turned away, her eyes were wet.

"My husband worked for five dollars a week when we came here, did you know that?" she cried. "We lived in one room, but it was better than the hut and the fear that we had in Poland. Then after a while, we had a store, and then a bigger one, and then this one. We bought this house and hired people to keep it clean and plant flowers outside. But we have always been strangers here, do you know that? We were naturally not invited by the Christians, but even the Jewish people were divided; the German group is ashamed of us because we're not educated. Do you think I don't know what they say about this beautiful house? They say I have no taste. What am I supposed to know about taste? I was glad to have a bed to sleep in."

Adam, listening to this lament, had the sense that he was the elder and the stronger of the two.

"It's a funny thing about people," he said gently. "Take those two old friends of mine in the store. Reilly tells me sometimes that you can't trust the British, that they're a cold lot. Archer talks about the Irish hanging out in the saloons."

This remark drew a wry smile as Mrs. R. replied, "Weren't they a sloppy pair, those two?"

"Not anymore."

"No, you've smartened up the place, you've certainly done that. I've noticed everything. I've never said anything about it, but that was only because I make it my policy never to interfere."

No, Adam thought with some amusement, as long as the money comes rolling in, you don't interfere.

Still, hostility, like smoke, had been quietly blown away. So it was time, it occurred to Adam, to return to basics, and he asked whether Emma and he were now free to see each other without any subterfuge.

"Because we are going to do it, anyway," he added with a smile.

Mrs. Rothirsch sighed. "All right. But nothing, nothing at all is settled here tonight. Remember that Emma has to complete her M.A."

"Of course, Aunt. I'm leaving the day after tomorrow."

The old lady sighed again. "Emma is all I have, Mr. Arn—Adam. She was my husband's favorite niece, only a baby when she came to us."

He did not need Emma's quick glance to understand that this fiction would have to be respected; if Sabine had been younger, a different fiction would have been used, and Emma would have been presented not as a niece, but as a daughter. An hour ago, he would have thought it impossible that he could feel such compassion for this fractious, pathetic old woman.

When the clock struck nine, he rose to go, leaving behind him an atmosphere totally different from the one into which he had entered. Who would have believed that the terrible-tempered Mrs. R. had actually been won over? She would deny it, but he knew with certainty that she had been.

Chapter 12

It seemed to Adam that he had always been worried about something. Now suddenly, his worries had evaporated into bright air. Pa still had a heart condition, but he was under a doctor's good care and his condition was stable. Leo was still Leo, holed up in his room with books, sulking and sullen as ever, but he did seem to be getting over his crushing rejection by Bobby Nishikawa's sister. And Doris, who had been on Adam's conscience because he had misled her and misled himself, too, now had another admirer and was no longer on his conscience.

The happy news was even happier. Jonathan was starting to send out applications to medical school. His letters were filled with reports about his work, and glowing descriptions of his darling Blanche. And

Emma, whom he would keep as a secret until the proper time, was coming home.

No, he could ask for nothing more, only that life might stay like this.

Sabine had wanted a celebration of Emma's double degree in Music Education and Performing Arts. At the long dinner table, he faced the enormous candelabra, the heavy silver, and the clustered roses, aware that his inclusion among the guests was a sign of acceptance on Sabine's part. Of course, the crowd at this party was a motley one; the only people there who belonged to what Sabine considered "society" were her lawyer, Spencer Lawrence, and his wife. The others were old widows, a few elderly couples, the family doctor with his wife, and half a dozen college friends of Emma's, two of them accompanied by prosperous young husbands.

"Theo Brown isn't here," said Emma, possibly in answer to someone's question. "There's illness in the family, and he had to go out of town."

Theo, an old friend by now, would have been the one guest with whom Adam had very much in common. Nevertheless, the party was interesting, it being his first formal dinner complete with catered French food, elegantly served in one of the ugliest dining rooms a person could imagine.

He was seated next to Emma not far from the hostess, at the table's end. The talk was, not unnaturally, of world events.

"Regardless of Wilson's promise," said Spencer Lawrence, "we are going to fight. It's inevitable."

He spoke with authority. Tall, earnest, with lean, haughty features and appropriate gray at the temples, he even looked authoritative. It must have cost some effort on Sabine's part, Adam thought, to introduce the likes of me to Spencer Lawrence. No one else but Emma could have forced her to do it. And he wondered whether Lawrence could possibly have recognized him from those occasions when, in Francine's luxurious brothel, he, Adam, had stood inconspicuously among the outer circle that liked to hear what was being said by the big names.

It was of course a long time since he had been there; never once since Emma . . . He wondered why in the first place so many married men patronized it. Years ago at home, the men who went to Gracie's had been almost all young and unattached. He thought of Pa and Rachel, doubting whether if Pa had been able to afford the extra cost, he would ever have gone there. But then he thought: Am I naive?

Well, naive or not, he could not ever imagine himself wanting any woman other than Emma. And he tried not to let this yearning show too boldly whenever his gaze fell upon her bare shoulders and her bright hair.

Dr. Macy remarked, "I was interested to see last week the column of Jeff Horace's where he talked about Cace Clothiers and the Rothirsch store. I often wonder how the dickens he gets all his details. He seems to know everything that's going on. Anyway, it sounds as if the merger will be a jewel in our downtown."

Adam was amused. He was a nice fellow, the doctor. Jeff was another nice fellow, always helpful when asked to be.

Lawrence scoffed. "The man's a gossip columnist, nothing more."

"Of course," the doctor conceded, "though sometimes he is interesting. This was about the architecture, about plans for a courtyard with a retractable glass roof. Very unusual, I thought. Very attractive."

Was it possible, Adam wondered, that Theo Brown had let someone see the plan Adam scrawled one day when they were having a sandwich lunch in his office?

Lawrence scoffed again. "Worthless chitchat. None of his business."

Well, any plan that Adam had scrawled was indeed not worth anything; he was far from being any architect, even though he did like to conjure up plans for fun.

"He needs to fill space," Lawrence continued. "So many dollars for so many lines."

Now Adam began to have toward Lawrence a feeling of intense dislike. The man seemed to snap words out of his mouth as if he were an angry judge quoting the law from his bench.

Dr. Macy was not frightened into silence. Half laughing, he returned to the subject of Jeff Horace.

"If you know Jeff well, and I do, he can tell you a whole lot of interesting stuff that doesn't get into the papers. He's got stuff about Francine's place that could fill a book if anybody wanted to write one. But nobody would, because who would print it?"

Mrs. Lawrence wanted to know what Francine's place was. "It sounds like a French dress shop."

"Is everyone ready for dessert?" Sabine interrupted. "They're meringues, and they do get soggy if they have to wait."

Even Adam knew that this was not true. Sabine was mortified by the doctor's subject, and became more so when he answered Mrs. Lawrence's question.

"It's a house of delight, with very beautiful young ladies who entertain gentlemen."

"Oh!" cried Mrs. Lawrence. "I'm sorry—I had no idea. It isn't—it surely isn't here in town?"

"Not very far away," the doctor replied.

Theo Brown, good-hearted and open-minded, would be getting a kick out of this, Adam thought, stifling laughter.

"That's disgusting! A woman should certainly divorce her husband if he ever . . . I certainly would."

Two of Sabine's elderly lady friends agreed at once with Mrs. Lawrence, while a third reconsidered. "A divorce is nothing to be proud of, either, my dear. It's very messy."

Another woman objected to that. "Only in America. In England the best people get divorced if they're unhappy, and it's no disgrace there as it is with us."

Sabine's poor face was purple with distress as this perfect party seemed to be deteriorating, and so Adam spoke out.

"More importantly, Mr. Lawrence, I read yesterday that there were definite signs in Washington that Wilson is weakening about this war."

Emma agreed at once. "It does make sense, doesn't it? I mean, six of our ships just gone down, all the men drowned. It makes you shudder. I don't think it can go on."

So the conversation was adroitly steered into another direction. The meringues, surrounded by strawberries, appeared a moment later, and Adam was left with the pleasant thought that Emma and he had saved the day for Sabine.

Over demitasse in the living room, she made an announcement. "Let's all go to the music room. I haven't asked Emma, but I'm sure she'll be happy to play something for us."

"Oh, please not," Emma said. "Nobody wants it. This is a party, Aunt Sabine."

"They've never heard you play. They'll all love to hear you."

Emma glanced at Adam, her lips moving without sound over the words *I'm sure they wouldn't.*

"Just one piece. Anything you like, Emma."

Sabine was so proud of her Emma! He would never have expected to be on her side, but he nodded to Emma: *Do it.*

There was scarcely enough room for everyone to stand in the music room, where the glossy black piano took up a third of the space.

"It's a concert grand, not a baby," announced Sabine. "I bought it for her," she added, extending her arm, "when she was this high."

Emma paused before announcing that she would play a Beethoven sonata called "To Therese," straightened her position on the seat, and began to play, while Sabine nodded approvingly and whispered to the Lawrences that they would love this piece.

"I've always loved it, all my life. It's one of my favorites."

Adam did not miss the interchange of

glances between the Lawrences. A smile twitched and died on the man's stern lips.

"Just look at those hands," Sabine whispered. "I'll never understand how she does it. She loves to play Mozart—no, Schubert, I mean. He has such a distinctive style, don't you agree?"

Mr. Lawrence did not reply. He was seeing the ignorance and the rudeness of Sabine's loud whispers while the music was being played; he did not see the pathos. And in the next instant, Adam knew that he did not like the man. He could at least have nodded and smiled a little, the cold fish; he was the kind of person who would begrudge someone a piece of ice at the North Pole. This poor old woman—and could he ever have thought he'd be taking her part?—knew nothing about music, and the respected counselor-at-law despised her for it.

Emma's fingers were racing across the keyboard. Adam managed to move nearer, where he could watch her earnest frowns of concentration, the slight sway of her body, and the strand of pearls, so long that the end must be hidden beneath her dress, between her breasts. Never in my life have I heard such music, he thought. For when and where could I have heard it? The piano sang. It rejoiced, it pleaded, soothed and seemed to soar; he could feel the beat of a small bird's wings as it lifted itself above the trees, and returned, and went away again.

Then suddenly he had the feeling that Emma was speaking to him through the music, speaking only to him. He wanted her to finish, wanted all these people to disappear, evaporate and be gone, so that he could be alone with her when the music ended.

They walked down the familiar front steps and stood in silence, with their arms wrapped around each other, within a grove of spruce at the end of the lawn.

"I don't trust myself to be in the same room with you," he said. "Oh, Emma, how long will it be? I think of you every day, every night, all the time."

"Give it a few months, and it will solve itself. She is already getting used to the idea, although she's not quite ready yet to admit it."

In a path of moonlight stood the bulk of that grandiose house, the house that would someday belong to her. There was no breeze, and the night was still, enchanted and still. For the last half hour, all through Emma's music and now under the moon, Adam too had been enchanted.

Yet there was a solid foundation beneath his mood. Final arguments were being drawn up by Spencer Lawrence and Cace's lawyers. Theo Brown called the merger a "bonanza." Liking the word, he often repeated it.

"There's real prestige in this bonanza, along with a pile of money. Of course, the old lady has to add a bit more, but she understands that. And you'll get a great promotion, Adam, a dandy raise, no question about it."

Well, that was fine. No charity from Mrs. R. would Emma's husband ever accept, but a salary that he knew he well deserved was a very different matter. And thanking his stars for all these gifts, he kissed his Emma.

"You've been worrying all year," she said when he released her. "Aren't you all over it now?"

"Yes."

"Honest?"

"Yes. Honest."

"We'll have the wedding soon?"

"Very soon. We both want it, and we need it."

And he walked away down the hill, whistling softly to himself.

Chapter 13

Adam was at his desk in the office one morning, when to his surprise, Emma, who had never before been above the selling floors in the store, came in. He saw at once that she was agitated.

"What's the trouble? What is it?"

"Sabine. She's beside herself. Theo Brown phoned and told her to forget about the deal with Cace. It's off. The figures don't add up, and anyway, he'd been having his doubts about it recently and had been intending to tell her so. Now Cace has come up with new figures that she can't afford, or should not spend. Something like that."

"New figures? How much?"

"Half a million dollars, I think. But she was so upset that I couldn't make sense of the story."

"It doesn't make any sense. I'll call Theo right now."

His heart sinking, Adam picked up the telephone.

"Hello, Theo? Emma Rothirsch is here with a story about the merger. Something about more money. Did you tell her aunt that it's off?"

"Yes, after all the negotiations, I hate to tell you, it's fallen through the cracks. The Cace people need more money, much more money, to do it the way they want it done. And your side simply doesn't have enough."

"I'm astonished, Theo. I don't understand it. We had enough all along, so what's happened now?"

"Well, since they're giving up the store in the capital, the way the neighborhood there is changing, you know, they want to buy that extra piece of land next to the store here, and—"

"All of a sudden they want it? I never knew it was for sale. In fact, I don't believe it is."

Theo sighed. "Even if it isn't, they want you to come up with another half million, or more. They've got very elaborate plans."

"This is the most unbusinesslike, last-minute, crazy thing that I've ever heard of,"

Adam said furiously. "It's not even decent. It's crooked."

"No, no, no. It may be indecent, but it isn't crooked, Adam. These things happen all the time. You've just not been out in the competitive world, but I'm an old hand and I know what I've seen."

The feeling in Adam's stomach had moved to his head, where it seemed a small hammer had started to pound. The rosy future, the marriage, the promotion he had hoped for in order to support Emma . . .

"I've got to talk to you, Theo," he said. "This is too important to leave to the telephone. I'll be right over."

"Adam, I'm sorry, but I just can't do it now. I'm up to my ears in work that a client needs by noon, and on top of that—you remember my father was sick a couple of months ago? He's in the hospital again. My mother's frantic, and I've got a two-hundred-mile drive before I can get there. I'll see you in a few days and explain it all, if he doesn't die. I'm awfully sorry, Adam. I hope you understand."

Adam hung up. Understand? No, I don't, not at all. He could give me fifteen minutes more before he leaves.

"Wiped away," he said to Emma. "All our plans, the future, wiped away. Just like that."

She flew across the room to his desk. When he looked up, he saw that her eyes were blazing with indignation.

"What do you mean by 'all our plans'? You surely can't mean our wedding?"

When he looked at her without speaking, she cried out, "You can't mean it! Are you saying that we—that you and I together—can't exist without Cace Clothiers?"

"I'm saying that you and I can't live on what I earn here, and I have no idea where I could go to get a better salary than what I have now."

"So?"

"So we can't live on what I have now! I live in two little rooms that are barely large enough for one."

"Adam Arnring, listen to me, you don't know what you're talking about. I'll show how I can live there with you, and love it, too."

"It's you who don't know what you're talking about," he said sadly.

"All right. We'll get three rooms. I can

make plenty of money with my piano lessons."

"I'm sure you could. But I don't want to depend on my wife's earnings. What kind of man do you think I am?"

"That's nonsense. Don't be silly. The time is coming when it's perfectly acceptable for a woman to help support a family."

"Maybe. But that time isn't here yet."

"Can you stop me from giving piano lessons if I want to give them?"

"No, but they wouldn't pay the bills, anyway. I have obligations, my brother, my father . . . I wish money were not so important! Does it have to rule the world?"

"It does. Unless we go back to trading. I'll give you a bag of potatoes if you'll shoe my horse."

"Don't make jokes about this!"

There was a long pause until Emma said, "I'm not joking. Think about that house of Sabine's. And this place where we're standing is all hers, too. She loves to give, and she has nobody else to give anything to. Why shouldn't we take advantage of it?"

"She can give it all to charity. I don't want it. I will not take it."

No matter how much compassion I have

for her, I will not live like a pet dog under her care.

"Fine, then, if that's how you feel. I don't need much, Adam. You may not believe it, but I don't even *want* much—a little house, a very modest house in this town is enough for me. I've lived all my life out of trunks and suitcases. I want to settle here and live simply, and stay in one place."

"And have children?"

"Of course. Children most of all, and you know why."

She had no idea what things cost. She had never had to pay a bill. Yes, she bought modest clothes, but those pearls she wears, and the price of food—how well he remembered the grocery store! Children, sons who'd need to go to college. And if Emma was any example, daughters, too. She had no idea what she was talking about.

"Well," he said, "I have work to do at this desk. I'll think about this later."

"And I have to go home. You know how emotional Sabine is. I would never have guessed what this means to her pride and prestige among her old-lady friends."

When Emma had left, he sat thinking

about Theo Brown. Their conversation had been so short; actually, it had been strangely perfunctory, considering this abrupt demise of what had been a very healthy proposition. People didn't usually shrug off a defeat with such easy acceptance. To be sure, Theo was a cheerful, hearty man, a brisk optimist who could probably shrug things off faster than many other people do. He could have given me a few more minutes, Adam thought. Of course, if his father was in a hospital a couple of hundred miles away . . . naturally he needed to go. But this was such a terrible blow! Everything he had been counting on had vanished. Adam sat there, let the mail lie unread, and stared into space.

After a while, he got up and went downstairs, thinking that maybe an early lunch might revive him. Reilly was walking down the street when Adam caught up with him.

"You look as if you'd lost your best friend," Reilly said.

"Not quite, but I've had an awful disappointment. You'll never believe it, but the Cace merger is off."

"Don't tell me! How so?"

"I don't know all the details yet. I have to wait for Brown to explain."

"But there were lawyers working on it! I read it in Jeff Horace's column."

Sometimes Reilly could say such stupid things.

"Well, of course lawyers," Adam said, a bit impatiently.

"So why don't you go ask them? They would know more about it than Brown does."

"Fine, fine. I'll do that."

He walked on toward a sandwich shop where he usually ate, looked into it, decided he wasn't hungry, and continued around the square past a row of expensive stores and a small brick building filled with lawyers' offices. Something in him recoiled at the thought of going in there to see Spencer Lawrence. That sarcastic snob wouldn't give him more than five minutes of his valuable time.

Back at work, Reilly approached him. "I saw you heading toward the square. Did you see a lawyer?"

"No, I didn't."

"Well, you should. Brown is an accountant, not a lawyer."

Exasperating idiot!

"I know that, Reilly. I really do know that."

Up in his private quarters again, he had just returned to the mail when the telephone rang.

"I'm having a time here," Emma said. "She can't understand what's happened. All that extra money they want! Where is it to come from? Sabine is not the national bank. I called Theo Brown, but he's left his office. Sabine thinks maybe you would be kind enough to ask Mr. Lawrence? She's too upset to talk to him."

"I have people here, Emma. I can't talk now. I'll call you later."

When he had hung up the telephone, he took out the directory, called the office of Lawrence, Wiley and Wills, and asked for an appointment with Mr. Spencer Lawrence.

He could have predicted the style of the office: eighteenth-century furniture, a dignified, middle-aged receptionist, and above the mantel, a traditional portrait, undoubtedly of an ancestor, given the resemblance to Spencer Lawrence's stern, frosty face. And again he had the feeling of intense dislike that had risen within him the first time he had met the man.

"Please sit down, Mr. Arnring. I had intended to speak with Mrs. Rothirsch this afternoon about the Cace merger. Unfortunately, I was unable to do it earlier today because I was in court. However, here you are. And since I have permission from her to explain the entire unfortunate matter, I shall do so."

"Then it really is 'unfortunate'? I had hoped not, Mr. Lawrence."

"Well, I daresay that from Mr. Brown's point of view it is quite fortunate."

A little smile flashed across Lawrence's lips and vanished without a glimpse of teeth. A hawk. A predatory bird looked like him. . . .

"Why is that? I don't understand."

"It's rather complicated from a legal standpoint. Since you are a merchant and not a lawyer, I shall put the matter in layman's terms. Mr. Brown has formed a syndicate which will pay far more than Mrs. Rothirsch can pay to satisfy Cace Clothiers. These people have tempted Cace with a plan that will quadruple the size of the property. They plan to make Mrs. R. a buyout offer that she will be unable to refuse."

It took only a minute for Adam to grasp the essence of this description. Then it took several minutes more, during which time he was silent, to absorb the fact that the instigator, the organizer of this scheme, actually was Theo Brown. He was stunned.

"But Theo and I," he stammered, "we're friends. He was one of the best friends I've ever had. Are you sure? . . . I mean, can there be any mix-up, any misreading? . . . Sometimes things get confused in the telling."

"No misreading. Do you remember a dinner we attended? I was annoyed, perhaps visibly so, by all that mention of the Cace deal. It is very unwise to have such matters bruited about in the yellow-dog press that imbeciles read. That business about the courtyard, the retractable glass roof—"

Adam almost jumped out of his seat. "That was my idea! I made a sketch of it one day when I was in Theo's office. They have something like it somewhere in Europe. I remember a photo—"

"A sketch? But nothing formal? No blueprint, no basis for a lawsuit?"

"No. It was just a passing thought, a doodle. Theo Brown was my friend," he repeated. "I would have sworn by his loyalty, his kindness, his honesty—"

Lawrence waved his hands in rebuttal. "Then it's a good thing you aren't practicing law," he said.

Adam, filled with grief and sensing the end of the interview, had to ask a final quick question. "Is there anything, anything at all, that can be done?"

"Nothing. They're quite within the law. Unless you can come up with enough money to outbid Brown's syndicate, you have to accept defeat. That's life."

With a sinking heart, Adam asked how much Mrs. R. would need. And after learning that half a million dollars might possibly do it, but only possibly, he thanked Mr. Lawrence and went out with his sinking heart down close to his boots.

The way home took him near to the park where Emma and he had met in secret on that summer day that now seemed so long ago. She, who was not an angel—and here in spite of all the troubles, he had to smile— had looked like one in her white dress and her hat with the single rose.

Next he had to pass the store. The green awnings and the flower boxes were still there where he had once placed them, and he remembered the simple pleasure he had felt on the day he bought them. The fine facade of the old building had been cleaned so that it now gleamed white in the sun. At the right-angle turn around the corner, he went past the addition that had been added three years ago. Here at this entrance the name Rothirsch was permanently carved beneath the cornice. He thought of some brief remarks that had gone between the architect and himself when he, Adam, had observed that it might be good to make this entrance match the old one. It had been no business of his to speak out on that subject, and he had a moment later regretted what the architect had every right to resent: a suggestion from someone like Adam. But instead, to his surprise, the man had accepted the suggestion.

"You know, Mr. Arnring, as I think it over, I do believe you are right. It would look better. Yes, you are right."

He drove out toward the highway. Here was the boardinghouse where he had spent those first weeks among the lady school-teachers. Who could have predicted how his life would change over the next few years?

Somebody knocked at the office door, and spoke. It was Reilly's voice. "Adam? Archer's here with me. We'd both like to see you."

Adam said wearily, "Come in."

What could they want, those two? After all this time, and the true affection he had for them both, they were still a pair of simpletons from a comic strip.

Reilly began. "Remember what you said a couple of days ago about the merger, and I said you should go to a lawyer? Well, we've got some information that you need to hear. I heard it last night at the bar near my house."

"Notice, he said 'I,' not 'we,'" objected Archer. "Because I don't go to bars."

"Sure, we know. Don't interrupt me. I need to tell Adam. Some guys were talking about that big deal. This one, I don't know his name, I don't think he lives in town, as a matter of fact he doesn't, I think he lives in Rosedale—"

"Go on," said Adam, already starting to fidget with impatience. "Go on."

"Well, this guy drives a car for a rich guy here, I forget his name, but he's a friend of our accountant, and he and Theo Brown were in the car, and they were talking, and you're right about what you said, Brown's cooking something up."

"I still can't believe it!" Adam cried. "So natural, so warmhearted—it doesn't make sense."

"It makes sense," Archer said gloomily. "You're still young. You'll find out when you've lived a little longer."

"So? What are you going to do about it?" asked Reilly.

"There's nothing to be done. Anyway, it's Mrs. R.'s business, not mine."

Reilly, with a gesture of complete dismissal, retorted that Mrs. R. was the last person in the world to manage such an affair; she would only put a monkey wrench in it, and the niece had no business getting mixed up in it, either. What did she know, a woman, and a young one at that?

"Well, that leaves nobody," Adam said.

"I was thinking," Reilly went on. "I didn't sleep last night, I was just thinking. You re-

member that man back east who gave you
the idea you should leave home and start up
for yourself? The man who played golf?"

"Mr. Shipper? What's he got to do with
anything?"

"Nothing, I guess. But he must have
thought a lot of you, the way you told it, at
least. Didn't he work in a bank or something?"

"He was an investment banker."

"Oh. I don't know anything about them.
But if he thought you were so smart, and the
way you built up this business here, he's a
banker, so maybe he'd lend you some
money and you could beat Brown at his
game."

The proposal was so absurd, and at the
same time Reilly's expression so anxious,
that Adam was touched. Reilly truly cares,
Adam thought, and recalled the time he had
said: *Pretend I'm your father.*

"The man hasn't seen me in almost nine
years, Reilly," he answered gently.

"Well, that's not so long. What does it cost
to try it?"

Plenty. All those records to be collected,
an expensive journey to New York, precious
time away from the job, and in the end, he

would only have made an embarrassed fool of himself.

These two kindly innocents, Reilly and Archer, were looking at him expectantly. Wanting to get rid of them and their foolishness, he said that he thanked them more than he could say, which was sincere, and that he would think about their suggestion, which was not sincere.

Yet when morning came and he went about the usual routine, he became aware that their idea was lying at the bottom of his mind like a discarded letter, or more accurately, like an insect bite or an itchy woolen sweater. For the next two days it kept irritating him; he neither mentioned it to Emma nor allowed himself to give it any serious consideration, but kept the itch to himself.

Then in the middle of the third afternoon, something said to him: Shipper *did* take an interest in you, this defunct store *has* prospered under you, this merger *would* be what my turncoat friend called a "bonanza," and Shipper *is* in the business of lending money for profit.

With these thoughts in mind, Adam returned to Spencer Lawrence's office, half expecting to be cruelly and courteously dismissed. Instead, Lawrence listened for more than half an hour to his story.

"Mr. Shipper is someone I used to know, you see." Adam's eyes drifted from the smooth rubber plant in the corner back to Lawrence's impassive face. "I was his caddy, and he liked me. I have no idea whether I could even get an appointment with him. I ask myself: Why should *he* do anything for *me,* when Theo Brown, who was my good friend, the salt of the earth, as my father used to say, is betraying us all?"

"Too much salt can kill you," Lawrence said wryly. He paused. "You mention your father. What is his business?"

"He has a little grocery store. It makes a bare living. He started out as a peddler when he came to America after the Civil War."

"Arnring. What kind of a name is that?"

"Jewish, from Germany."

"You've had two strikes against you. Poverty and being Jewish, like Mrs. Rothirsch."

"But she's not poor anymore, Mr. Lawrence."

"She's been up and down, on a roller coaster. She was on the way down when you came along. You've built something for her. It couldn't have been easy. She has her ways." And again there came that wry smile.

Adam, stifling a chuckle, agreed that certainly she did have her ways. But then he found himself defending her.

"Apart from poverty, she's had a lot of hardship in her life."

"So I've heard. Well, she's done a lot of good in her time. She's done a lot of charity, and she adopted that niece—a lovely young woman, don't you think?"

"Yes, very," Adam said.

"Well. To get back to you. I don't know if you'll accomplish much with Mr. Shipper. That's one of the two most important investment banking firms in the country."

"Am I a fool to try?"

"No, it never hurts to try. Nothing ventured, nothing gained. Isn't that true? I'll give them a phone call and find out whether it's worth your while to take the journey. If it is, I'll send them all the records, all the documents, yours and Cace's. I'll also take the matter up with Mrs. R., but I doubt there'll be any objection on her part."

Hardly, thought Adam, so astonished that for a moment he could hardly speak.

"I can't tell you, Mr. Lawrence, how grateful I am," he said finally. "Even if nothing at all ever comes of this, I'll always remember that you gave me your time and effort."

Lawrence nodded. Did he ever show a real smile? Enough to show his teeth?

"You know, Mr. Arnring, I have had a very privileged life, as did my father and grandfather. Every advantage was given to us. So I have a great deal of respect for any hardworking, ambitious man who hasn't had these advantages, and if I can help in any way, I will. You are a fine young man. You are well-spoken and mannerly. You are a gentleman. Mrs. Rothirsch is a very difficult woman with honest, good qualities, and I do not like to see her being tricked by Theo Brown, a person she and you both trusted. It's a very dirty affair."

Then, rifling through papers on his desk, Lawrence dismissed Adam. "Well, I have a lot of work to do here. I'll get back to you in three days."

Whoever could have thought it? Critical,

chilly, stiff as a ramrod—or was he, really? Was that only an outer manner, natural to people of a certain type and class? He surely had a great heart. Who could have expected it?

When Adam looked toward the window and raised his eyes, the Woolworth Building was there, a spear that cut the sky in two. It was the tallest building in the world. Below him was Wall Street, one of the richest streets in the world. On the other side of an enormous, carved desk sat Herman Shipper, one of the most powerful people on that street. Here in the midst of superlatives sat Adam Arnring, an average man.

"You haven't changed," Shipper said, "except for your clothes," and he winked. " 'I'm a man of the world,' that suit says."

How I wish it! Adam thought. What did he know or what had he ever known of "the world," in which, after you have scrambled for a toehold on the rock, it crumbles under your toe?

"Have you been back in the old hometown at all since you left?"

"Just once, four years ago when my mother died."

"I thought your mother had died long ago."

"Well, yes. But this one raised me, so I—"

Mr. Shipper nodded kindly. "Of course. Tell me, what's happened to the brother who was such a fine student?"

"He's getting ready for medical school."

"And you're still helping him?"

"I have to. I want to."

"Not easy, is it?"

"The hardest part is getting accepted. The Jewish quota, you know."

"What else is new? It's only been two thousand years." And Shipper sighed. "At least he stands a better chance than if he were one of those eastern Europeans, those Russian types. We don't want them around us ourselves, don't want them in our clubs, do we? We want to be with our own kind."

Words flashed through Adam's mind. *The upper-class Jews don't want Sabine . . . Archer says Reilly's got a hangover from last night. He's a fine guy, the best, but the Irish, you know, they can't keep away from the drink . . . Reilly says, I've lived next door to*

Archer for the last twenty years, and he's a fine guy, but still he's cold. That's some funny thing about the British.

Mr. Shipper continued, "They have no polish, no background, no taste. They give us a bad name."

Poor Sabine Rothirsch . . . No polish, no background, no taste.

Adam, clearing his head, returned to the business at hand. "The heart of the matter is that she wants the deal but is afraid to spend what's required. She's old, scared, and not sufficiently competent to understand that the business is flourishing well enough to handle a debt."

Shipper nodded. "I know. I had a couple of conversations with Mr. Lawrence. Look at this pile of documents that he sent last week. What startled me was the record of profit that changed in the very first month after you took over."

"It was a challenge. I enjoyed it, and I still do."

"That's what Lawrence said about you. Sort of a stiff-upper-lip type, isn't he? But very helpful, very thorough, and answered practically all my questions before I asked them."

Shipper leaned back in his chair, offered Adam a cigar and, being refused, lit his own and savored it for a minute or two. While the smoke rose, Adam waited in suspense. Yes or no, Mr. Shipper, so I can go home.

"You told me yesterday, Adam, and Mr. Lawrence also said that Mrs. Rothirsch wants the deal, but will not advance the money. Let me ask, what if you had to undertake the debt yourself?"

"I, Mr. Shipper? However could I—"

"Very easily. I discussed it with Lawrence. We would make you a loan at five percent. We then own your proportion of the new firm's stock. You would be a part owner. It would take a very few years, if all goes well, and there is no reason to think it will not go well, for you to pay us back."

Adam responded hesitantly, "I don't understand. You'd trust *me* with over half a million dollars?"

Shipper laughed. "You know better than that. You're surprised, and that's why you're asking a foolish question. Look here, if you don't repay me, then I will become a stockholder in your firm. That's putting things in simplest terms. I assure you, I'm not worried in the least."

"I don't know what to say."

Adam's eyes began to fill. He blinked, and hoped that Shipper would think it was the cigar smoke's fault.

"Say nothing. Just continue to do a good job and be well. By the way, you didn't say. Do you ever think of marriage?"

"Well, yes, I have been thinking, but—" and apologizing for his eyes, he added, "The smoke. My eyes get funny."

"Oh, I'm sorry. I didn't realize it bothered you."

"No, just keep the cigar, please. I don't mind, it's nothing."

"Mr. Lawrence was really quite enthusiastic when I gave him my idea about you. He said you are very, very worthy."

"This is all too much for me to believe," Adam said.

Mr. Shipper laughed. "Well, believe it. Our lawyers will be in touch with Mr. Lawrence tomorrow."

Somehow or other, the lengthy meeting came to a close. After handshakes, best wishes, and the most earnest thanks that Adam had ever bestowed upon anyone, he found himself down on the street, staring up at the Woolworth Building. Then he went to a telephone, spoke a few halting, gleeful words to Emma, and made his way to the westbound train.

Chapter 14

Adam was stunned, and he was not alone. In no time at all, once he had received his check from New York, the merger papers that Lawrence had long ago readied for signature were signed. The news spread through the city, and a handsome sketch of the proposed new building was printed in the newspaper, accompanied by a Jeff Horace feature article.

"It seems like a dream," Emma said. "I'm so glad for you, Adam."

"Be glad for us both." He wondered whether in time he would take it all for granted. Not wanting ever to forget where he came from, he relived the events of these last days. He considered the actors in this drama: Brown the betrayer, Lawrence the righteous, Shipper the generous, Sabine the incredulous, Emma the joyous, and the last, who could well be counted the first, that old friend, Reilly.

How ironic that Reilly, of all people, had steered him in the right direction. So what did that prove? Never assume. Never dismiss.

"The first thing I'm going to try for when I have some say in the combined store is to get a raise for all the employees, the women especially. They don't earn nearly enough. And Reilly and Archer have been there since Rothirsch opened the store, so there should be something very special for them."

A tremendous excitement was stirring. It was amusing to see its effects on various people: on Theo Brown, who, pretending not to see Adam, had crossed to the other side of the street; or on Sabine, who, having heard Spencer Lawrence's high opinion of Adam along with the news that Adam was now a stockholder (even though a small one), now fully accepted him as the man whom Emma was to marry.

"I was thinking," she remarked one evening at the dinner table, "that you might suggest a change of name. Instead of Cace Rothirsch, wouldn't it sound better to have Cace Arnring? I've always thought that

Rothirsch was an awful name. People can't spell it, and they can't even pronounce it."

"I'm only a very small stockholder," Adam protested.

"But I'm a big one. And I can have my say. It's my name that would be the one changed. And as for you, Emma, wouldn't it be nice to get rid of Rothirsch? Emma Arnring. That's much better."

What some money and a bit of prestige can do to change an attitude! Adam reflected.

They were determined not to give in to Sabine's urging that they live in her house.

"Five empty bedrooms! It's ridiculous for you two to spend money when all this space is going to waste," she protested, up to the very day on which Adam signed a contract to purchase a house.

It was an old one in the historic district, not far from the circular house that had so fascinated him when first he arrived in the town. Two acres of grass, cottonwoods, and an old red cedar sixty feet tall surrounded it, and there was space in the rear where a room would be added to accommodate Emma's piano.

She was elated. "I can close the door and give lessons while you read in the front room, and you won't be disturbed at all."

"I shall never be disturbed by your music or anything you do," he said gravely.

She wanted a gas stove. The old coal range was a treasure for cooking and for warmth, but the gas range was modern, and they would have both.

He teased her. "So you are going to be a domestic wife as well as a piano teacher?"

"Why not? I love both, and I can do both. Darling Adam, you have a lot to learn about me."

If happiness can be called "divine," then Adam and Emma were divinely happy.

Dear Family, he wrote, electing to write one letter to all three to save time.

The work on the new building is going along at top speed. The foundation is laid, and the steel for the structure arrived this morning. Three huge truckloads of it. Do you remember when I wrote about the glass-roofed section that I dreamed up? It's going to be done. The people at Cace were delighted with the idea. They're all tremendously enthusiastic about our joint venture. It has surely taken long enough to be born, but the result is worth all the delays. Mr. Lawrence, the lawyer who I said wouldn't give away an icicle in January, has turned out to be my guardian angel. As the lawyer for Cace Arnring, he has assured me that I will be part of top management with a very nice salary, this in addition to being a stockholder.

It's hard to believe, but I need have no more concern about my job or about money in general. Compared with a lot of people around here, I certainly have no fortune, but I do have enough now to satisfy my needs and yours, too. Pa, you always say, "Nothing," when I ask you what you need, so I will not ask anymore. I will just send. Please take care of your health, and write soon. Love,

Adam

The tip of his pen wanted to continue with the story of Emma, but somehow it would seem, he thought, just all too glorious on top of so much good fortune. So he stopped the pen. Better to wait until the house was ready and the wedding date set. Better to let Jonathan and his Blanche occupy center stage for a while; she was wearing his little ring, she was the most wonderful girl, and Adam must come soon to meet her and see for himself.

In March it seemed as if the question of war with Germany that had so long been debated in the newspapers and on street corners was about to be answered: Yes. In February, diplomatic relations had been severed; now three American ships, homeward bound, had been sunk by submarines. England had three weeks' supply of food, and the Allies had a death toll in the hundreds of thousands, with no end in sight. So, on the sixth of April, the President appeared before a joint session of Congress and asked for a declaration of war.

Men between the ages of twenty-one and forty-five were subject to the draft. Jonathan was called, while Adam was not, at least not yet. He had complex feelings about the difference. Should he or should he not volunteer? He decided that if he was needed, he would be summoned. But since he was obviously not needed immediately, he would go on with the work at Cace Arnring and the repair of the house.

"Jonathan expects to sail in early June," he told Emma. "I'll have to see him before he leaves."

When she offered to go along, he declined. "I haven't even told anyone about us," he explained. "And since I'm still here with you and he's leaving his sweetheart, it would seem rather unfeeling, don't you think so?"

Emma did think so. And therefore on a fine May morning, Adam boarded a train crowded with draftees and relatives on their way to the eastern coast.

A sense of strength and accomplishment rose in Adam. There was no trace of arrogance in the feeling; indeed it was largely made up of gratitude. Here he was in his old hometown, in its best restaurant, taking his

family to dinner and able to give them almost anything they might need. At the head
of the table he sat and observed them.

His father was aging too fast. Men twenty
years older than Simon often looked
younger. Stubborn as ever, he held on to his
little store and fretted that Adam's check
was too generous.

"Pa," Adam said, "do you realize how long
it is since I went west, and you've never
come to see me, although I've kept asking
you to, especially during this last year when
I could take such good care of you? There's
a nice small hotel, brand-new, right
nearby—"

Simon waved him away. "No, no, Adam. I
don't want to spend a couple of days and
nights on any train. Besides, I can't leave
the store in Leo's charge. And he doesn't
want to visit, either. Do I have to explain any
more?"

No, he did not need to. Leo had even refused this evening's dinner because the restaurant was on the same street as the
Nishikawas' house, and he had vowed
never to walk on that street again.

As for the two lovers—well, they glowed
as lovers do. They were sure of each other,

and they had the same plans that Emma and he had been making. The difference was that they were about to be separated, while Emma and he were not going to be, unless the war should last long enough for him to be called up, too. In the meantime, in the circumstances, he certainly was not going to mention Emma to anybody here.

He could not help but make comparisons. Beauty, as the saying goes, is in the eye of the beholder. In Adam's eye, Blanche was not beautiful, but she was interesting. She was tall, with gleaming black curls that escaped from her pompadour; she had searching, intelligent eyes and the thin, beaked nose of a Roman aristocrat. She had poise and the sophistication that Jonathan, in spite of his knowledge, had never had. In fact, Adam reflected, there was a certain innocence in him that he had never noticed before. But Blanche had had a hard life, and she was unafraid. She would make sure that nobody took advantage of Jonathan. It was not, as far as Adam knew, that anyone had ever done so, but who can foresee the future? Look at his own experience with Theo Brown! While a man like Jonathan was at work in his laboratory or the library, Brown would have walked away with the whole business.

"Leo is so upset," Pa said. "It's not that he's eager to join the army, but the rejection insulted him. Too short, underweight, poor eyesight, and flatfeet. He's still furious."

"I admire your patience with Leo," Blanche observed. "Many people would not have so much."

"What would they do?" asked Jonathan.

"I can't answer that. They just wouldn't be as patient."

"Well, we can't turn him loose and forget about him."

"Because he is ill, you're saying?"

"I don't know whether he's ill. He's certainly different. Difficult. But illness? I don't know."

"Freud would say he's neurotic," Blanche said. "When I lived in Vienna—"

"Not everybody agrees with Freud." When Jonathan was earnest, as now, two parallel lines formed on his forehead. "With all that is unknown about human behavior, it could be anything. It might be something that some medicine, as yet undiscovered, can repair."

"You will be a fine doctor," Pa observed. "You have a heart along with your mind.

Now I need to ask something of you, of both of you. If anything happens to me, I want you to take care of Leo. Remember that you are brothers, and he may need you."

"You can depend upon us," Adam said.

Blanche remarked that the subject was too sad for a night like this one. Adam was not sure whether she meant that the evening was still bright and fragrant, or whether she was thinking, as he was, of Jonathan's departure to France.

"I'd like to take a walk after dinner," he said. "I'd like to see what, if anything, is new in town. Who'll come with me?"

Pa was not coming. "You young folks go ahead. After this big dinner, I'm going home to my chair and the morning paper. I haven't read it yet."

Blanche reminded him, "Your warm milk, Pa. Don't forget it again. It makes him sleep well," she explained to Adam.

Jonathan smiled. "I told you she's already a part of the family."

There were changes on the streets. More cars, and many more trucks, more doctors, dentists, lawyers, real estate offices, and every kind of shop. There were flags, and a band marching down Main Street to the sound of song: *Over there, over there . . . the Yanks are coming—*

"Do you know who gave all the flags? Your friend, Herman Shipper," Jonathan said. "First thing we knew, right after April sixth, the whole crew was out putting up flags, a hundred of them, all over town. A remarkable man, Herman Shipper."

Yes, remarkable. Not only the man in that office on the fourteenth floor with a view of the Woolworth Building, but the man who had once told a boy just out of high school that he had "a head for business," and would go far.

"How about walking over to the beach?" he asked.

The grand houses, Shipper's white one beside the neighbor's Tudor, were the same; yet now he did not wonder about them as he had done then. He did not even desire one. Nor, as he regarded the Tudor that he had so easily, proudly been able to identify, did he long to be an architect.

Jonathan suggested that they sit down in one of the pavilions. "Might as well enjoy the ocean. I never get tired of it, whether it's gray and angry, or olive green before rain, or sapphire. When summer comes, you can hardly get a seat here."

Adam began a description. "In the summer, bathing huts look like sprinkled confetti on the beach. And in the winter, it's deserted. All you see are gulls. These railings are covered with snow. A few kids and a few hardy old men have it all to themselves."

Blanche smiled. "You're forgetting that this is the start of my fourth year in this town. I am beginning to feel like a native. I know the ocean in all its moods. I might even feel more at home here than you do, Adam. You've been away so long."

"But not as far away as you are from Vienna."

"That's true. The difference is that I have nobody there and not very much that's nice to remember, as you have here."

She had a lilting voice. *Her voice was ever soft, gentle, and low, an excellent thing in woman.* Shakespeare said so in some play that Adam had forgotten.

"Tell me about Vienna," he said. "I've only seen pictures of it."

"You have seen pictures of the palace and parks, and the carriages driving along the Ringstrasse under the lime trees. To me, too, though, they were only pictures. I did alterations in a fine shop there, but I never drove there or walked there, except to walk home to the tenement where I lived. Two rooms for a big family, and always extra relatives, including me. No plumbing. A pump in the courtyard. In winter, the water froze. My father was killed in one of their foolish wars. When my mother died, she left me enough to pay my passage to America . . . Still, it was beautiful if you could afford it. The emperor rode out in his carriage behind white horses. We used to stand on the sidewalk on Sundays and watch. And now all the blood being shed because an angry man killed the archduke. They should get rid of them all!"

"We'll do the job," said Jonathan. "But still, it's never that simple, is it? Of course Pa wants us to win. Yet even he said something the other day about the cousins he left behind. He rarely writes to them or hears from them, yet he's thinking about their wearing our enemy's uniform, while next week I'll be putting on mine."

There was a silence until Blanche broke it. "I can't believe it's only a week before you leave."

"I'll be back sooner than you think, my darling. It'll be a short, quick war."

"And after that, four years of medical school," said Blanche. "It doesn't seem fair that you have to work your whole youth away, poor man."

"And after that, a few more years of being a student's wife, while I go on into a specialty."

"Have you any idea which one?" asked Adam.

"I don't know. There's so much that's fascinating, surgery, neurology, or a combination of them. But I've only just finished with college. I don't have to decide right now."

"It seems to take forever to become a doctor," Blanche said. "You're middle aged before you start living."

Her tone was sad, trailing off like a note in a minor key. And why not? Faced with this parting that must be almost unbearable? While I, he thought, am going home to Emma. . . .

Jonathan laughed. "Oh, it's not all that bad, darling. Remember, everybody can't be a tycoon like my brother here. Have I shown you Pa's sketches of the plans for the new shop?"

"You have," said Blanche. "Very, very handsome, Adam. Do you handle many imports?"

"Yes, some. We've ordered some Paul Poiret a few times."

"And Vionnet? And Lanvin? They're not as fussy as he is. Not as formal."

Jonathan laughed and said teasingly, "Ah, Adam, listen carefully! She'll tell you everything you don't know about fashion."

"Then she'll have a lot to tell me. I leave fashion to the buyers. I only supervise the hiring, and sometimes the firing."

"I can see," observed Blanche, "why Leo resents you so. It's envy, pure and simple."

"Not simple," Jonathan said quietly. "Very far from simple."

"Very complicated," Adam agreed.

What relationship isn't complicated? he thought. What of Pa's guilt about my birth? I often think he favors me because of it; I often think Leo reads the family relationships that way. I've taken the place as eldest son that rightly belongs to him. Ah, my God, it's all too complicated . . . Emma and I began with enough complications, but, thank heaven, they're over. I'd like to tell Jonathan about us, but—not just yet. Now's not the time.

"When are you leaving us, Adam?" asked Blanche.

"Tomorrow. I'd like to stay longer, but I need to get back."

"Of course you must. You need to watch your investment. There's always a schemer of some sort who's ready to nibble away at it."

Adam laughed. "It's not quite as bad as that, although I can't say you're entirely wrong."

"That's one thing I don't ever expect to worry about," Jonathan said. "If I make a decent, modest living as a doctor, I'll be completely satisfied."

He had moved and was sitting now with his arm around Blanche and his hand clasped over hers. They made a romantic picture against the surf and the pink light.

"It's getting chilly," Jonathan said to Blanche, "and you have no coat. Take my jacket."

"Absolutely not. My dress is heavier than your shirt. He's so good to me," she told Adam. "Your father calls him 'the salt of the earth.' "

"That's Pa's favorite saying. But he exaggerates," Jonathan said. "Come on. The wind's churning the ocean. Besides, it's Adam who's the salt of the earth." And he turned to Adam. "I know I've said this often before, but you have to hear it again. Going away, leaving you all, I need to say it. So hear me out. I thank you with all my heart for everything you've done for me, and for everything you are. And I'm so glad about all your success. When I get back after this war, we'll go out to visit you and see it for ourselves."

For a moment the three stood, listening to the crash, murmur, and crash of the incoming tide. The sun was about to sink, leaving just enough pink in the sky to light the way home.

At the corner of her street, Blanche and Jonathan left Adam.

It's a good match, he thought as he watched them walk away. They'll do well together. God bless them both.

When Sabine had wanted a huge, glamorous wedding at her house, Emma had pointed out that they did not know a huge number of people to invite. But Sabine had assured her that now, with all of Adam's new contacts, it would be easy to have at least two hundred fifty guests.

"I'll have a dance floor laid on the back lawn with a tent if it rains, or then we could easily move indoors. Goodness knows, the house is large enough."

"Do you like the idea?" Adam had asked Emma in private.

"No. And I wouldn't like it any time, but especially now with the country at war. It doesn't seem fit. Let's have a small wedding and invite only the people who mean something to us."

Adam telephoned to his father. "By now you must have my letter," he said, "so you know all about Emma and me. And you understand why I didn't mention her in front of Jon and Blanche that evening. But we want to get married very soon and have some time together before I may have to go where Jon is. Do you want to tell Blanche? Tell her she's invited if she wants to come. I don't know her as you do, so I can't decide what's best. I don't even know whether you and Leo want to come to the wedding, Pa. I'm saying this because I want you to tell me truly. You won't hurt us if you say no."

"I've been looking at Emma's picture. I hope she is as good to you as she is beautiful. And I can't tell you how glad I am. But I guess you know. You didn't have a great start in life. I still think about it, God forgive me. Surely I want to be there to see you married, but it just doesn't seem possible to work out. I can't bring myself to mention the subject to Blanche. She is so miserable, poor thing, so lonesome for Jon. She worries me. And you know Leo would never go to a wedding, not yours or anybody's, or to any other social event. He only likes to come home from the store and hide with his books."

Jon wrote:

On the fourth of July we marched down the Champs-Elysées, our bands playing "The Battle Hymn of the Republic," crowds on either side cheering, women throwing kisses. It touched our hearts and our pride. These people believe we will save the day for them, and we will save it. I'm sure you get the cable news and all the papers, so you know what's

going on over here. It won't be long.
After a couple of battles, we'll wipe out
the Boches and probably be home
before winter comes.
   Save some time for my wedding. I
cannot begin to describe how I miss
Blanche, but I guess you can imagine.
She is with me every hour of the day.
Please take good care of her, in spite of
the distance between you. Keep in
touch.

On a rainy fall afternoon, promptly at half after four because Sabine had looked up the proper hour in a book of etiquette, a group was assembled in her long drawing room under the glowering stare of the late Rothirsch. The guests were mostly those who had sat at Adam's first grand dinner in this house: two each of Sabine's old ladies and Emma's college friends, Jeff Horace, who would report the occasion in glamorous terms, although Adam had already begged him to "keep it simple," Reilly and Archer with their wives, Rudy and Rea, who had known Emma since she was two years old, and the Spencer Lawrences, who had procured a judge to perform the ceremony

that would satisfy Sabine—more or less—
and completely satisfy the pair who were to
be married.

Adam was thoughtful as he waited for the
bride. A sense of unreality came and went
while he looked around at the guests, the
small table before which they were to stand,
and the wall of white chrysanthemums in the
background. Rea, perhaps remembering the
bicycles hidden down the street, caught his
gaze, smiled, and winked. Archer's unhappy
wife Edna, a plain woman drably dressed,
looked wistful. There was no mistaking that
Reilly's wife Bridget, standing with his arm
around her shoulders, was happily dressed
up in pink for a grand occasion. Mrs.
Lawrence was attractive and impeccable in
dark blue with a single narrow diamond
bracelet on her wrist. Now and then, he reflected, whenever he caught a glimpse of her
with her two young daughters at the store, he
would have another swift mental glimpse of
Francine's place and wonder how and why a
man with such a family, an otherwise honor-
able, decent man, could bring himself to
such a place. He would never be tempted to
do the same now that he had Emma.

There she was, walking in from the hall

with Sabine at her side, for Sabine was to give her away. Dressed all in white as she had wanted to be, her expression was grave. A penny for your thoughts, darling Emma.

Sabine, decked with bracelets and necklaces, was teary, smiling, and happy. Surely this must be the crowning event of her life in this house.

The judge, looking properly solemn, stepped forward and began to speak. His words, which Adam barely absorbed, were solemn, requiring only brief and solemn responses, just one answer really: *I do.* Adam had forgotten that he had a ring in his pocket until he was asked to produce it. He could not take his eyes away from Emma's. Then it was over. *You may kiss your wife,* the judge said, so they kissed and went out among hearty smiles and hearty good wishes into the dining room.

Laughing, Reilly said, "You're in a fog, Adam."

"I don't know what's the matter with me. I don't seem to know where I am. It's not real."

"It'll be real tonight. You'll know where you are and what to do," Reilly said, still laughing.

"Oh, stop," his wife chided, "don't embarrass them!" But she was laughing, too.

Sabine had summoned a quartet to play during dinner. The music, which had no doubt been selected by Emma, was airy and joyous, so that between it and some very good champagne, all gravity faded.

Pa sent a telegram, a long one unlike his usual few frugal words. "Make merry," it ended.

Make merry. So they did, and the champagne flowed.

Then Emma went upstairs to change into a traveling suit. And in a rain of rice, they went down the steps to the car that was to take them away.

"I've waited so long for a bed together," Adam whispered.

"Oh," said Emma, "I have, too. We could have done it long before this wedding, darling Adam, if you weren't such a cautious, proper gentleman."

Two weeks later, Adam and Emma were met at the railroad station by Rudy in the Pierce-Arrow, without Sabine.

"Where's my aunt?" asked Emma.

"She's coming by to your house later."

"You know something," Adam said when they were alone in the backseat, "I hate this car. It's so stupid to be sheltered here while the driver's outside in the weather."

"Do you remember the time you were the chauffeur, and I sat in front with you? Sabine was furious, but she controlled herself."

"I take it that you won't ask me for a Pierce-Arrow? Not that we can afford one."

They were both laughing when they drove up to the little house that, incredibly, was their own. In the afternoon sunshine, its fresh paint glistened, the cottonwoods were bending to the mild fall wind, and a pair of rosebushes at the front door were still in bud. For a moment before he opened the door, Adam went to peer into the dining room window. Having spent his life eating his supper in a kitchen, he had always pictured a beautiful room and a beautiful table large enough for family and friends. Now he had one. He had dreamed of a really big front porch with beautiful chairs on it, and of a home with shelves for all the beautiful books he wanted to buy. Now he had them.

The key turned easily in the lock. He put down a suitcase, while Rudy brought in the rest of the luggage, set it in the hall, and said good-bye.

"Wasn't he strange? Hardly a word to say," remarked Emma. "Not like him at all. Oh, here's a letter in the mail slot. Look, it's got an odd postmark. It's from your brother, Jonathan."

"Dear Adam," he read aloud, "I cannot say where I am or what I'm doing, but I can say what anyone with a brain in his head already knows: War is hell. I find myself thinking so much about you. My brother! I have no friend in the world like you, except, of course, my Blanche. I think about that night at the shore and remember you told me how lovely and how beautiful she is. Please take care of her while I'm gone."

He did not recall having made any remark about Blanche's beauty. But nevertheless, he was touched by reading Jon's words. And having finished the short, precious letter, he put it away in a safe place to be brought out someday and shown around as a memento of the war.

Emma was reading it when the telephone rang for the first time in the new house. "That you, Adam? This is Jeff. Jeff Horace."

"Hey, you're the only Jeff I know. How's everything?"

"I called Mrs. Rothirsch. She told me you'd be home around now. Do you mind if I come over?"

Adam glanced at the luggage that waited to be unpacked. "Why, no. We just got in, but—"

"I'll be right there."

"That's odd," Emma said. "Oh, well."

"I don't know why I feel uneasy, as if something's going to happen."

"You're a worrier. He's got some surprise, a house gift, or—I know what! His article about the wedding!"

When, a few minutes later, they opened the door, Jeff was there with Sabine. Then there followed a moment when four people stood looking at each other.

In an instant, Adam knew, or thought he knew, something. "You have something to tell me. It's about my father."

Jeff, turning away, looked toward the opposite wall, or simply into the air. He said, very quietly, "No, it's about your brother."

"My brother?"

"The news came to your father last Thursday. Somebody called Mrs. Rothirsch. I don't know how to tell it . . . The telegram came to your father's house from the army. You know what they always say: 'We regret to inform you that your son . . .' Oh, my heart breaks for you, Adam! My heart breaks."

"Jonathan? He's been hurt?"

"Killed in action, Adam."

"Jonathan," Adam repeated.

When he said "brother," I thought he meant Leo.

"Mrs. Rothirsch asked me to call your father," Jeff went on gently. "They had a doctor, a heart specialist, who took care of him. Mrs. Rothirsch has been on the phone. She'll tell you. The neighbors, the whole neighborhood, she says, has been so kind, so helpful to your father and your brother. Leo? Is that his name? It was the first war death in the area, they say, and people are stunned. Leo has gone to pieces and Blanche is falling apart. They've given her pills to calm her down."

Calm her? Calm Leo? What about Pa? Ah God, my poor old father . . .

Adam knew that Sabine and Emma were looking at him, their eyes full of horror and pity. He was having a queer sensation, as if time had stopped, and there was nothing to do but stand there looking at each other.

"I think you should speak to your father," Emma said, gripping his arm. "Let me get the number for you."

"Yes, yes. I've got to leave here tomorrow, first train out."

But that was not to be. "No," Simon insisted. "Stay right where you are. You've just been married! I can manage."

"What about your coming here to us?"

"Soon, but not right now. Don't worry about me, Adam. There's nothing anybody can do except bear it. Jonathan would be the first to say so."

The voice wavered and the telephone clicked.

Nothing to do but bear it.

He put the receiver down. Then he walked to the window, for no reason except that something was bursting in his chest and he needed to move. He stood there looking out into the bright afternoon, where some boys on the way home from school were racing, swinging their school bags. Over there, an ocean away, a boy not much older than they lay dead in the mud.

Why? Why of all people, Jonathan? Why?

Something struck at him, choked in his throat, and tore at his gut. He fell onto a chair and sat there weeping, pounding his knees with his fists, until Emma put her arms around him, and led him away.

Chapter 15

As Shakespeare says, *The rest is silence.* For by comparison with the roar and wreckage of a tempest, such as an unexpected death in a family, the resumption of ordinary, daily life is almost like a silence and a relief.

So, a little more than a year later, Adam and Emma met Simon and Blanche at the train. "Pa," Adam said. "I thought Leo was coming. He told me he would when I visited you."

"He didn't want to. Changed his mind at the last minute. You know him. But I hired a young fellow to help him out at the store. Already knows more than Leo does, so he can have plenty of time for his books and his friend Bobby."

Adam introduced them to Emma, and after hands were shaken and cheeks kissed, they all climbed into his new car, a Maxwell.

Pa was looking around and craning his

neck to peer down the cross streets. "Town's bigger than I thought," he remarked.

"It's growing every day. Would you like to have a quick ride around downtown before we go to Sabine's? Sorry we can't have you both sleep at our house, but the furniture for the extra bedroom hasn't come yet. We've only got ours and the nursery. The crib and stuff arrived yesterday."

"You don't show much," Blanche observed, glancing at Emma.

"I'm going into the ninth month, but I have this loose duster on. I must tell you my aunt Sabine is a wonderful hostess, and she loves having guests, so you really mustn't feel uncomfortable about staying with a stranger."

"Except for Pa, you are both strangers, too."

A cool answer, Adam thought, almost rude. But he didn't like to criticize her after what she had been through.

Swinging the car around the corner, he stopped and pointed out the store. "Here, folks, is Cace Arnring, getting ready to open its doors."

Everything, the cool, dark shrubbery, the

tall windows in their ornamental niches, the white stone, all gleamed in the noon-day sun.

Pa whistled. "I never imagined! It's a whole lot bigger than the old store, isn't it?"

"Three times bigger. We've got menswear now, small items like shirts and ties. Gifts, too, and jewelry, stuff we didn't have before. Oh, and fine linens, tablecloths, imported, handmade. It's a luxury store."

Pa nodded. "Yeah, well, there must be a lot of money around here."

"There is. The wealthy folks used to buy a great deal when they traveled. Now they don't have to, at least not as much," Adam said modestly.

Blanche nodded. "This does have ele-gance. It's better looking than Printemps in Paris."

"Oh, I thought you came from Vienna," Emma said.

"I did, but I passed through Paris when I emigrated. I stayed a week, in fact. It's amazing how much you can see in a week."

"Emma lived there for a whole semester," Adam said, "studying piano."

"Oh, that's interesting."

"She has a teaching degree. She teaches

a class at the university here, and gives lessons at home, too."

"Oh," Blanche said.

Again he felt that twinge of annoyance. He hadn't meant to make her feel foolish in comparison with Emma.

"Well, here we are," he announced as they arrived before Sabine's dark fieldstone pile. "I hope you're hungry. Emma's aunt sets a great table."

Indeed she had done so. There was enough food for a dozen people, and excellent food, too. At the head of the table Sabine presided in a gracious, kindly mood as she welcomed the poor grocery man and the poor immigrant to her grand house. For by this time Adam knew her well enough to read in her the emotions that she might not even know she was feeling.

"That's a beautiful dress you're wearing," Sabine told Blanche.

The dress, like the wearer, was slender. Black cloth, narrowly striped in white, was belted at the curving waist. On her head she wore a turban with a band of fur.

"Very striking, very unusual. And I love the hat," Emma said.

"Thank you. I made them both myself. The

fur was left over from a coat Berman the tailor was altering."

"They're beautiful, Blanche. Really beautiful."

"Well, the piano for you, the needle and thread for me."

"Right now I wish I knew how to use a needle and thread. They're having a company party next month for the grand opening, and I have nothing to wear."

"You shouldn't go there, anyway," Sabine said firmly. "It isn't seemly in your condition."

"Allow me to disagree, dear aunt," Adam objected. "I don't believe most people nowadays feel that way about it. And she can easily buy a wide skirt for concealment."

"Men!" Sabine exclaimed. "What do they know? Do you even know that people haven't worn hoopskirts since the Civil War?"

Pa laughed. He was enjoying this kind of talk. It was a long time since he had been present at any conversation that was so free of gloom.

Blanche asked whether Emma had any

dress that she would wear if she could fit in
it.

"Well, yes, I have several in bright colors,
and I have a black and a gray-and-white."

"We could take the black," Blanche said
positively, "cut the whole front out, and
cover it with small ruffles. Small, narrow
ones, pleated. It would conceal, I think, and
it would be quite handsome, maybe in pale
blue."

Emma, considering this for a few minutes,
replied that it seemed to be a wonderful
idea. "Except," she said, "that I can't think
of anybody who would be skillful enough to
do it. It sounds too much like Paris."

"I could do it," Blanche said.

"But you won't be here long enough."

"It would take a good week's work. No,
close to two weeks. But I'd be willing to stay
and do it if you'd like me to."

"Blanche!" Simon warned. "I said five
days, you remember? I have responsibilities
at home."

"I could change my ticket, Pa. You go
home without me, and I'll be back a week
later. How does that sound?"

Simon frowned. "Are you serious about
this?"

"Of course I am. I haven't been doing any real work for a couple of months. I've been moping around ever since . . . Now I feel like doing something that will take my mind off things."

"You're absolutely amazing!" cried Emma.

"Well, if that's what you all want, go ahead. I'm happy," Simon said.

It was good to see a cheerful expression on his father's face, Adam thought. This pleasant atmosphere, the women's talk, and the sense of family—things that had for too long been missing in the old man's life—must have brought about the cheer.

Really, it was very generous of Blanche to make this offer, and Adam was sorry that he had almost misjudged her.

The candle flames that flickered on the table flickered again upon the glass roof. On a small dais in one corner of the long space, a string quartet mingled its music with the hum of voices.

"Like our wedding," Adam said.

Emma was radiant, flushed pink with the marvel of this night. He understood completely. For him the sensations were possibly even more intense. For he was at the launch of a substantial enterprise in which he, Adam Arnring, already held some small authority, and would probably hold a great deal more. And here he was, too, with the only woman he had ever loved, who loved him and who was to bear his child. He had had very little to drink, but he was already drunk with wonder.

When the music stopped, it was time for another speech. When an elderly member of the new corporation's board stepped forward to speak for Sabine, who had turned down the honor in utter terror, Adam with hidden humor was thinking that those board members must have been in terror that she might accept.

A penny for your thoughts, Sabine, he said to himself as he glanced in her direction. You, too, have come a long way, a much harder way than mine. Seated between Emma and Blanche, she looked almost magisterial in a dark satin dress. For once, she was not bedecked with jewelry; he wondered whether it had been the advice of Blanche that had sent her out of her house with only one pearl choker, one pearl bracelet, and one diamond ring.

Blanche herself could have stepped out of a fashion magazine. Emma had lent her a ruby velvet dress, too short for her, but Blanche, with what Emma called her "magic needle," had added a matching silk flounce that reached the floor. A wave of pity went through him as he watched her smile and nod and listen politely to the droning from the podium. She should have been having Jonathan's child. . . .

The speaker was calling out names, giving recognition to the new staff in the new store. Smiling their thanks, men stood, and their wives stood with them. Gallantly, uninhibited by a round of respectful applause, Emma in all her charm stood up with Adam.

Jonathan Arnring was born at home. In the sunny upstairs bedroom, Emma, propped up by pillows and surrounded by a room filled with flowers and boxes of extravagant baby clothes, was carefully examining his ears, eyelashes, and toenails. He was already one week old, and she was still exulting over this marvel.

"Isn't he beautiful, Adam? I know every mother must say that about her baby, but I really believe this one is unusual. Some babies look all squashed and red, if you know what I mean, but he doesn't. You can really see his features."

"Just how many new babies have you seen in your lifetime?" Adam demanded through his laughter.

"Well, to tell the truth, none," she said, and now both, a little bit teary, were laughing at themselves.

But how, how could a woman take this tiny, soft life, wrap it up, and leave it on a doorstep? What kind of human being could she have been, Emma cried to herself. How could it not have broken her heart to do a thing like that?

But as Adam had said to her, who really knew whether it had broken her heart or not. And she had understood that he himself must have been recalling that night when, through his brother's words, he had first learned that he was a bastard.

She caught his hand that was resting on the blanket, his warm hand with the blue veins and the strong fingers that could be so gentle. And raising the hand to her lips, she kissed it.

Oh, enough! Here is our wanted, welcomed child, our Jonathan. I suppose he will be called Jon. He has such lovely blue eyes! The doctor says that eye color often changes after birth. I hope you will look like Adam, or even like Adam's brother, the one who died in the war . . . and she tried not to think of the other one.

"I'd better go downstairs," Adam said. "Blanche is coming with another gift from Sabine, who is still not over her cold."

"Another gift! This baby has enough clothing to fill the infants' wear department at Cace Arnring. Blanche is going home soon, right?"

"The day after tomorrow. She was waiting for the baby's birth so she could tell Pa about it. And I guess she likes being at Sabine's, which must feel like a luxury hotel."

"I suppose so. Poor Blanche has had a hard life. I'm awfully sorry for her, and I wish Sabine wouldn't keep saying she's better off than thousands of young widows with children in the bombed-out villages over there."

"It sounds as if your aunt isn't overly fond of Blanche."

"Well, you know Sabine and her tart opinions. She can be very nice to people—and she is very nice to Blanche—without liking them. She says Blanche flatters and caters to your father, poor old man, and he falls for it. He's so grateful that he'd give her the shirt off his back, she says."

"Well, since he hasn't got much more than a few shirts, the old store, and the old house, she's wasting her time. But the truth is that I don't believe Sabine. She's just having one of her spells, being her cranky, old, bad-tempered self again. Shall I send Blanche up to you when she comes?"

"No, I'm sleepy. Put the baby in the bassinet while I take a nap."

The green-and-white living room was filled with flowers not yet faded that had been sent by their many friends, from the Lawrences to the Reillys and the new neighbors across the street. In one corner was a pile of gifts, still to be sorted and acknowledged, gaily ribboned boxes of baby clothes and toys. The most recent one was in a box on the sofa next to Blanche.

"It's a nursery clock that Sabine couldn't resist. My gift hasn't been made yet. I'm going to start work on it as soon as I get back home.

It's going to be a patchwork quilt with characters from fairy tales."

"A big job, I should think."

"True. But it will fill my lonesome evenings. I often go down the block and keep your father company. He's a good man, as my father was . . ."

From the kitchen, where Rea's friend had come to help out in the house, came the clatter of pots, followed by a dreary silence. Blanche, with head bent, was examining her fingernails.

"You're a young woman," Adam said gently. "Life will begin again for you."

Blanche sighed. "I suppose so. But Jonathan is hard to forget."

"He will be with me till the end of my days."

"I keep thinking of that evening when we sat in the pavilion and looked out at the ocean, talking about the future. I could never have imagined what it would bring."

There was no answer to that, and Adam gave none. What could he say to her except to repeat, "Life will begin again for you." Intense pity filled him. It was a hard thing for any human being to be all alone in the world, but especially hard for a woman, he thought.

"What are you looking at?" Blanche asked him. "My hair? I saw a picture of Irene Castle dancing the tango, and she had bobbed hair. That's where I got the idea. Soon everybody will be doing it. Do you approve?"

"I hadn't noticed, really," he replied, taken aback.

"Nobody notices it very much on me, because my hair is so curly. It looks like a hat when it's bobbed."

He gave a short laugh. She's terribly nervous, he thought. And this conversation is making me uncomfortable.

"I don't suppose Emma will ever cut that marvelous hair of hers," Blanche went on.

"I hope she won't," Adam said.

"It's lovely. And she's lovely. And her music is lovely." Blanche said all this so blandly, and yet . . . Adam thought he heard the sadness behind the words.

"Yes, it is. When the back door is open, you can often hear it when you're in the yard. The neighbors sometimes come outside to listen."

It would soon be dark, and he was beginning to wish that Blanche would make a move to go back to Sabine's house.

"Tell me, how is it that you never even mentioned her to Jon and me when we met?"

"Oh, that's easy. Because Jon was going overseas, and it was your time to get all the attention, not ours."

"Well, now it's yours, with a new house, a new baby, and a new business. Wonderful!"

"I'm grateful for all of it."

"The store is really magnificent. The day after the party, Sabine took me through it. Even though you still haven't got all your merchandise, I could see the potential. The aisles are wide, people have room to browse, you have beautiful cabinets for separate displays, the dressing rooms are spacious—yes, it's as nice as any store in Paris or New York."

"You talk like an experienced manager," Adam said.

"No, just an experienced looker. I love clothes."

"Well, you certainly saved the day—the evening—for Emma. She calls those blue ruffles a stroke of genius."

"Oh, they were relatively simple. How do

you like this suit I'm wearing? Or haven't you even noticed it? I'll bet you haven't."

When she stood up, he realized that he had noticed, in spite of having a head full of other concerns, that Blanche, dressed in soft, rosy wool, looked very smart.

"Hobble skirts are finished in Paris. Next year they'll be finished here, too. Skirts will be short enough to show the ankles. Paquin and Lanvin already have a new, very slender silhouette. No more whalebone and corsets. We are always a year or so behind, you know."

Adam, amused by this tone of authority, asked where she got all her information.

"There are plenty of French magazines to which you can subscribe. I copy a lot of things in them."

"Without a pattern you do that?"

"One can figure it out. It's not hard. Maybe you don't get it exactly like the original, but you can certainly get the effect."

After a pause, Blanche continued. "Sabine took me around that neighborhood on the hill where the golf club is. There's plenty of money up there. Where do those women buy their clothes?"

"They buy a whole lot from us. If they want

something special, they buy our yard goods and have their seamstresses make it up."

"The dressmakers go to their homes?"

When Adam nodded, she seemed to be thinking for a few minutes, and then, speaking slowly, she remarked that she had a much better idea.

"Why don't you hire your own dressmakers to work in the store for wages? I'm sure you would find plenty of them who'd be glad not to be traipsing from house to house. They'd have a comfortable place to work in and a dependable income that they don't have now. Your store would have some more traffic to be tempted by other things on display, the shoes, the shawls, and the whatnots, to match the dresses. Right? What do you think?"

Not bad, he was thinking. Pretty clever ideas. This woman has a good head for business. She seems dependable, too. He recalled his first impression of her as a good wife for Jonathan, who had never been what one might call practical. Would she, perhaps, want to stay here and supervise these dressmakers? Maybe she would. He wouldn't exactly be hurting himself, either, by walking in with a brand-new idea so soon after his promotion.

He watched Blanche now as she walked across the room to pick up her cape, which matched the rosy wool of the jacket. She was really very attractive—not pretty, but still better looking than he remembered. She was not the kind of woman who usually appealed to him—in the days before Emma, of course—but she could be a fine advertisement for Cace Arnring.

"Well, you do have an interesting thought," he said. "Of course, I'll have to talk about it with the people on top."

"Naturally."

"If they like the idea, would you personally want to consider getting it started? No promises, of course."

"I understand. I don't mind staying awhile, a couple of weeks, let's say, until you decide." Blanche smiled. "Sabine likes my company."

No, she doesn't, he could have told her. But instead he said, "I'll get my car."

"Don't get your car. It's not far, and I enjoy the walk back."

For a moment he stood at the door and watched her. I really don't like her, he thought, or is it that I don't quite trust her? Why don't I trust her? She's done nothing wrong. And life has beaten her down. I should only be sorry for her.

Chapter 16

After the armistice, after some months of lag and uncertainty, the economy, nourished by oil and beef, began to bloom over the next few years.

This could be clearly seen on Cace Arnring's main floor, where imported British shirts, hats by Reboux, French perfumes, and a hundred other fine luxuries were on display. Although Adam's office, three times the size and grandness of his former one, was situated in an administrative area on the third level, he still spent much time keeping track of business on the selling floors. He knew the merchandise, the sales staff, and many of the customers, as well.

"When you think of what this place was on the day you and I met, it seems impossible, doesn't it?" Reilly said. "All that mess, and the yelling, the place folding up? It's like a dream." They were standing in front of the shoe department, where Reilly was now the buyer in charge, and earning more, no doubt, than he had ever dreamed of earning.

"I'm glad you can feel that way," Adam replied.

He was asking for no credit, but he knew all the same that a good part of the credit belonged to him. That longtime saleswoman over there, who used to worry about her young sons home alone, and that thin spinster behind the glove counter who used to worry about the myriad things a solitary woman worries about, had each received a decent raise and were feeling more secure than they ever had before. It was still not good enough, he thought, but it was better, and he intended to keep on trying to make it better still.

"That Madame Blanche keeps pulling the customers in," Reilly said. "She's put this store on the map, the great big map, hasn't she? 'Madame Blanche'—sounds funny, doesn't it?"

"Women love anything French."

"Seems like it. You have to get up early in the morning to get ahead of her. Got enough vigor and vim for three people."

Yes, she did, except, of course, when Jonathan was mentioned.

"It's more than vigor," Adam said. "She's an artist. Clothes are a kind of art. Some women live for clothes. My wife doesn't, but a lot do."

"Your wife looks like a doll. She always did, even when she wasn't much taller than a doll. Oh, look! Look at that display cabinet! What kind of crazy hat is that? It looks like a pot."

"It's called a cloche. That means 'bell' in French."

Next to the hat stood a photograph of a woman wearing such a hat, along with a handwritten card in Blanche's pointed European writing: This is how you are all soon going to look.

"A clever woman, Madame B.," Reilly said. "I didn't know what to make of her at first, but now she has my respect. And when you get used to her, you begin to see that she's a good-looking woman in her own way. Don't you agree?"

Having many other things on his mind, Adam was in no mood to get into one of Reilly's long conversations about trivial matters. He replied that he was in a hurry to get home, which was true.

Emma had planted redbuds in the yard. Why were they called "redbuds," Adam wondered, when they had lavender flowers in the spring and yellow leaves in the fall? He must ask her. She was one of those people who took pleasure in simple things like those redbuds, or the gardenia plant that flourished in the dining room window, or the corn muffins with strawberry jam that he liked with his breakfast coffee.

In the side yard the nanny rocked James in his carriage; at seven months he was sitting up and shaking a rattle in his hand. Jonathan, now three—and where, as people always ask, has the time gone?—was running around with a neighbor's four-year-old. He was tall, already taller than the four-year-old, Adam noted with satisfaction. Deep within him had lurked a fear that he had never confided to anyone, certainly never to Emma, that the wayward strain, the one that had produced Leo, would reappear in a child of his.

Faintly, out of the room at the far end of

the hall, came the sound of the piano, first a halting, dissonant phrase, and then the phrase repeated as it was supposed to sound. Emma was giving a lesson.

On the kitchen counter stood a pot of her favorite fish soup, cooked these days without wine so that Jonathan might have some. Beside the pot stood a cup of real wine which Adam might add to his if he chose to. She always said that of course the soup wasn't the same as when the wine had been there from the beginning.

He wondered how she found the energy to cook after giving piano lessons at home, teaching two music classes a week at the university, and putting in an hour of practice every day for her own advancement. She ought to have some help. Sabine said so, and Sabine was right.

The trouble was that the house was too small to hold another inhabitant with any comfort. As soon as I have finished paying my debt to Shipper's bank, he thought, we'll have to move. One of those places on the hill near the golf club would be nice, not that the club would ever admit a Rothirsch connection! He smiled to himself. He didn't play golf and had no desire to learn.

In the small den, surrounded by walls of the books that he could never resist, he sat down at his desk and began to write an overdue letter.

Dear Pa,
Thank you for remembering our
anniversary. We love the beautiful,
leather-bound album with all those
old pictures of us boys in our
knickerbockers and black cotton
stockings. I often think we should be
grateful for the way that time's passing
helps us cope with our grief, so that I
can actually bear to look at a picture of
Jonathan.
So you were surprised when the
neighbors showed you our ad in
Foibles. I have to confess that was
Blanche's doing and not mine. I've had
ads, but never a double page, which
costs a fortune that you'd never
believe. But she says that's the way to
get national recognition, and that it
won't be long before Cace Arnring will
have a fashion show in New York.
Do you remember how we all felt so
sorry for Blanche? Emma swears that

*she will be on her way to a career like
Chanel's. If you don't know about
Chanel, let me tell you she's famous.*

*Remember how Sabine always
boasted about Emma's being famous?
Well, Emma doesn't want to be! She is
very happy making music and caring
for our beautiful boys.*

*When are you coming here to see us?
We keep on asking you. And please tell
Leo that we really expect him to come,
too. Love,*

Adam

The children slept and the house was still,
as the last notes of a Chopin sonata died
away into the night.

"It's not every man," Adam said, "whose
day can end with a little music of his
choice."

"Unless he listens to the radio."

"No comparison! Oh, come on upstairs,
let's go to bed. I've been thinking about it for
the last hour."

In the bedroom, Emma opened the closet
door and took out a dress wrapped in a pro-
tective bag.

"First you have to have a look at this. I brought it home from the store today."

This was an evening gown of pale green velvet. A narrow diagonal panel of darker green crossed the skirt, while the bodice was low enough to display bare arms and naked shoulders.

"It's for the governor's inaugural ball. Do you like it?"

"You bet. The color is wonderful with your hair."

"Blanche is amazing, isn't she? She gets it right every time. I didn't ask her, but has she been invited?"

"No, it's for names, politicians and businesses that have contributed to the party. You know how it is."

"Maybe she feels overlooked. Maybe I'm wrong, but I thought she was just a trifle cool toward me today."

Adam shrugged. "Why would that be?"

"I wonder whether she's been lonesome since she's been in that little apartment by herself. But Sabine laughs when I say so. She says Blanche can get all the men she wants, any place, any time."

"Well, she can certainly make more contact now than she could living with Sabine."

"I thought you didn't think she was that attractive."

"Well, maybe she is, in a way. She's just not my type. Put that dress back in the closet, will you, and come here?"

Out of the blackness, a thin white light fell through the slatted blinds, laying stripes upon Emma's breasts and her thighs. The bed was fragrant, not with any perfume, but with the natural scent of her lips and her hair. And Adam lay there holding her to himself, not letting her go until they both fell asleep.

Chapter 17

The country had certainly known prosperity often before, but never anything like this in the year 1928. One had to wonder whether blue-ribbon stocks like Standard Oil and General Electric would simply keep on rising forever. Property values soared, too, and there was hardly a street in town or a road out of town where somebody was not either constructing or improving something.

Adam kept his investments within his own company, where he was able to have a little control or at least some knowledge of affairs. Having paid his debt in full to Shipper's bank, he owed no man.

From back east, Pa wrote,

You wouldn't believe what's happened to real estate here. They've built a grand road in from the suburbs, and my store is right on the four corners, along with a big new gas station, a pharmacy, and a Woolworth's. I never dreamed how a grocery store could boom. I'm having it modernized, inside and out. I've hired two men dressed up in white jackets to wait on my fancy suburban customers. Leo is keeping the books for me, going to the bank and the stockbrokers, doing a really great job this time, Adam. Really great, you'd be surprised. He's taking some classes at the new state college, he's busy day and night, and I hardly see him, so we don't have time to argue.

Adam had his doubts about putting Leo in charge, but he hoped his father was right. He would always help his family back home if they needed it. But for now he had plenty of people right here to take care of.

Emma was pregnant with their third child. This tiny house was too crammed with people and all their goods—nursery furnishings, baby carriages and strollers, bicycles, books, and concert grand piano—to say nothing of the one-car garage for a two-car family. So the time for a move, long postponed, had arrived.

Reilly always talked about "real money up on the hill, ranches, cattle, and oil. It's not the kind of money doctors and lawyers have, but big money. Real big. Bigger than Mrs. R."

Adam was unimpressed by the hill and the people on it. He was interested only in a certain piece of land on the other side of the hilltop, a plateau with a view of long, level miles, where corn and grain were growing and cattle were grazing. There, the distant horizon was blue-gray, like the one that rims an ocean. There was a great calm.

The wreck of an old farmhouse, half burned out, was still standing, as were the graceful elms that had once shaded it.

"They look like green flower vases," said Emma.

The new house could be built on the foundation of the old; it would stand with its back to the town and the daily bustle of the great store. Standing in a silence that was broken only by birdsong and the rush of wind, Adam and Emma planned their home.

No doubt their architect was surprised when they gave him an outline of their idea. They were not interested in any grand display of what Reilly called "real money." They wanted a simple house, much like the oldest ones in the town below, but more spacious, with room for everything that they and their children owned and did, along with rooms for Pa, when and if he should come to stay.

The architect smiled. "A farmhouse, you said?"

"Well, not exactly," Emma said. "Something very comfortable, but surely not one of those awful 'look-at-me' things that we sometimes see. You know what I mean."

Adam knew, too. Please, she meant, nothing like my aunt Sabine's house.

They pored over magazines and cut out pictures of nurseries and boys' rooms, and of a terrace with a movable roof to use when it rained. The kitchen must have one of those new refrigerators, and there must be a telephone closet in the front hall. Emma made sure that the piano room would be far removed from household noises—meaning, of course, the boys. Adam had some vague vision of a large white room until he realized that somewhere at the back of his mind, there must still linger a picture of Mr. Shipper's white parlor.

So slowly and surely the house took shape. First in their heads, then on blue paper, and finally, on the very day when Emma gave birth to their third boy, the bulldozers dug the first hole in the ground.

On the morning after the housewarming party, Adam sat down at his new desk and wrote to his father.

Dear Pa,
We had our party yesterday. When I say that everything, even the weather, was perfect, you can believe me. Neither Emma nor I wanted such a big housewarming, but somehow it just happened. All kinds of people came: my bosses at the company, old-timers like Reilly, whom you met at the store, and a whole crowd of friends.
You were missed. I know I haven't been east in two years, and I'm sorry, but honestly, the days are very short for all I have to do at work, and now with the new baby, the move, and the settling into the house, there hasn't been a free minute.
I'm glad things are quiet between Leo and you and that he is busy, which is

good for him. Emma joins me in begging you both to visit. You will love the house, and there are beautiful rooms waiting for you.

You always ask about Sabine and Blanche. Sabine is her generous self. She can't do enough for us. I don't think she is very well because her cranky moods have been coming on more often. Of course, she's pretty old.

Blanche continues to be the great success that you already know about. Although we work for the same company, I rarely see her. She sent a very nice house gift, but didn't come to the party. We don't blame her because she probably had a date. She really should have a husband by now!

Now the best for the last. Our boys are wonderful. Right this minute Emma is going over fifth-grade math with Jon and James is playing a board game here on the floor beside me. Our Andy is having his nap. Did I tell you that he has Emma's hair? What a waste on a boy! It's barely grown yet, and Emma is already dreading the day it will have to be cut.

It doesn't seem possible that we have been married more than eleven years. I suppose time flies faster when you are as happy as we are. Write soon. Love,

Adam

Chapter 18

Sabine, on days when she was feeling morose, often liked to quote the Bible, particularly the warning about the seven fat years and the seven lean.

"That doesn't mean only harvests or prosperity, you know. It means life, all the things that can happen to people, their health, their spirits—everything."

These words came to mind on that morning when Rea telephoned to say that Mrs. R. was "bad."

"I heard her about three o'clock this morning. She fell in the hall outside her room, and I helped her back into bed. I wanted to call a doctor or an ambulance, but she wouldn't let me. She screamed at me. She wouldn't even let me call you, but Rudy said I must. So I'm downstairs, where she can't hear me."

"We'll be right there," Adam said.

Dressed in a satin bed jacket, Sabine was sitting up in bed when they arrived. She was having breakfast and was annoyed by their visit.

"Such a fuss over nothing! I slipped in the hall because I was coughing my head off and didn't look where I was going. But Rea has always been a worrywart. Why, once when you were about six, Emma, I remember—"

Emma interrupted. "Have you got a fever?"

"How do I know? I never take my temperature."

"Well, you should. Where's the thermometer?"

"I don't own one. Oh, do go home. Thanks for coming, but do go home."

Nevertheless, they sent for a doctor, and from him learned that Sabine simply had a cold with the usual fever and sore throat.

After the usual treatment and improvement, she sent for them. Still in bed, she was as talkative as ever.

"I've asked you both to come over this evening because I want to settle things. It's time. I don't want any uncertainties after I'm gone."

"You're not going anywhere," Emma began, and was interrupted.

"Don't be silly. I don't mean right away. I'm strong as a horse, but at my age, it's time to look ahead.

"The first thing is this house. You've been very considerate in keeping your thoughts to yourself, but you can't believe, can you, that I haven't known your opinion of this house? So what I want you to do is give it away as a temporary home for children who don't have a good one, or perhaps not any home at all. You understand?" she asked without looking at Emma.

"I do," Emma said quietly.

"Next comes Adam. If anything should happen to you, and I pray that it won't because you have made my Emma so happy, I have asked Spencer Lawrence to watch out for her and the children."

"Dear Aunt," Emma protested, "God forbid that I should lose Adam, but I could take care of the children just as well as he could if he were to lose me. And Lawrence is such a—a stick, anyway."

"A sturdy stick," Adam said in defense. "If a person ever had to lean on it, it wouldn't break."

"Don't argue about it." Sabine spoke sharply. "No discussion about anything, Emma, because I've already made up my mind. Now, next. Most of what I own, natu-rally, is stock in the business. But I also have government bonds because I don't believe in the stock market and never did, in spite of Theo Brown's advice. Goddamned crook, that's what he was."

Sabine never swore, so this last was sur-prising.

"I have left a fair share, about a quarter of everything, to you, Adam, because I have total trust in you, and because life hasn't been easy for you, with one brother dead and the other so sad and unfit. The rest is Emma's, except for a good-sized amount to each of the children. They should have the best possible education, but they should also be charitable and thrifty, and appreci-ate the value of a dollar. Above all, they should not be spoiled."

Visibly moved by these words and by the feel of finality in the room, as if the booming old voice were already speaking from the grave, Emma tried to lighten the mood.

"Spoil!" she cried. "That, from you? Who is

the person who has loaded them with toys, books, and clothes enough for an army?"

"I'm not finished," Sabine responded as if she had not heard Emma. "You need better help in that house with those three children and your teaching. So I have asked Rudy and Rea to go to you and be to you what they have been to me."

"Oh, you haven't!" cried Emma. "Why?"

"They may have other plans for themselves," Adam pointed out gently.

"Well, they haven't. They love you, and they love the house, too. Frankly, I don't know what they see in the house. There's nothing to it. Even Reilly said so the last time I was in the store. 'There's no decoration,' he said. 'Nothing pretty or fancy. It's too plain.' "

The conversation was, happily, taking a turn away from death, and Adam readily joined in.

"He tells me so, too, whenever I see him. I get a kick out of him, and then out of Archer, who tells him, very seriously, that he doesn't know the first thing about architecture. 'The house is a Georgian country house,' Archer says, and of course he's right."

Funny thing, Adam thought. If it hadn't

been for Reilly, plus Mr. Shipper and Spencer Lawrence, we wouldn't be in that house. Well, maybe we would if I had gone elsewhere to earn a lucky living or won big at the races or something.

"I'll make you both feel better," Sabine said. "There's another person who admires your taste. Blanche. She stopped in after work yesterday. I told her I didn't think it was very nice of her not to come to your house-warming that time."

"You've got a long memory, Aunt. That was a year ago."

"I don't care. It was wrong. It was wrong after the opportunity she found here. She's making a bundle for herself."

"For all of us, too," Adam reminded Sabine.

"That's true, but I still don't like her. Never did. I can't say why, but I don't."

"Poor Blanche," Emma said. "With all her success, it must be an empty life. No Adam, no Jon, no James or Andy—"

Mischievously, Adam asked, "Wouldn't you rather be touring the world giving piano recitals?"

"Ah, you're teasing me," Sabine interjected. "Where's Rea? I asked her to bring some coffee and chocolate cake. She baked this afternoon—ah, there you are, Rea."

"Nobody ever leaves this house without first having something to eat," Rea said. "I'll put the tray on the table right next to you. Let me just fluff your pillows before you eat."

Adam was moved. With all her foibles and flare-ups, there was something in this old woman that made people care about her. In a way, he thought as he watched, she reminds me of a light that flickers, flares, flickers again, and is about to go out. She will be missed, Adam thought.

And one week after that, under the fair April sky, after the last solemn words had been spoken at the cemetery, the same thought returned to him.

"She will be missed," he said to Emma, who was wiping her tears. "Yet, in a way, we never knew her."

To that, Spencer Lawrence, who had overheard, responded, "Do we ever know anyone?"

The summer seemed to be especially beautiful that year, having just the right amount of rain and the right amount of sun, enough of each to keep green things flourishing and humanity comfortable.

"I was thinking," Emma said one Sunday afternoon in August, "that maybe next summer, we could load up the station wagon and take a trip to the Grand Canyon and Yosemite. Andy will be old enough then to get something out of a trip like that."

Adam, engrossed in the newspaper, answered briefly. "Nice idea. Let's talk about it when it's next year."

"You look as if something's bothering you. What is it?"

"Well, to tell you the truth, I think this country is on the edge of a huge disaster, and doesn't know it. Look here," and he tapped the paper, "stocks have reached the highest prices in history, and the highest volume of trade. This professor of economics says it will go on forever. The economy has never been as prosperous, he says."

"It's true, isn't it? Look how people are buying things. Look at the car dealers in town. Look at your own store."

"Stock pools. I hear men talk. The other

night at that dinner party, a couple of brokers were getting a pool together. Pump the stock up, way up, and then sell to the poor suckers who go out and borrow to buy it. I am telling you that there's going to be a day of reckoning. There has to be. What goes up eventually comes down."

"Well, you don't have any stocks except in your own business. So don't worry."

"But my father has. In every phone call he tells me where his stocks are. Rudy and Rea have stocks. They ought to sell. I've told them all, but they think I don't know what I'm talking about. Listen, back even in 1926, Hoover, who was then the Secretary of Commerce, said there was too much speculation."

"Oh, it's too nice a day for such talk. Let's sing." And through laughter, Emma, as she aped an operatic soprano, began, "My God, how the money rolls in!"

She could be cute and funny, but right now Adam was not in the mood for humor. He got up and went inside to make a call to his father.

"How's everything, Pa?"

"Good. Good. I was at the beach with my new neighbors. Nice people, very friendly, but I think it was too hot for me. I had to take a nitroglycerin and go home. The heat, I guess."

"No, not the heat, but your heart. You'd better see the doctor in the morning."

"He can't do anything besides give me the medicine. I'll see him anyway, though, just to make you happy."

"There's something else you can do to make me happy. Sell your stocks tomorrow."

"Sell my stocks! Are you out of your head? AT & T and GE? They've doubled and tripled, even more than that, since I bought them."

"There are too many crooked deals on Wall Street. I don't like what I'm hearing. Take your profit and put it away."

"Leo would really think I was crazy if I should tell him to do that."

"The devil with Leo. What's he ever done with his life?"

"Okay, okay, Adam. You mean well. I'll think about it."

He'll not even think about it, much less do it, Adam told himself as he hung up.

❈

October arrived. Pumpkins and Halloween skeletons appeared in store windows. At the table, Jon recited an autumn poem that he was supposed to memorize: " 'Season of mists and mellow fruitfulness,'—What's that about mists, Mom?"

"It's a British poem. England has much more rain than we do here, so— What's the matter, Adam?"

"The stock market. It took a terrible drop just in the last hour yesterday."

"Watch, it'll go back up again. Want to bet five dollars?"

The next day, Tuesday the twenty-third, Adam handed Emma a five-dollar bill.

"You see? I was right. Jumped right back up again. I knew it. I shouldn't even take your five. It was too easy."

"Wait," he said.

That night he went again to the telephone and called his father. "Sell," he roared. "You've had your warning."

"What makes you such a fortune-teller?"

"I can't say. It's a feeling. It's common sense."

There was an element of selfishness in these calls, he admitted to himself as he fell asleep that night. For who but me is to take care of Pa and Leo if the worst should happen?

The worst came in sections. *Black Thursday,* they called it on the twenty-fourth of the month. All the rest of the week, things dangled: up a bit and down a bit. Then on Tuesday, the twenty-ninth, they hit the bottom. Disaster came over the radio; one could listen to the panic in front of the Stock Exchange, the police in front of the banks, the crowds hysterical or stricken into a silent contemplation of their own ruin.

From back east, Pa sobbed over the telephone. "Why didn't I listen to you? We had the best broker in town. I had confidence in him. Everything was bought on margin. The phone's been ringing with the margin calls that we can't pay. Leo has locked himself into his room. He says it's his fault. He wants to kill himself."

"He won't," Adam said. "Hold on, Pa. Use your nitroglycerin. I'm taking the train tomorrow. Hold on till I get there."

"It's not only about harvests," Sabine had said. "It's about other things that happen to people, their health and hopes and spirits. It's about everything, lean or fat."

There was no doubt about the nature of the year that ended with Simon and Leo's arrival in Chattahoochee. During his two-week stay back east, Adam had straightened out as many affairs as he could. Since Simon was the owner of the stocks and his only other possession was his meager little home, it was, so the lawyer explained, a simple matter to turn the house over to the broker, which was repayment along the lines of one dollar on a five-hundred-dollar debt. The store had long ago been signed over to Leo, so he would have a small income from rent. That left him modestly cared for, but his father not cared for at all—except by Adam.

It was, in spite of all efforts to enliven the atmosphere, a disheartened group that assembled on that first afternoon in Adam's house. Perhaps it was Simon's appearance, shrunken, bowed, and pale as he was, that brought thoughts of death into their midst. Perhaps it was Leo's scowl at having to accept his brother's favors that depressed them.

And yet the old man's eyes lit up at the

sight of his grandsons. He gave them each a hug.

"Three of them! Hey, Adam, you're copying me. No girls in our family! Never mind, I love boys best—except for you, Emma, you beautiful lady, and you, Blanche, another beautiful lady and my old friend besides. You know I still take my warm milk, Blanche, just as you always told me to."

He was delighted with his room. "My own bathroom! Flowered tiles—this is fit for a king."

"Look at the view, Pa," Emma said. "Of course, this is January. Wait until spring! And, Leo, we have an equally nice room for you, with two big closets and shelves for your books."

"Thank you, but I won't be staying here," was the stiff response. "I thought I'd get a room for myself, go into town, where you must have a library. And isn't there a university near the capital?"

Adam felt a spurt of anger. He could at least stay for a couple of nights and be sociable before moving on. But then, he had never been sociable.

Blanche, suggesting that Leo might like to

find a nice two-room apartment in her neighborhood, offered to drive him there.

"You can spend the night in my place, and tomorrow I'll show you around."

"Thank you, Blanche. What a good idea."

He would stay with Blanche, but not his brother? Ah, just as well. Why pretend?

"I have two big cases of books," Leo continued, to no one in particular. "When they arrive here, I'd appreciate it if you would send them on to wherever I end up. Of course I will give you the address as soon as I have it. Do you want to leave now, Blanche? I'm ready if you are."

"Well, of all the cool characters," Adam protested when Leo and Blanche had left and the boys had gone upstairs with Simon. "I should think that he, even he, might be a little humble after what he's done to his father. A lifetime of grueling labor, and I mean grueling, with nothing left. Nothing. Pa trusted this fool to deal with the broker, who didn't give a damn about safety until he called up to collect and found he couldn't collect because they had been wiped out. You'd think at least that Leo would be a little bit humble," he repeated.

"Thousands of people did the same,"

Emma pointed out gently. "You wouldn't be as angry at anyone else as you are at Leo."

"What makes you defend him, may I ask?"

"Well, I can see that behind his rudeness, he's afraid of his own shadow."

After a pause, Adam said, "Perhaps you're right. Now listen, we'd better talk to James. He whispered to me that Uncle Leo is 'awfully funny-looking.'"

"I'll talk to the boys tomorrow. Let's have dinner and spend the evening in front of the fireplace. Pa will feel strange going to bed in a strange place tonight."

"Do you think so?"

"Well, wouldn't you if you were here as a dependent who was going to die here?"

There was a moment of silence until Adam said gravely, "You understand people so well, Emma." Then smiling, he added, "Even me."

On the mantelpiece a fine old mahogany clock stood between two pots of miniature roses in bloom. Above it hung a large watercolor of fishing boats in moonlight. Below it, the fire crackled and snapped.

"A palace," Simon murmured as he looked

around the room. "A palace." He sighed. "Look what Leo is missing."

In this second week he was still in awe of the house, still mourning his losses, still unsettled.

"You remember what Mr. Shipper told me about 1907," Adam said. "It was a calamity. Banks failing and stocks falling, but the country recovered. And it will again, Pa."

"I don't expect to see it. Look at AT & T. It was three hundred ten. Now it's one hundred ninety-three. General Electric was four hundred three. Now it's one sixty-eight. RCA was one hundred fourteen. Now it's twenty-six. Ah, life is all troubles. Something goes along fine for a little time, and then before you know, it rises on its hind legs and pushes you over. It's all an accident, like your finding this spot on the map. You had never heard of it. You could just as well be freezing in Alaska tonight. All you had to do was close your eyes and put your finger on a spot."

"It's not quite like that," Adam said gently.

"Yes, it is. Look at poor Blanche. One bullet, a small thing not as big as your finger, and look what it did to her. It ruined her life. That was a real, true love affair. When she tries to help Leo, she's thinking of Jonathan, because he would want her to. She'll never get over what happened to him. None of us will."

"Leo's books got here today," Emma said, "and I sent them on to his apartment. There must have been a hundred of them in those crates. What can they possibly be?"

"I don't know." Simon was obviously impatient with a question that he had often before been asked. "He's been doing this for years, that's all I can tell you."

"Pa," said Adam. "I know you must be thinking of our big store here, and I wish I could offer Leo some kind of position in it. But I am not the supreme boss by any means, Pa, and Leo would have to make his own offer and his own impression."

"No apologies, Adam. It's all as plain as the nose on your face. They wouldn't take him. And he wouldn't take their job if they begged him to."

Later, Adam proposed that before going up to bed, they should go outside for a look at the stars.

Looking up from the terrace, Simon was awed. "This is the largest sky I've ever seen."

It was one of those nights that was bright with untold numbers of stars. Emma remarked that even after reading some of Adam's huge books of astronomy, she understood nothing.

"Nothing except their names, but not what they mean. What do you think, Pa?"

The old man thought for a while before he replied. "As it says in the prayer book, I pray that it may someday be given us to understand."

It seemed strange that Sabine, who had been so sturdy, had suddenly, in fewer than ten days, died, while Pa, who had been sick for several years, still lingered and might well go on, as the doctor said, for many more years.

He was even becoming acclimated to the life of the house. He called Emma a treasure and told Adam to take good care of her because she was "one in a million." He praised the comfort of his room and swore that he had never enjoyed such cooking as Rea's. He was in love with his grandsons, especially with Andy, whom he called "the redhaired rascal." When Emma was giving a piano lesson, he sat in the living room with the door open so that he might enjoy the music. As spring approached, he strolled outdoors and found the first daffodils pushing up toward the sun.

Visitors came, and it pleased him if they came to see him. It pleased Adam, too, when Reilly and Archer came on Sunday mornings, when Blanche occasionally spent an evening, when Cace Arnring's top executive spent a half hour with Simon Arnring, or when an old lady, one of Sabine's surviving friends, arrived with a box of cookies for Adam's father. Leo, too, sometimes visited—in the afternoons when Adam was not home.

One day there came a change. On a Sunday filled with wind and rain, Simon stayed in bed. As he entered the room, Adam saw at once that this was one of those rare times when Pa was going to break his reserve and speak his mind.

"On the bottom shelf of that closet," Simon began, "there are things you'll want to keep. You've seen them all, the albums from when the three of you were kids."

Yes, of course he remembered the black cotton socks, the high-laced shoes, and Leo standing between two tall brothers.

"I had a copy made of your mother's photograph. You might want to have some more for your children."

There was a long pause. Adam's eyes went to the window, where rain was spattering the pane.

One photo, and nothing more. If he had loved her, wouldn't there be more? Wouldn't he have married her if only to save her from shame? And how many times have you asked yourself this, Adam?

Then his father, resuming, went through a list.

"There's Jonathan's college diploma and that box of the stuff returned by the army, his watch, his safety razors, and a picture of him in uniform with his buddies, all the stuff you've seen. There's also another photo of Blanche. Give it back to her."

"Shouldn't she have his other things, too?"

"No. Blood is thicker than water. They're for you and your children. I also have letters from some cousins in Europe. Of course, I've never seen these women. It's always the women who write. Men don't bother, do they? But I answer them, even though I hardly remember how to write in German. One of them died in the influenza epidemic in 1918. So they've had their hard times, too. You might want to ask Leo to tell them about me when I go. He can manage a little German, I think."

"Pa," Adam said, "you called me here also to talk about Leo. I know you did. What is it you want to say?"

There was another pause before Simon replied. "I suppose what I want to say is that I wish I could know what he's thinking."

"I wish I did, too. Tell me, does he keep in touch with Bobby Nishikawa?"

"I don't think so. Not since Bobby got married and moved away. It seems to me that all those books have taken his place."

"Tell me this, too, Pa: How is it that he cared so much for Jonathan and never at all for me?"

The answer came so softly and so wearily that Adam barely heard it. "Because Jonathan was weak, and you are not. You're different."

"You thought Jonathan was weak, Pa?"

"Yes, in a way, he was. And that had nothing to do with his bright mind. Nothing."

"I don't understand. I never saw any weakness in him."

"You didn't know. You were away from him too long and never knew him as I did. You're very strong, Adam. You solve problems. You manage. I believe that's what Leo holds against you. That, and the fact that you had a different mother."

"Is all this a reason for him to hate me? Because I believe he really does."

"It's not a good reason, but if people want to hate, they invent reasons. Hatred, Adam, is a fact of life, especially within families. And now I'm tired, Adam. I think I'll sleep."

Quietly Adam left and closed the door.

So Pa, overburdened by daily cares and often remote from the family, had in truth been watching them and drawing his own conclusions. Simon Arnring, psychologist!

A few days later, Simon died mercifully in his sleep. They thought of burying him not far from where Sabine lay next to the husband she had not loved. But in the end they decided to bury him back east, next to the wife he had loved.

From blocks around, the neighbors came to the graveyard, along with the rabbi and the Protestant minister, who lived at the end of the street.

"He was a simple man," they all said. "A kind and simple man."

Kind, indeed, but not as simple as I once thought, Adam said to himself, while his heart ached more than he had ever thought it would.

Chapter 19

Life, indeed, was not as simple as Adam had once believed it would be if only one had enough to pay one's bills. For now he was one of the senior vice presidents, with so many responsibilities and so many eyes upon him that he rarely got home in time to eat with his sons. Sabine's house had not yet been totally emptied of forty years' accumulation, and Emma could not do it all without some help from him. That left the weekends in which to sort out, sell, and give away everything from the cumbersome furniture to Sabine's jewelry, most of which was, with great joy, received by Rea.

"I don't know why I'm so terribly tired," he said to Emma one day. He had been watching her at the park tennis court teaching Jonathan to play a game that he himself had never had the time to learn. In her pleated skirt and white blouse, with a band keeping her bright hair in place, she looked no older than eighteen.

"It's been a terrible year," Emma observed, "one of the lean years, as Sabine used to say. Sickness and death began it, sickness and death ended it. There was the house to clean out, then James's broken arm—no end, it seems."

"You had to suffer through it, too, and look at all your energy!"

"But I can take a little rest in the middle of the day. You can't. I can sit down with a book, or go for a good walk. You can't. Why don't you take a trip, go someplace for a few days? Maybe go fishing with Spencer Lawrence?"

"I wouldn't mind, but Dan Cace has asked me to do him a favor. He's supposed to go to New York for the spring showings. Our Madame Blanche is to be one of the big names. It's grand publicity. But since Dan has to go to his sister's wedding, he's asked me to go in his place."

"Absolutely, you should. How would it look to say no? I ran into Blanche downtown the other day. She was all enthusiastic about some new connections for Irish woolens and French silks. You should go, Adam. It'll be a change."

"For Pete's sake, you know I haven't got a thing to do with fashions, Emma. My job starts and stops with the building, the plant, and the equipment. You think I want to watch a lot of skinny women parading their silks and woolens?"

"You might enjoy it more than you think," she said mischievously. "You're just cross and tired today."

"Well, I'm darned if I'm going to stay a whole week. I'll put in an appearance at the big show and a couple of lunches, or whatever Dan is supposed to do, and then I'll come home."

"I have been looking all over for Mr. Cace," Blanche said over dinner at the hotel, "and now I discover it's you who has to fulfill this obligation! Poor Adam—I know you have no interest in fashion! It's Dan who knows all about fashion shows. He wants to start having a little show once a week at home, did you know that?"

"I heard something about it. I think it's a great idea, but maybe not once a week. An event stops being gala when it happens that often. I would make it four times a year, as the seasons change. Put out a red carpet, have music, flowers, and refreshments, with Madame Blanche as the star."

"Chanel and I!"

"Why not? You don't have to be French to be a star. By the way, what's the story with your skirt? I noticed it when you walked into the lobby."

The skirt of Blanche's black suit hung midway to the ankles; a pale, light blue blouse was matched, not by the familiar cloche, but by a little hat that nestled far back on the head and was framed by her curly hair.

"It's the newest look. You can't have read my elegant card on the display case when I foretold this change as long as four months ago."

"I didn't see it. But I do remember that other time when skirts were long and you predicted that they would soon be short."

"That was a hundred years ago."

He thought he heard a mournful tone in her voice even though she smiled. And in a flash, he saw himself as he must look to her: a man not much older than herself, with a marriage, a house, three children, and above all, stability. She's not over Jon's death, he thought, as he often did, and perhaps never will be.

The restaurant was crowded with men and women in formal dress. "They're on their way to the theater," Blanche explained. "Monday night is theater night in New York."

"I wouldn't know. I guess I'm a country boy. Pearls by the rope length and diamond tassels in the ears—all this jewelry dazzles. You wouldn't expect it with times as bad as they are."

"There are always people who prosper, even in bad times. They can still buy anything they want. How much has Cace Arnring suffered? Think about that."

"I do think about it. That's why I put in the lower-price department years ago. But since you don't work there, you probably don't even notice it."

"I notice it whenever I see your wife. That's where she shops, except for a few 'big event' clothes."

"Yes, that's Emma. But should she wear one of your suits to give a piano lesson?" he demanded.

"I'm not criticizing, Adam. She always

looks lovely. Is she ever going to bob her hair?"

"She doesn't want to, and I don't want her to. Why should she?"

"I didn't mean that she should. I only asked, Adam. Only asked."

He had not meant to be short with Blanche, and now, feeling that he might have been so, he apologized.

"I'm tired from that long train trip. Anyway," he added ruefully, "I am not the gentle soul that Jonathan was."

"It seems to me that every time we see each other, which isn't often, we bring his name into the conversation. I suppose that a major tragedy scars you forever."

"Yes, we share the grief, you and I. You two were like two fingers on a hand together."

She did not answer. Changing the subject, he asked what time the showing was to start tomorrow, where the dinner to which Dan Cace had given him the ticket was to be held, and who the guests were to be.

"Some of the biggest manufacturers go to Paris every year to see what's happening over there. Mr. Cace thought I should meet some of them because it might be a good thing for me to take the trip, too, sometime."

Adam was doubtful. "We're only a department store, not a factory. I wonder whether we should spend that much money."

"I could pay my own way. It would be worth it to see Europe again. I sold all my stocks at the top a month before the crash, so you see I'm in very good financial shape."

"Smart woman. I tried so hard to get my father to do it, but it didn't work. It still upsets me to think of his whole life's savings gone down the drain."

"You have to put it out of your mind, Adam. What's the use?"

"You're right. What's done is done."

"Well, not everything. Some things can be undone, or redone."

"That sounds like a crossword puzzle."

"Shall we go? Tomorrow's my big day, and I need some sleep."

The afternoon took too long. Down the runway they came, the skinny girls with their peculiar strut, whirl, and strut, while the designers beamed and the audience applauded. Carefully, Adam wrote down the information that Dan Cace would want and sat after that in a fog of indifference until, now and then, a truly astonishing piece of information woke him up.

Two hundred fifty dollars for a dress! It was a Madame Blanche design in the bright pink that was lately known as "shocking." Now wide awake, his eyes and ears alert, he felt a new enthusiasm sweeping through the audience. Behind him, paper rustled as pens scribbled and voices whispered.

". . . not lamé, it's a chiffon lamé . . . one narrow necklace . . . doesn't detract from the gold skirt . . . mink border . . . berthas are finished . . . don't use trains, too Patou . . . a ski jacket . . . the new sport."

"Marvelous taste," said the man next to Adam. "An original, this Madame Blanche."

The man beyond that one had more to add. "She's a whole lot better looking than those flat-chested gals on the runway. I wouldn't mind getting my hands on her. I'll bet she . . ." The voice dropped away.

None of my business what she does, Adam thought. *It's her life. But what an asset to the store! Her name will be in every fashion magazine after this. We'd better make sure that our name is in great big letters. She'd better get a raise, too—a fancy one. Bring it up first thing at the meeting next week.*

At dinner last night she seemed to be a trifle touchy. Or maybe I only imagined it. Maybe it was my fault? We'll be sitting together at dinner tonight, and since we're the only people from the store, I'll make up for it.

"How does it feel to be a winner?" he inquired, and before she could answer, informed her that she looked beautiful.

Thanking him, she went on to say that he looked rather fine himself. "I haven't seen you in a dinner jacket since the opening of the new store, the night your wife wore the maternity dress I fixed for her."

Again he had the feeling that there was a double meaning in her words. Was she perhaps feeling that they had excluded her in some way from their brilliant social life?

"We don't live an exciting social life," he explained truthfully. "Our friends don't go out in formal clothes every week."

"That's not what your brother Leo says."

Blanche laughed. "He puts you on a par with the Prince of Wales."

"My brother Leo? What does he know about me? As a matter of fact, I've scarcely seen him since Pa died. He used to visit the boys a lot, but he hasn't done it much lately."

"Do you know why? Because Rudy said something about your boys growing tall. 'Tall, like your daddy,' he said, 'and smart like him, too.' And Leo took that as a slap at him, so he stopped visiting your boys."

"Good God," Adam groaned. "Poor Leo. How often do you see him?"

"Fairly often. He lives only three blocks away from me, so he walks over. We like to speak German together."

"German! He knows it through broken sentences that he picked up at home. That's all he knows."

"On the contrary, he speaks an excellent, fluent German."

"He does? Are you sure?"

"Of course I'm sure. Why else would I say so?"

"This is all a puzzle to me. Not that that's anything new, because Leo has always been a puzzle that no one seems able to solve."

"One thing I can tell you. He needs a woman."

"Surely somewhere he should be able to find one."

"He wants a pretty one. There's a girl in his apartment house who would go out with him, but he says she's too homely."

Dumbfounded, Adam could only shake his head.

"He wanted to kiss me until I made it clear that I would be his friend and nothing more."

"So you're still his friend?"

"Why not? He's no bother. He always telephones before he comes over, so if I don't want to see him, I simply say he can't come."

"Maybe you can find out what he's doing with all those books."

"I've tried, but he won't tell. He refuses to tell me anything about himself."

Under the glittering chandeliers, the great room was filled with animation. People moved among the tables, greeting one another; waiters bustled about with platters of food and glasses of champagne; the orchestra's lively tunes brought couples to dance in the cleared space at the center. This was neither the place nor the time for sad speculations about Leo Arnring, and thinking so, Adam drank down the champagne and invited Blanche to dance.

She began to sing along with the music. *Who stole my heart away . . . you stole my heart away . . .* The lilting voice lifted his mood and cleared, if only for a little while, the tangle of his thoughts: death, stocks, Cace Arnring, and James's poor little broken arm. Just dance, feel good.

"You're a wonderful dancer," he said.

"You haven't seen the half of what I can do."

When she smiled, he seemed to be seeing a double row of upper teeth; then it occurred to him that he had perhaps had too much champagne, and he told her that he'd better sit down.

"I'm not much of a drinker, Blanche, never was. But I don't remember having so much tonight."

"You didn't. It works fast, though, faster on some people. Let's finish dinner, have plenty of coffee, and leave. It's been a long day."

❋

Adam had not been more than five minutes in his room when the telephone rang.

"I hate to bother you," Blanche said, "but the tiny hook and eye at the back of my neck is caught in the lace. I can't unfasten it without tearing everything, and I hate to tell you what that lace cost. So can you help me?"

He was tired and he had already taken his shirt off, but he couldn't bring himself to refuse. So he replaced his shirt and went.

The room was perfumed with flowers. Dan Cace would have seen to that; when a company had a winner like Madame Blanche, it held on to her. All kinds of feminine frivolities were spread around: a jewelry case, a sheer yellow nightgown, and a pair of marabou slippers to match.

In a corner, in the pink light of a lamp, Blanche stood while he labored over the hook and eye. When he had finally succeeded, the whole dress, fragile top and heavy silk skirt, fell slithering to the floor. Three pieces of silk, each one no larger than a tiny handkerchief, covered her nakedness.

Adam stared. "Well!" he gasped.

Her eyes laughed. Like black opals under a light, they shimmered and glowed.

"Well?" she replied.

✳

Awake in his room, he lay trying to reconstruct the scene. It seemed to him at first that what had happened was simply an unthought, automatic reaction to an abrupt situation, much like the use of the brake to avoid an oncoming crash. The difference was that this time, the brake had failed. And now the aftermath was nausea, fear, and a leaping heart.

Soon it would be time to get up and face the day in which he was supposed to keep Dan Cace's appointments. There was nothing difficult about conferring with a few manufacturers except that his head was churning. He remembered his father's explanation of his, Adam's, birth: *Things happen. It's nature.*

He remembered, too, that someone had told him Blanche was a "pushover." In fact, there had been several such people, on several occasions, who had told him so. But how did that excuse *him*? A little wine, a little music . . . that hardly excused what had happened.

And what if she should be pregnant as a result of "nature"? Vaguely he recalled that she had murmured something about love. Could she really believe herself to be in love with him? Or even worse, believe him to be in love with her?

Somehow, he got through the day. In the wholesale offices, at least, he would not be encountering her. But sooner or later he would have to face her, and face what he had done.

He was not yet ready for the inevitable meeting. He needed time to think things through. Therefore, he would not risk any accidental encounter in the hotel's restaurant. Instead, he went to a double feature at the movies, only to find that neither Charlie Chaplin nor Harold Lloyd could make him laugh.

He had only one more of Dan's appointments to keep. An intense need to get home—as if there could be any salve to his conscience there—overwhelmed him, and deciding to catch the early train in the morning, he got ready for bed. He hoped he would be able to sleep. He tried to tell himself that he had only done what many men did all the time when they were away from home. But he didn't feel any better. He wasn't just any man.

There came a knock on the door. Something said to him: Don't answer it. But he couldn't keep avoiding Blanche. Sooner or later, he would have to face her. And maybe it was better here than at home.

The knock, light but persistent, was repeated.

He opened the door and there she stood, wearing her black winter cloak that was lined in red velvet. She was naked underneath it.

"No," he said.

Her eyes seemed to sparkle at him. "You don't mean that. You know you don't."

He was not sure what he meant. A queer feeling flashed through him; if I run I can get across the street before the light changes. . . .

"We've got a long night ahead of us, Adam. We can make it a night to remember. Go on, don't keep me standing here. There's a good boy. Let me in."

✳

Late the next afternoon, when they met in the crowded lobby after another showing, he told her he was sick. "I have a fever. I'm taking the train tonight."

"For home?"

"Where else? I was able to get a compartment, so I won't spread whatever it is I've got."

"Oh, I'm sorry." She kissed him slowly on the cheek. "Take care, Adam. I'll be back Friday. I'll see you then."

The train clicked, clanked, and rattled its way west. He did not recognize his own body as it sweated and froze through the meaningless hours and the dreary landscape that, the nearer it reached home, became more ominous.

He realized that he was desperately afraid of Blanche. He knew that he would have to make it clear to her that there would be no further relationship between them, but he kept thinking of the old adage about "a woman scorned" . . . and the words she had very definitely spoken the previous night: "I love you."

Love! Love had had nothing to do with what had passed between them the last two nights. Not for him. But for her?

So now he was Blanche's creature. She could break him. She could break Emma.

Then, after a while, he remembered how she had loved Jonathan. Perhaps he might speak of that love and ask her never to let anything slip from her lips, even by accident, about what had happened. Yes, that's what he must do. He would go to her and make his honest appeal, in memory of all the goodness that was in Jonathan.

At the railroad station, Emma was wearing a particularly lovely smile.

"I feel as if you've been away for a year," she cried. "I couldn't wait to give you the surprise. Darling Adam, we're having a new little addition to our family. I wasn't sure about my dates, so I didn't want to say anything to you until I had seen the doctor. But it's true. Next December, in time for your birthday."

He felt . . . he didn't know what he felt. But he leaned over, kissed her, and chuckled as people do when they're given a wonderful surprise.

"Congratulations to us. Do the boys know?"

"No, it's way too soon. They'll have to wait so long that they'd get bored with the whole business. I'm praying for a girl because I know you want one."

"Yes, it would be a change, wouldn't it? Dolls instead of trucks and guns."

He must be joyful, glad to be home, delighted about the baby, and prepared for questions.

"The paper had some marvelous photographs of Blanche's show. Ball gowns fit for a princess, and ski jackets. Skiing's the new sport, isn't it? She really knows something about the haute monde, doesn't she? I think she'd love to be a member of it herself, don't you think so?"

"How would I know? I hardly ever see her, much less talk to her."

"I can't help thinking how lucky I am. First I think of Sabine, who would have given anything to have a baby of her own. And then I think of Blanche. She's still young enough, but has no husband. With all her success, I still feel sorry for her. Sometimes she seems to look wistful, or discouraged or something. I think that's why she never visits us anymore. Haven't you ever noticed?"

"No. I just said I hardly ever see her. How's

James's arm? Did they say when the cast will be off?"

"Next week. The bones heal fast at his age."

Past the crest of the hill and down toward the plateau on the other side, it was often a pleasure to slow the car midway for a view of the house. As if gilded, it lay now in this afternoon's sunlight, but the pure joy that the sight always brought was not there.

It was early, so the boys were still in school. Having had a sleepless night on the train, Adam lay down on the terrace and closed his eyes. Some men, especially those who keep a mistress, would laugh at his fears, but many others would not; he wished he knew one of these well enough to talk to him. He condemned himself. He had lost his integrity. She could cause him to be the butt of whispered jokes, or unthinkable ruination, if that crazy episode should come to Emma's ears.

Emma! The other half of himself from whom nothing, nothing at all, is ever hidden! He lives in the world. He looks and listens and reads, so that he knows how rare is a marriage like theirs.

And now comes that woman, whom he

neither likes nor dislikes, that woman who means nothing to him, who has no shame . . . She laughs, she dances. She laughs in front of his eyes, and he cannot get rid of her.

He drowsed and woke in horror from a dream that she had just told him she was pregnant and that she hoped for a girl.

The boys must be home from school because the phonograph needed to be rewound; it sounded like a person who is starting to yawn. They were always putting on records and forgetting about them.

It was time for him to jump up wide awake, and be a father to them, a jolly, strong, and fearless father.

Blanche's room was what one would expect, both comfortable and elegant, very French and floral, peach-colored, brown, and green, with well-tended plants at the windows. Blanche, who expected him, was wearing a negligee. A thought passed through his mind as he took his seat: I would rather be having dental surgery.

They looked at each other. He wondered whether he would always envision her, no matter how she might be dressed, as she had looked without her clothes. Then he wondered whether she might be thinking the same about him.

"So," she began, "I suppose it is you who deserves my thanks for that nice bonus I'm to have."

"Not at all. It was a unanimous decision. You earned it. You put your name, and the store's name, in all the newspapers, and next month, in the magazines, we'll have all the photographs."

"True, but I'm still sure you had a whole lot to do with the bonus. You did it to buy me off, didn't you?" And the black eyes twinkled.

Rarely, perhaps never, had Adam found himself without the right words to meet a tough situation. Anything, anything would do, if only to break this awful silence. And he said the first thing that came into his head.

"I never buy anyone off, as you put it. I've never needed to."

"But you need to now, don't you? Come on, Adam, loosen up. It would be quite a mess if your wife were to know, wouldn't it? Proper ladies like her usually get hysterical when these things happen. You wouldn't like that at all."

This is the enemy on the dark street, the man with the gun. Don't argue with him.

"No, I would not like it, especially now. Emma is pregnant."

"Domestic bliss. How nice for you. Shall I congratulate you?"

This is a bitter woman. Why should she hate me so? What have I done to her? Ah yes, I distanced myself from her after we returned home. I made it clear that I did not love her. And that I did not want her.

"Let's talk about you," he said. "I have news for you. It's still confidential, but I trust you, so I'll tell you. We're going to open a store in New York. The custom-made salon there will undoubtedly be yours."

"Do you have to spend all those millions just to get rid of me?"

"Don't be ridiculous, Blanche."

"It's you who are being ridiculous. What makes you think you can move me around as you please? I don't care whether you open a New York store or not. I don't want to go to New York. I like it here. I never thought I would, but I do. I'm satisfied."

She was teasing him, prolonging the

game, enjoying the game until she was ready to give the blow that would end it.

"I'm glad you're satisfied here," he said. "But—"

"But nothing. What I'd like is to hear something about your satisfaction."

"Mine? I don't understand."

She was laughing. She was going to have her story all over the store from highest to lowest, if she hadn't already done so.

"Your satisfaction. How was it the other evening . . . when the hook got caught in the lace? And then the next night—our night to remember? Did you enjoy it?"

My God, he thought again. What had he done to deserve this? A little music, a little wine, and now this woman had such power over him. He wanted to say, "You disgust me," but he didn't dare. Perhaps he disgusted himself.

And he looked around the room at the picture frame, the calendar, and all the gold-rimmed objects that had come from Sabine's house, then back at the woman, who was looking at him with amusement in her face.

Sabine hadn't liked her. . . .

"Let's get to the point," he said. "Just tell

me what you are going to do so I can pre-
pare myself."

"Do? Why, Adam, what in the world do you
think I'm going to do?"

"I don't know. That's why I'm asking."

"Well, dear man, I'm not going to do anything. I have no intention of washing dirty
linen in public, as they say, although frankly,
I don't consider this particular linen to be especially dirty. But many people would say it
is, and certainly your wife would, so I'm not
going to do it. You can rest easy."

He was stunned. Should he believe her?
He asked her whether she truly meant what
she said.

"Oh, I certainly do. You're a very decent
person, one of the best, and everybody
knows it. Your wife has always been nice to
me, but it's really for the children's sake that
I will not embarrass you. Besides, you've
had enough troubles in your life. You lost
Jonathan, and for God's sake, you still have
Leo. So you see, Adam, I do have a heart after all."

This sudden inclusion of Leo was startling.
"Why? Is Leo making any trouble? I thought
he was still immersed in those books."

"He is. But that doesn't mean he won't make plenty of trouble before he dies."

"Well, I can't worry over that. One trouble at a time. Can I truly depend upon what you've just said, Blanche?" he pleaded.

"For your children's sake, you can. I had a miserable childhood, and I will never hurt a child in any way, or disrupt a child's home. Never."

Looking at her, he saw that her face was earnest. The taunting had been her vengeance. . . . But he had to believe these last words about the children because the alternative was to live in anguish. He decided, then, to believe.

When Blanche stood up and extended her hand, he took it.

"Let's have a truce, Adam. You've been sick over this foolish business, haven't you? But now go home and forget it. I'm sorry that I worried you. It was a nasty mean little game, and I shouldn't have played it. I was merely amusing myself."

There was a lump in Adam's throat, a mixture of emotions: the receding fear, the relief, the gratitude, and, abruptly, a thought of Jonathan. Was this really the woman his brother had so loved?

You were an adult, you were in the world and met all kinds, the good ones who do terrible things and the ones who seem bad but do good things. How is one to judge? How is one to know?

Tired beyond description, he thanked her again, and breathing normally now, went home.

Chapter 20

✳

Adam stood looking down at the bassinet. This birth was different. He could not express in any way that would not sound foolish to modern ears how the female-ness of this little person affected him.

"So fragile," he murmured. "I'm almost afraid to touch her."

Emma was laughing at him. "No more fragile than the others."

"They're boys, and a girl is more vulnerable."

"Aren't you straight out of the year one! Except for a few muscles, she will be as ready as any man to face life."

Let her believe so. She wouldn't be so complacent if what he still thought of as "zero hour" with that other woman had ended differently. Even now when he passed Blanche occasionally on his way to his office, he felt a jolt. God only knew what

she would say to Emma if she should ever
have a change of heart. But she had kept
her word . . . so far.

"Are you sure you haven't changed your
mind about the name?" he asked.

"No. Unless they're really awful, I think
names should be kept in a family. Eileen is
rather nice, and it was your mother's name."

Not many women would be giving that
honor to a person she had never known.

"I want to tell you something," he said,
"only I don't really know how to say it properly. Words can't—" and Adam made a
small, helpless gesture.

"Well, try."

"I love you, Emma. I love you. That's all I
can say."

That was the summer when they found a
nurse who would come for a few weeks to
care for Eileen while the rest of the family
took the long-promised trip to the Grand
Canyon and Yosemite. Business, moves,
deaths, and births had filled the years
since the October wedding that sometimes
seemed to have happened only yesterday.
So, after kissing Eileen's bald head, waving

good-bye to Rudy and Rea, and climbing into a station wagon loaded with snack food, cameras, swimsuits, sweaters, umbrellas, and everything else they could think of, they headed west.

Even with three noisy boys in the back of the car, this was a reminder of their honeymoon. The mountain roads, the log cabins where they had slept, and the fragrance of pines were still there.

"I need to remember everything so I can tell what I did for my summer vacation," James said. "You're supposed to do that when school starts again. I'm going to put some words down to remind me. How do you spell 'Indians'?"

"You read so many of these articles about car trips with bored, whining, fighting kids," Emma whispered, "that you almost dread to try it. But these three have been angels."

"Angels? Hardly," Adam said, remembering the uproar when James had put two beetles in Jon's bed. "But they are very interested in everything. They're lucky, and we're lucky."

Returning was, in its way, as exciting as departing had been. As was their tradition, they stopped the car on the crest of the hill.

"Look, boys," Emma cried. "There's home! And what on earth is that thing on the lawn?"

"The baby carriage!"

"Rudy and Rea and the lady with the carriage!"

"Can Eileen talk yet?" Andy asked.

"Dope!" James said. "She just got born."

"Well, how long does it take to talk?"

"In about a year and a half she'll start to say something," Emma explained. "It takes time."

"What do you think she'll say, Mom?"

"Well, maybe she'll say she's very happy and very lucky to be in this family."

"Why?"

"Well, because we are all together and we all love each other."

One quiet Sunday afternoon, many months later, when Adam was working at his desk in the home office, Rudy came to announce that some people were at the door asking to see Mr. Simon Arnring.

"Did you tell them that he—"

"Yes. It's a man and his wife. They want to see some other member of the family. He knew your brother Jonathan, he says. They were in the army. In the war."

More useless pain, thought Adam, or else maybe it will be one of those semihumorous, loving anecdotes and reminiscences told by relatives and friends at funerals in order to put a more cheerful face on death. But he went to the front door, greeted the couple, and invited them to come in.

They looked like country folks, the man in his best suit, while his wife was no doubt unaware that she had left a roller in the hair at the back of her neck.

"Steve Woods is the name, and this is my wife, Margie. Gee, I feel funny, barging in on you like this, Mr. Arnring. But Margie here kept after me to do it. Sorry to know you've lost your father."

"Yes, I'm the one who made Steve come," the little woman said nervously. "We moved last month, and we had all this stuff in the attic, stuff we hadn't looked at since Steve came back from France twelve years ago. You know how it is, how things pile up and you never open some boxes and bags for such a long time that you forget you have them. But when I saw this, I thought right away—"

"Get to the point, Margie! I looked up Si-mon Arnring again and got this address from the post office. I guess you folks got all the stuff the army sent, all the things from the war."

"Yes, we got them."

The package that Pa had left was still in the attic. Would he ever forget it? There was the watch, the graduation present, the leather folder with the family snapshots taken by their neighbor with the old Brownie camera, and then the photo of Blanche, with her curved lips and her cheekbones that re-minded him of exotic Asia. Now no doubt these people had some more photos to show, maybe of Jonathan himself in a group of grinning soldiers, perhaps to show the folks at home that things were not so bad: *Don't worry, we're winning the war, I'll be home soon—*

"Well, I knew I had this thing in my pocket that I took from him when—when they brought him in. And Margie says, I guess she's right, I ought to give it to you. The thing's been bothering me, although I'm still not sure what good it will do for you to have it, except that it sure doesn't belong to me, either, does it? We live only one hundred seventy-five miles north of here, so we thought we might as well take a weekend instead of putting it in the mail because you might want to ask some questions, although there's not much I could tell you. It's a short story."

Having delivered this explanation, Steve Woods handed over to Adam some creased, folded sheets of paper that had once been crisp and pale blue.

Dear Jonathan,
I hope this finds you safe and well. It's awful to see that the war is still going on, but with 1917 half over, we have been reading lately that they believe it will be won by Christmas. I hope for the whole world's sake that that is so and that you will be home to start medical school and be on your way.

I have been thinking a great deal about what an unusual person you are. So many people seem to choose a profession in a halfhearted way, for the reason that they see somebody else who has made a lot of money in that profession, or because they have a relative who recommends it, or because it seems prestigious. Only now and then do you see a man who is really born to be a teacher or a lawyer or a doctor, or any particular thing. Well, you were born to be a doctor, that's sure. Not only do you have the intellect for it, but you have the understanding of it. Forgive me for mentioning this, but I have to tell you how I admire your patience and your forbearance with your so difficult brother, Leo. Having seen that, I am less upset about what I have to say next.

Perhaps it is a good thing that you and I were forced by this war to be separated. It has given us time to think, with much of that time apart while you were in college. When you are in medical school, there will be what amounts to four or more years of separation because, though we would be living under the same roof, you will be spending almost all your working hours at school or in the hospital. So when you are finally finished, we would still not have had a chance to find out who we really are. That would certainly not be fair to either of us, and so, not the right way to be really married.

I am not, I swear to you, thinking only selfishly of myself. I am thinking more about you, Jonathan, because you owe more to yourself than a risky, halfway marriage. If I did not love you, I would go ahead, marry you and let you take your chances. But you deserve better. I want you to enjoy your training with a free mind, get your medical degree, and then find somebody whom you'll have time to know well before you make a final decision about love and marriage.

I do this for your good, and in sorrow. But I know, because you are the man you are, that you will understand and will be much happier in the end. Much love,

Blanche

Adam laid the letter on the arm of his chair and looked at the two people who, with curious yet troubled eyes, were watching him. Then he took up the letter and read it again. When he had finished it, with his voice sounding strange to his own ears, he asked, "So what else? What else?"

It seemed to him that they had something more to say. When he had cleared his throat a few times, Steve Woods made a gesture with his right arm to indicate height and explained, "The top of a trench is way taller than a man's head. Well, naturally, it has to be. A kind of ladder is there so you can go over the top. Geez, it's years ago, and I still get the shakes thinking about it. We were only a couple of hundred yards from the Krauts' trenches, and we were all waiting for the next barrage and wondering who's making the next attack. Our turn, or theirs? It's so quiet, just waiting.

"Geez, I can't think of it even now . . . Your brother read the letter, and read it again, just the way you did just now, and then, before any of us guys could stop him or even notice what he was doing, I guess, he started to race up the ladder. When we saw, we yelled like hell, and a couple of us started up to pull him down, but it was too late. His head was already above ground level, and he was waving his arms toward the enemy. He wanted them to see him. And he was yelling, 'Come get me.' Well, you've seen

pictures and you probably have an idea—
except that unless you've been there—"
Woods finished with a shake of his head.

"He wanted to die," Adam said, still in that
queer-sounding voice.

Eight million men died in that war. Could
any of those have wanted to die?

"Yeah, he did. He wanted to die. And for a
woman. Can you beat it? Can you beat it?"

"Poor boy," murmured Margie. "I hope—
oh, Mr. Arnring, did we do something awful
coming here with this letter?"

She was so fearfully anxious that Adam
said quickly, "No, you did the absolutely
right thing. The truth is the truth."

Thank God that Pa left us before he could
know this! He never had had a clear road to
travel with any one of his three sons, had
he? Me and my little-girl mother, then poor,
pitiful Leo, and now this cruel, wasteful, stupid death. If he had at least died fighting in
the good cause! But this, this . . .

"The bitch. The bitch."

Outdoors on the lawn, the two bigger boys
were playing ball. Their voices, still soprano,
faded off down the hill, while the little
brother was most likely trailing after them
and getting in their way.

Three great sycamores and oaks give shade. Out of a placid sky the sun shines on their innocence. And Jonathan, who so loved life and who had so much to give, has missed it all.

The bitch. The bitch.

Steve Woods broke the stillness in the room.

"I never knew till I read this letter that he was going to be a doctor. Come to think of it, he never did talk much about himself. Worked in his dad's store, he said. He was a nice, all-around guy. He was the kindest guy. I remember how when one of the guys was wounded, he picked him up and carried him and talked to him. We were a mixed bunch when this happened. Farmhands from way down south, a schoolteacher, a couple of stuffed shirts, and some quiet ones. Some of the guys liked to argue a lot. You know how it is. But he never did, I remember. He only liked to listen. He got along with everybody. Afterward they said it couldn't have been just the letter. He must have lost his marbles."

In that one minute, he did lose them.

"Geez, over a woman."

"It happens."

In the hallway, the screen door banged and three pairs of feet raced up the stairs. But two dogs, catching sight of the strangers with Adam, came flying into the room to investigate.

"Good-looking pups. Some kind of hunters?" asked Woods.

"No, they're poodles. The big one, the black one, is a standard. His name is Buster. And the little one, Billy, is my wife's favorite."

"We have a couple of 'coon hounds home. Wouldn't be home without dogs, would it?"

Mrs. Woods remarked, as she stroked Billy under the chin, "They're all the same. They just stand there as long as you'll keep doing this under the chin. They love it."

Adam went suddenly all soft inside with the choking that is so close to tears. The goodness, the simple, honest goodness in simple people! In some of them, anyway.

"My wife's upstairs with the baby," he said. "But she'll be down in a minute. We'd like to have you stay for some supper with us."

But the Woodses were already standing. "No, no, thanks, we've got a long ride and want to get home before dark."

"You're sure? You're very welcome. You've

been so kind, going to this trouble. I can't
tell you how I appreciate it."

They had seen his struggle. He had shed
no tears, but they had understood. At the
door as the three shook hands, Woods said,
"Just need to tell you one thing more. He
didn't feel any pain. It was over in a second."

Adam watched them go down the drive-
way and into their car. They waved, he
waved back, and then he turned, went to
the foot of the stairs, and called out.

"Emma? I forgot some papers in the office
downtown. I won't be long."

The Packard roadster, a luxurious present
for this year's anniversary, a happy toy for
two, raced along the road. It roared down
the hill, past Sabine's old mansion where,
under a tree, a child in a wheelchair was
reading a book. It skimmed down the street
where Cace Arnring, in the silence of Sunday, presented its dignified face.

Almost blind with rage and barely enough
in control of himself or of the car to know
how sick he was, Adam finally slowed it
enough to prevent a crash, and then
stopped along the curb to collect himself
and go on.

Some minutes later, he entered the farther suburb of Chattahoochee. And passing through the street where Leo lived, he wondered for an instant how that troubled soul would react to this awful news. For an instant, too, but only for an instant, he wondered what might be the purpose of this undertaking, or even the wisdom of it, given the circumstances. She had committed a crime, but how to punish her? Then he saw the picture that Woods had painted, or had mercifully not painted: Jonathan had been shot in the face.

The bitch. The bitch.

Then he stopped in front of the apartment house where Blanche lived. He had forgotten—had wanted to forget—the number of her apartment, so he had to read the list in the lobby. Second floor. Ah, yes, down the hall on the right-hand side. He pressed the bell.

"Who is it?" she called.

"Adam. I need to see you."

She opened the door. The foyer was papered in rose-colored toile with bucolic scenes, a castle on a hill. She was wearing a robe, chiffon lamé, pale yellow, not new; had she worn it that night in New York?

"You killed my brother," he said.

"What are you talking about? Is this a joke?"

"I am not joking. Do you hear me? I am not joking. *You killed my brother.*"

"Stop it. You come here on a Sunday afternoon with this nonsense and bother me, when I'm getting ready to go out. What are you doing?"

"You killed my brother," he repeated.

"How many times are you going to say it? Listen, Adam, I want you out of here—no, don't come in! Get out! You're crazy."

"You weren't even worth his little fingernail, do you know that?"

She laughed. "I do hope you don't mean Leo, the crazy one," she retorted.

"I mean the other one, the kind and patient one, who would never have allowed you to use these words about Leo. I mean my brother Jonathan, whom you loved so little that you sent him to his death."

Blanche stared at him. "I do believe you are serious about this. Are you feeling all right, Adam?"

"My head is functioning, if that's what you mean."

"I don't want to hear any more. Look, I'm

being called for at five. I have an engagement for dinner at the Hotel Empire, and I have to do my hair. That's my dress over there. Whatever nonsense this is, please save it for another time, Adam."

Abruptly, the rage departed. The fire went out, and in its place lay a poisonous hatred. This time he spoke quietly.

"You told him you had changed your mind about him, and so he killed himself. That's the whole story." And withdrawing the letter from his pocket, he gave it to her. "Here. Read."

Her lips moved, and her eyebrows rose as she read. He could not bear to look at her face, and turning away, found himself staring at the dress that lay on the back of the chair. A few years ago the dresses hung to the knees. They were calf length this season. Blanche was a fashion expert. Imbeciles! Idiots! Spending a lifetime draping their bodies!

"Whatever did he see in you?" he cried.

Blanche laid the letter aside and looked up. "The same thing you did," she said.

"For God's sake, Blanche, you and I never loved each other. Never, not for one moment."

"Speak for yourself. Read the date on that letter. What is the date of your wedding? Did I know when we met in June 1917 that you were already planning a wedding? We spent a whole day together, and an evening on the beach. You never once mentioned Emma. Even Jon didn't know."

"Jon was going to war. Should I have displayed my own happiness in front of him? Anyway, you didn't fall in love with me after those few hours. No, you simply got the idea that I was richer than Jon would ever be."

"You didn't exactly marry a pauper, did you?"

"You know better than to say that. But why should truth ever stand in your way? Sly and cruel and cold as a snake, you are. Money is all it was about, and nothing else."

"You know there was much more to it than that. You were what they call a catch, and you still are. Good-looking, decent, intelligent—you can have all the women you want."

"Thanks for the compliments, but it happens that I don't want any women except the one I have."

"Yes, and don't you love to tell how you fell in love with her the first time you saw her sitting on the step? Or something like that? So why couldn't it happen to me?" Now, as her eyes filled, she burst into a tirade. "Oh, how I've hated her! Not hated exactly, because she never did anything to me, but because of what she had. Rich parents, rich aunt, Paris, London, Rome, God knows where else, universities, husband, children—all dumped into her lap."

So this is it, or part of it. Perhaps if another man had taken Emma away and I had been living alongside of them all this time, I might feel the same?

He was profoundly uncomfortable and filled with a sense of futility. Her face in its frame of black curls repelled him, and yet at the same time he could feel pity. He wished she would disappear so that he would never have to look at her again.

"I'm truly sorry about Jonathan," she said, wiping her eyes with the back of her hand. "I never dreamed that he would take it so hard. Thousands of men got letters like that, not as thoughtful as mine was, either, and they didn't kill themselves."

Thousands of men were not like Jonathan, Adam thought.

"What are you going to do?" he asked.

"Are you asking me whether I plan to stay? You don't think I'd want to stay after this?"

"Well, then, how soon do you plan to leave?"

"I'd leave today if I could. If you think this will be an unbearable hurt for me, you're making a mistake. For a long time, I've been getting tired of this place, sick of these flat prairies and this boring little city. And this whole country, if you want to know. So if you think I'm crushed, you're wrong."

What was the use? Why go on with this useless bickering?

"You can make your arrangements with the company's lawyers and with your own," he said quietly. "I'm sure that the terms will be fair all around."

He stood up, prepared to go, but Blanche, also standing, had one more thing to tell him.

"Be careful of Leo."

"Careful? What do you mean? I hardly ever see him except when he comes now and then to visit my boys. He doesn't even seem to like being with them as much as he used to."

"He's your enemy. Other than that, I'll say good-bye to you and good luck."

"Good-bye, Blanche," he replied.

Behind him the door closed with a soft thud, a finality that reminded him of the curtain going down on the third act of a solemn drama. Passing the street where Leo lived, he knew he ought to go and give him the news, but admitting to dread and cowardice, he decided to postpone the task until tomorrow.

When he reached home, he found to his surprise that the fateful letter was in his hand; without thinking, he must have picked it up from the little table where Blanche had discarded it. Wordlessly, he handed it to Emma.

When she had read it and read it again, she only shook her head as if there could be no suitable comment. And then she said that somebody had to tell Leo.

"Let me do it, Adam. It will be better that way for you and for him, too. I'll go now and be back soon. You go rest."

For some reason Leo liked her, or perhaps it might be more accurate to say that he disliked her less than he disliked other people.

Adam was still sitting with an unread book when Emma returned and reported that it hadn't been as hard as one would expect.

"I simply told him the fact. He wanted to see her letter, but I hadn't brought it with me, and anyway, it's just as well. Frankly, I think it would be best to destroy the sad thing. I was surprised that he let me kiss his cheek. That's when I got close enough to see that his eyes were wet. I asked him to come back here and stay in Pa's room as long as he liked, asked him to come back with his brother, but he said no, that he is all right where he is. He has a long table covered with books and papers, so I guess he's doing something or other that is meaningful to him. He said he was going to take a sleeping pill tonight so that he could get through till morning and go back to work. So that's it. Now tell me about Blanche."

Then he told her what he could, omitting along with much else the fact that Blanche had spared their children from hearing some ugly things about life that children should not hear. After that they spent some little time in reminiscences of Blanche and analyses of her character; then, reaching no conclusions, they went upstairs to bed.

Early the next day one of the secretaries reported that Madame Blanche was not feeling well and would be staying home for a few days. Not surprising, Adam thought. Then, wondering when and where she was going to go, he decided that she would probably go to New York, that being the logical place for anyone with her reputation. It would be easy for her to open a shop for custom-made clothes, or to design for some major house. In either case, she would be far enough away from him.

Two of the dressmakers, believing that she must be quite ill, went to visit her, and reported, surprisingly, that she was quite well. Then, quite naturally, rumors spread: that she was secretly married, or that she had a lover somewhere, or that some other company had offered her more money.

By the end of the month, during which time she did not appear at the shop, it was reported by some who had thought themselves her friends that she had emptied the apartment and left without saying good-bye or where she was going. For another month or two, the tantalizing puzzle remained. But then, since it was unsolved, it ceased to be so tantalizing.

The designer salon was as busy as ever. Adam hired two excellent buyers, customers seemed to be well satisfied, and business, even now as the country fell into depression, still flourished.

"She made an enormous fortune in the stock market, you know. Sold out two weeks before the crash," a man said one evening when they were at a gathering of friends.

"She was a strange person," a woman remarked. "Very talented, very polite, but cold underneath, I thought, not that it was any business of mine. I never could decide whether I liked her or not."

"Oh, I liked her," Emma said. "Even though I never got to know her very well. As time went on, especially during the last couple of years, we hardly ever saw her. She was so successful, and yet I always felt a little sorry for her. I wonder where she is now."

Blanche has come home just in time to miss the rain. Now, as she stands at the window, the singular fragrance of wet leafage rises to meet her, making her feel almost happy.

"I am Blanche," she says aloud, "and I live here."

Here is one of the oldest streets in Paris. A well-dressed couple passes below, sharing

an expensive umbrella, an elderly gentleman walks a pair of expensive dogs, and a
tourist shields his expensive camera under
his raincoat. No doubt he is on his way to
Notre Dame or to the Louvre. Years ago in
Vienna, the tourists used to follow the same
path, from the cathedral to the museums
and the shops.

Wouldn't it be quite an experience to go
back there for a few days now and find out
how it feels to be well off in Vienna? Rich,
with all these dollars in one's pocket, dollars
enough to dine at the best restaurants and
to buy things in shops one had never even
dared to enter?

And then after that, to walk past the tene-
ments, those gloomy prisons where life either shrivels or else erupts into rage, as
when a hideous man, the husband of one's
mother, does terrible, dirty things to a girl,
while the mother pretends not to know because he is the one who pays the rent. How
would it be to walk past those places and
know that one will never suffer like that
again?

No, not quite like that. Yet this much is
true: A child who has never been properly

loved will grow up without knowing how to love. And is that not a kind of torment?

First there was Jonathan, a good man. And then there was Adam, a better one. It wouldn't have been too hard to take him away from Emma, even after they were married. Proximity, novelty, and a few tricks, that's all it needs. And it happens all the time.

But to take him from his children is something else. One would have to have a heart of stone, and no memory . . . Still, it might be a blessing to have no memory and so not care about Adam's children, or about his poor brother, or anyone.

Ah well, enough of that. Turn around and look at this room, at the landscapes, very fine ones, that hang on the eighteenth-century paneled walls. A charming, modern touch was the octagonal glass table next to the Louis XVI chair. Everything is in perfect taste, perfect for formal entertaining or for an intimate evening with that interesting gentleman on the floor below.

It is a home, a nest, a permanent refuge, the first you've ever had. It is "upper class," poor old Sabine would say, and did say

when she gave away those gold-framed articles on the desk.

Even on a rainy day, they had a soft, rich
gleam. From inside the gold picture frame,
Blanche smiles back at Blanche. Below the
gold rim of the calendar, the date stands out
in beautiful Gothic letters: April 1932.

Chapter 21

Whenever Adam looked up from his desk in the office, the picture met his eyes. It never failed to brighten a dull day, to increase the pleasure of a pleasant one, to make him laugh with the joy of the scene, or in a more serious mood, to remind him that this is what life is all about.

There they stood, he at one end of the row and Emma at the other, with their children between them and palm trees behind them, all together on a beach in southern California.

They had just returned from a sail that day, and strangers, amused by the sight of three strong boys, one ready for high school, being trailed by a bossy two-year-old sister, had taken this picture.

They had attracted attention in many places during that vacation. There was a night when, at a country inn, the pianist in a quartet fell ill, and Emma, to great applause, replaced him. There was the restaurant where Eileen casually walked out onto the floor and danced a solo. There were the endless shops, where the boys squabbled over souvenirs for their favorite people, for Rudy and Rea, for Mr. Reilly and Mr. Archer, along with certain teachers, certain friends, and surely the basketball coach . . .

But now the outgoing basket as well as the incoming basket of mail were both full. He had just put down the telephone and was about to make another call when Miss Fitz, the secretary, appeared at the door and whispered, "There's a man here who says he's your brother. He wants to see you."

Brother? Leo? What could he possibly be doing here?

"He doesn't look at all like you, Mr. Arnring, so I wasn't sure. You never know."

Poor guy, he didn't look very much like most people. "Tell him to come in, please."

"Leo! How're you doing? We've hardly seen you in months. Three months, at least," Adam said cheerfully. "The boys miss you and ask for you. Don't be such a stranger!"

There Leo stood, a little man with the lined

forehead of a person years older than he, along with the uncertain, wavering glance and stare of someone less than half his age. A familiar wave of sympathy mixed with distaste passed through Adam.

"What brings you here this morning?" he asked, still cheerfully.

"Personal business," Leo said, with a slight, anxious frown.

"Personal? So why not visit me at home? We could talk more comfortably over breakfast, lunch, or dinner. You choose."

"You don't have to cajole me, Adam. I know perfectly well that you're a busy man and that I'm wasting your valuable time here at work."

Here we go again, the same old sarcasm, the same old hostility. Sighing, Adam suggested that Leo sit down and explain his problem.

"It's a simple problem. I'll give it to you in three words. I need money."

"Really? I thought you were nicely fixed with the rent from the store. They've been paying so much more than I ever thought you'd get."

"How much of an income do you think that is? I need a real income."

"I'm sorry, but I don't follow you at all," Adam said.

Leo gave his small, crooked smile. "Come, come, Adam. By now you've found out what real money is. That's what I'm talking about, real money."

"It seems to me you might get a job," Adam said, patiently hiding his annoyance. "People do. I did."

"Listen, Adam. It's time for you to be taken down a peg. You know perfectly well I can't do what you've done. Look at me! You didn't offer me any job in Cace Arnring, did you? No. Maybe if I had had some education, I wouldn't be sitting here asking for money. I never went to college; I worked in a grocery store hauling vegetables—"

"So did I, and I worked my way out of it."

"Look at me! What the hell are you talking about? Take another look at me, and spare me your pompous answers."

Huddled in the big leather chair near the desk, Leo looked like a wicked imp in a book of fairy tales. And Adam, putting himself for one painful instant in his place, said gently, "I'll help you out, Leo. What do you need?"

"Well, let's talk. Tell me, didn't this company of yours issue stock sometime ago at twenty-six dollars a share? And you as vice president, didn't you get many thousands of shares of preferred stock? You must have. I read and I know what you fellas earn."

Now Adam frowned. "You have no right to delve into my personal affairs, Leo."

"Well, maybe yes and maybe no. But when a man needs money, he can get desperate. And I need money. Here it is, short and sweet: I want to get married and set myself up in comfort. The lady comes of a distinguished old family; she's accustomed to a good home, nothing ostentatious or nouveau riche, just simple and refined. She happens also to be a beautiful woman, and I can't come to her with empty hands. That's my story."

A beautiful woman. Was she the reason for the well-tailored suit, the neat shirt, and the cuff links, when Leo had never looked like that before? It made no sense.

Adam stared at his brother. He makes no sense; it's some sickness, he thought, and in some alarm, was at a loss to deal with it. So they confronted each other in a tense and wary silence.

Then, with a sudden recall of Jonathan's

calm methods, he thought of something else. "All right, I'll make you a handsome wedding gift: I'll furnish your house and send you on a splendid honeymoon. I'll tell you what, come tomorrow to dinner. Emma, you, and I will sit around afterward and we'll give our advice. After all, we're old hands at weddings and houses by now. All right?"

Leo, with a vigorous shake of his bald head, indicating that it was far from being all right, continued. "Half a million dollars, and not a cent less, Adam."

"You're being ridiculous! Stop making a fool of yourself."

"You'll be surprised to find who's the fool if you don't give me what I want. The tables are turned, Adam. I've been at the wrong table all my life, and I'm sick of it." Accusing, complaining, the shrill voice rose. "Look at me! Well, don't look. You've all spent your lives trying not to look at me. Five feet one—"

"That's not fair, surely not fair to Pa. He was good to you. He stayed with you till the end—"

"He stayed because he didn't know what else to do with me. And I stayed because it was safe, a sure thing. But now I've waked up, you see?"

"You've let your feeling about your height ruin your life," Adam said, attempting to soothe. "But think, Napoleon was short, and—"

"Yes, and he vented his rage on the world."

"All right, so that's a poor example. But instead of venting rage, try to get rid of it. Rage can destroy a person."

"Easy for you to talk! Even though you had a father who never got over his guilt about not marrying your mother."

"That's a nasty, cruel thing to say to me. You always like to bring that up, don't you?"

"And as for Jonathan, he was going to be a doctor—doesn't every poor, blue-collar immigrant want his son to be a doctor? Poor kind fellow, Jon was a fool to kill himself over a fancy slut—yes, a slut, and you know it."

"I don't know anything about it, Leo."

"Oh, I think you know a great deal about it, Adam."

"Listen here, I have work to do. I have no time for this drivel. I have to ask you to leave."

"So let's get back to the subject, and I'll be only too glad to leave. Just give me what I'm asking for."

How to get this man—my brother, this impossible brother—out of my office? Call one of the salesmen? No, the ruckus will be all over the place if I do. Try again.

"Leo, be reasonable. I'm inviting you to my house. We'll talk in privacy about your affairs. Emma likes you, and she's the most understanding woman you could want. She'll listen to you and make practical suggestions—"

"But she won't like what I have to say if you don't give me what I want. How many times must I tell you? *Give me what I want,* Adam, or I'll open my mouth. I'll break Emma's heart, which I don't want to do because she's never harmed me and she has good kids—"

"What the hell do you mean, you'll break Emma's heart? What the hell are you talking about?"

"About Blanche, Adam. About the wife you love and would humiliate with a dirty affair in your office."

Just as one feels the hot flash of anger, one feels the white chill of terror as the blood drains, or seems to drain, out of the heart.

Adam sat down, two pairs of eyes met, and no one spoke. Out in the corridor, some women were laughing, their voices tinkling through the stillness; a horn blew in the street below, and a dog yapped.

Very quietly then, Adam asked, "What about her?"

"The Sunday afternoons, the weekday evenings. It was stupid of you. I saw you driving past where I live and I wondered what you were doing in my neighborhood, so I found out."

"For God's sake, she was an important part of the business! Once or twice—yes, exactly two times, no more than that, I went to her apartment to talk business."

"Come, come. Don't waste your energy talking nonsense. You've been lovers for years. You, the perfect husband and father. Amusing, isn't it? What about your little fun at the Waldorf-Astoria in New York? And don't deny it, because she told me herself."

"She—told you? It's a lie! She was hateful, she lied—"

"She was hateful because you took advantage of what she offered you, and then treated her like a leper. You who everyone thinks is so perfect! I know this was a time ago. I know that you would never have left Emma, but still, would you like me to tell her? A woman like her—she'd fall apart. She wouldn't stay with you. So it's up to you, Adam."

Adam's hands gripped the edge of the desk as though he would rip the wood apart. If he had had a knife or a gun, he knew what he would do with it, what he would not be able to stop himself from doing.

Break her heart. She'd fall apart.

"Blackmail," he whispered. "Oh, you are scum, my brother. Scum."

"Oh, no, I'm not. You know I'm not. I'm desperate. You had everything. You were the one Pa loved, you were the success, the benefactor, and didn't you enjoy it! But now the model husband has cheated on his wife, hasn't he? You can still have everything— everything but the half a million you're going to give me. Once you give it to me, I'll get out of your life. I'll get out of Emma's life. You'll never see me again. You'll never even know where I am, so help me God."

Before Adam's eyes, the room swayed,

the ceiling tilted, and he was too dizzy to stand up. But he was still able to speak.

"You ugly misfit! You've always taken out your rage at the world on your family. When you walked into a room you brought gloom with your bitter tongue. You made Pa's life miserable. And as for your treatment of me, the less said the better."

The procedure did not take very long. A bank check was issued—the clerk visibly startled by the size of it—and the two brothers were out on the sidewalk among the normal flow of normal people on their way to work.

"I don't feel bad about taking this," said Leo. "A man who can afford to give away a mansion like that aunt's, or to pay for the Children's Room at the library that I heard about last week, can afford to give a helping hand to his own brother. Thank you, Adam."

"I'll thank you to get out of my sight and stay out of it forever. And I mean forever. You're rotten, you're hideous, you poison the air with your stench. May God damn you. Get out of my sight."

"With pleasure. You'll never know where I am." And Leo bowed.

For a minute, Adam stood watching him scurry down the street where some young girls stared and laughed at him as he passed them.

Oh, he will take this money that I should be able to save for some good cause or for my children, and lose it as he lost Pa's savings. What a crazy story—a beautiful woman from an old family. Crazy! The poor creature! And could Blanche really have told him we were lovers for more than just that one time in New York? Why does he hate me so much?

Sometimes, Pa said, people just hate each other without really knowing why. Especially in families, it happens. It's a fact of life. And yet—and yet my heart aches to see those cruel girls laughing at him. . . .

He went in the other direction, toward the store. At a turning, he recognized his old friend Doris, climbing into a dusty car with a man, obviously her husband, and two little children. Although he hadn't thought about her in years, he recalled that someone had told him she lived way out in the country. Now he thought, wherever she lives, she is better off than if she had married me, as she had once obviously wanted to do.

His head ached. A man defeated in battle deserves a rest, and he decided to go home. At the crest of the hill, where the car always paused before the descent, he looked down at his house. It seemed to him that he was looking at a place destroyed, by fire or flood or some other horror that had passed through, leaving a terrible wreckage behind.

"You're back early," Emma said.

"I have a splitting headache. I'm going upstairs to lie down."

Shadows from moving leaves flickered over the ceiling. From below, barely heard, was the sound of the piano; Emma had started a lesson. The mailman's car crunched the gravel.

What if he returns and asks for more, or simply talks for the hell of it? I know he would gladly hurt me, but would he hurt Emma like that?

Please God, keep Leo away from this house and family. Please.

✳

The year rolled on relentlessly, broken only by the usual events, such as birthdays, holidays, school plays, and games, along with a growing audience for Emma's quartet. But still the heavy burden that Adam bore remained.

Inevitably, he would have to tell the truth about Leo. A family member, even one so rarely seen as he had been, could not simply disappear without arousing some questions. And so he explained to Emma as simply and unemotionally as he could that Leo had asked for money to finance some sort of undertaking, heaven only knew what, and that he, Adam, had given it to him and gotten rid of him.

"He was his usual disagreeable self. What else can I say? You've seen him. And I really don't care whether he ever comes back here or not, but I wish him well."

"Of course you do. I wonder what his undertaking might be. I have an idea it will turn out to be something that will surprise us. You realize that he's very, very intelligent, don't you?"

" 'Very, very'? No, I don't."

"Why, his language alone, his choice of words, should tell you something."

"The world is full of glib idiots."

"No, no. I'm talking about something entirely apart from glibness. Even our two big boys have remarked about it. Andy hasn't because he probably doesn't even remember seeing Leo. But Jon wondered the other day why Uncle Leo almost never comes here anymore."

"I'll tell him he went away on business, went back east. He missed his friends, or he wasn't feeling well, or anything. You do the same if they should mention it again."

"I will. But you know, I really think he went away to transform himself, to start fresh. I understand that you worry about him, Adam, but I have a feeling that he's going to make a life for himself and then he'll come back to show us."

How sharp she is! he thought. Independent, competent, talented—and yet how delicate, the softest human being you can imagine. And a brutal creature like Leo, venting his rage on me, also walks the earth.

During the Christmas season, Reilly, standing by the garlands, wreaths, and red velvet bows, hailed Adam as he passed.

"Here's a piece of news for you. Madame Blanche has been found! She's living in Paris, Mrs. McQueen says. The dressmakers got a Christmas card from her."

"Interesting. Anything about coming back here?"

"Didn't say. Just something about 'Noël,' which is what they call Christmas. You haven't heard anything?"

"Good God, no. The damn woman is sore at Cace Arnring. Not enough money, I guess. Well, good luck to her."

Adam was sick in the pit of his stomach. Questions, unanswerable, pounded in his head. What if she were to come back here? What if Leo and she were in touch with each other? But why should they be? he asked himself. Am I paranoid? I don't think so. I didn't *dream* everything that has happened so far. . . .

At home after dinner, he sat down with a book. It was a new one, *Look Homeward, Angel,* by Thomas Wolfe. He had heard much praise of it; besides, the title was alluring. Now, turning a page, he came upon lines that almost jumped up and struck him.

Which of us has known his brother? Which of us is not forever a stranger and alone?

But he, Adam, was not alone! He had
Emma, the other half of himself. But what if
they come—not today, but someday, maybe
a few years from now, or even next month,
and tell her that I have been Blanche's lover,
or tell her God knows what else they might
tell—then, then I really will be alone.

And what would that do to Emma? She
trusted him. They had brought four children
into the world.

Laying the book down, he got up and went
outside. It was warm for December, and not
yet dark, with the grass still cheerfully green.
Far in the distance, past long fields, a light
sparked on in a farmhouse. He wondered
whether the person who had turned it on,
whoever he might be, could possibly have
known the agony that was now his.

After a while, he went into the house,
where Emma had just come downstairs to
listen to the radio. He would have liked to
talk to the boys, but they were up in their
rooms now, doing homework. So he sat with
Emma, and listened, and heard all the words
coming from the radio without understanding one of them.

It occurred to him that the wisest, bravest
course would be to tell Emma, because

once she had heard the lies, his truth would come as a mere defense later. But the first few days went by, then a week, and after that the firm's gala, black-tie Christmas party for the executives.

Remarking that she almost matched the decorations, Emma wore dark red velvet, and praised the dress. "It's the last of Blanche's things, and I'll probably wear it for the next ten years. Her clothes last forever."

That was all it took for the people at their table to begin talking about Blanche.

"I can't understand whatever made her leave in such a hurry. She was doing so well, recognized in all the fashion magazines—"

"Making quite a little fortune for herself, too."

"I heard she had a beautiful apartment. She got the best of Mrs. Rothirsch's stuff, most of which was worthless, but Blanche inherited the good stuff."

"I heard that the women in her department thought she had a love affair that didn't work out."

"That's a laugh! One love affair? She had a whole series of them."

"No, I heard there was one in particular, some man she was crazy about."

Every nerve in Adam's body was being pulled to the snapping point, until he broke into the talk by asking somebody for his opinion about the coming election.

A day or two later, he contrived to have a seemingly accidental meeting in the shipping area with Reilly. He opened the conversation by asking about Reilly's new granddaughter, received thanks for the sum he had put in the bank for the baby's benefit, and gradually drifted into another subject.

"Is there really a lot of gossip going around about Madame Blanche? I was surprised to hear some at the dinner the other night."

"Where there are women, there's always gossip." Reilly shrugged. The shrug could mean nothing, or, if Adam wanted to find meaning in a hasty glance and another hasty glance at the floor, it could mean something.

And so he made his decision. Before the month was out, he would speak.

It could not possibly be done at home where anyone, especially the children, or even Rudy and Rea, should witness the inevitable scene. He tried to imagine how Emma

would behave. Stunned first with disbe-
lief . . . would rage or grief come next? Very
likely it would be a combination of both, he
thought in sorrow.

Maybe that bend in the river would be the
best place. There was hardly ever anyone
there except coots. And remembering that
afternoon, now long ago, when they had lain
together and he had withdrawn from her
while he was still able to do it, Adam cursed
himself for not having done the same on
those cursed evenings in New York; why, he
had not even *wanted* that woman!

It was another mild, unseasonable afternoon when they got into the car. Fighting an
urge to postpone the deed once more, he
had suggested some joint errands on one of
his rare days out of the office.

"Let's take a look at our river on the way,"
he proposed.

The trees and shrubs were bare, but there
must have been some fruits and seeds to
attract a fair number of birds, which Adam
pointed out when he had stopped the car.

"Plenty of bluejays and cardinals," he said.
"With the leaves gone, it ought to be easy to
see where they nest. I've often wanted to
find out where they go." With no nests in

sight, he walked a considerable distance away along the river's edge, feeling desperate for words, and also foolish, because he knew that Emma was probably wondering why he had taken this considerable detour to hunt for birds' nests. And those were the exact words that met him when he turned about and faced her.

"You didn't come this far out of our way to look for birds' nests! We're late as it is, so come on, unless you have something else on your mind. Have you? You look as if you have."

He looked down toward the ground where a small, black beetle was climbing onto the tip of his polished British shoe. Then he looked up at Emma and admitted that he did have.

"It's a messy business that I've been keeping to myself because I know it will hurt you. And if losing my arm could spare you any hurt, I would lose it, Emma."

So well did he know her that he almost expected the spritely reply that he received.

"What is it? Have you bought some overly extravagant present again for me or the kids, as you sometimes do? Like that bracelet I adore, even though it cost too much?"

"I wish it was something like that. No, it's a mix-up that has something to do with Leo and Blanche." He paused. "And with me."

Searching for apt words, he waited, and then, finding a few, began with a question. "Do you remember when I gave Leo some money a while ago? Well, it didn't happen quite as I described it. He threatened me, so I had to give him a great deal of money."

"Threatened you?"

"Yes. He said he would come here and tell you something about me that would cause you great pain. And because it is . . . or almost all of it is, a lie . . . I have struggled so much with myself . . . but I have to tell you the truth."

Now that he had come this far, to the very edge of the cliff, it was impossible to go back. So he plunged ahead.

"Something happened that time I was in New York. Blanche was there in the same hotel. And something happened that never should have. It's unexplainable. I feel sick when I think of it. I tell myself it was the champagne, not that I drank that much. I'm certainly not much of a drinker, as you know.

There was a hook, or something caught in her dress, and she wasn't able to take it off without tearing it. So she asked me to help her, and I didn't want to, but how could I have refused? So I went—"

He had started to ramble, to lose himself and tremble under the impact of Emma's eyes.

"Are you trying to tell me that you made love to Blanche?"

"Not love!" he cried. "It had nothing to do with love. But it happened, and it was over. . . . It was completely crazy. I can't explain it. I don't suppose anyone ever really can."

Now, turning away from him, Emma stumbled, and would have fallen if he had not caught her.

"Don't touch me!" she screamed. "Take your hands off me, you bastard!"

This is the second time in my life that somebody has called me that to my face. The difference is that this time, I deserve it, he thought.

"I think I'm losing my mind," Emma cried. "All these years . . . four children . . . and half a husband. Sharing my husband!"

"No, Emma, no. For God's sake, listen to

me. Please! Believe me, it was only that one time."

"Believe you? Why should I?"

"I swear by the health and lives of those four children. Look at me, Emma. Look."

"I don't care what you swear by. How could you—with her—all this time, I've seen her, spoken with her, and I didn't know! But *she* knew. How would you feel if you were to find out about the new cellist in the quartet? He's a very desirable man. Do you want to share me with him?"

"Emma, Emma, listen to me. I told you, it was one crazy time. Love the woman? I never even liked her that much. I felt sorry for her, if you want to know."

She whirled about, screaming, "Where is that witch? Where is she?"

"I'm told she's in Paris. Reilly told me."

"I wish I was dead," she said, with tears spilling over her cheeks. "What can a person believe in? One morning the sun won't rise, but I won't be surprised. One day five and five won't make ten anymore, and I won't be surprised. Anything can happen. Yes, anything. Oh, a woman like her—who killed that innocent brother of yours. No, not innocent, ignorant. Not to see through a woman like her. And you . . . And you . . ."

Emma sank down on a rock and covered her face with her hands. A scene flashed before Adam: that same flat rock, the bicycles on the grass, the basket with lunch and Rea's doughnuts. Wanting to hold her, in some way comfort her or even to cry with her, he bent over her.

"Stay away from me," she said, growing suddenly quiet. "I mean it. And now I want to go home. Drive home."

"No, let's take our time, talk this over some more, until you feel better. I want to help you. I want to help us get past this. I love you, Emma."

"You're only worried that someone will see me in this condition. You actually think I would frighten the children? I'm going to bed. I have a fever, maybe the flu, and nobody must come near me. That's it. That's all."

Back in the house, she ran upstairs. When, a few minutes later, he followed, he found her at the linen closet with blankets, sheets, and a pillow in her arms.

"What's this for, Emma?" he asked, speaking calmly, as if calmness might somehow be contagious.

"For me. I'm sleeping in there." And pointing to the room where Simon had slept, she added, "Tomorrow I shall move some of my clothes to that closet, but I'm too exhausted to do it all now."

Was it a mistake to tell her? Look what I've done to her with this confession, he thought. On the other hand—and there stood Leo, large as life in the air before him, Leo with his smile and his threats. Take it easy, he told himself, take it easy. It will come out all right.

"What about when the kids come home, Emma? What about dinner tonight?"

"I shall not eat with you all tonight, because my eyes are too swollen. But tomorrow I will be perfectly normal. I shall give my lessons, and live as I have always lived. The only difference will be that I will not share a bed with you. That's asking too much."

In the morning, her door was locked. Wrapped in a concealing bathrobe, she opened it when he knocked.

"You look better this morning," he said. "I hope you're feeling better."

"I'm feeling very well, thank you. My heart is broken, but otherwise I am feeling very well."

"What can I do for you? Tell me."

"You can tell Rea that I'm late this morning, but that I'm much better. You can make sure that the boys catch the school bus. Then take Eileen to nursery school. I'll pick her up. I will have pulled myself together."

"Emma, I know how this must hurt a woman—"

"You don't know anything. What can a man know about how a woman feels? Not long ago you all thought we weren't smart enough to vote. But I've been thinking, I lay awake all night thinking, and a lot of things made sense all of a sudden. That woman almost always had an excuse whenever we invited her here. When I went for a fitting of one of her gowns with their ridiculous prices, I sensed a coolness toward me. Very polite she was, of course, but cool. Now I know why."

Yes, and he knew, too. *She with her rich aunt, her Paris and London and her music, her house, her children . . .*

"I should have suspected. In the back of my mind, maybe I did suspect. After all, I wasn't born yesterday."

"Emma, I've told you the whole truth. It was one small, nasty episode that should not have happened. But women do forgive. They forgive a lot more than that. In France, women put up with mistresses. Even their presidents—"

"This isn't France. But still, maybe they're better off that way. Then the wife can do what she wants, too."

"You don't mean that."

From below came the sounds of a morning's commotion; the boys were happily scuffling in the hall, Eileen was calling for Mommy, and Rea was shrieking that they would be late for the bus.

Emma shut and locked the door in Adam's face; he ran downstairs to quiet the commotion; after that, he would try to quiet the commotion within himself.

All was in proper order. Eileen, who had graduated at the age of three from the high chair, sat comfortably on a pile of telephone books. Adam started the dinner with the usual invitation: "Let's take turns around the table and tell what happened to you in school today."

After each had reported, the conversation usually drifted in the parents' direction: news, sports, politics, friends, plumbers' bills, a movie, a book, or what the vet said about the little white poodle's teeth.

Lately, though, this comfortable pattern had changed. The remarks and observations traveled from everyone to everyone else, except between father and mother. And one day, Jonathan had something to say about that.

"What's wrong about you and Dad? You don't talk to each other."

"Why, nothing," Emma answered. "We're all talking to each other."

"Dad," Jon persisted, "are you and Mom angry?"

"I'm not at all angry at anybody," Adam assured him. "But people feel less like talking at certain times than at others."

And he sent a significant look in Emma's direction.

She understood the look. He was telling her that there was no sense trying to hide anything from an intelligent boy like Jon.

Then Eileen said, "I need a plate for Susie's dinner. And I need another dolly like her, only with a red dress this time."

"Ask Blanche for another. She gave this one to you," advised Andy.

"She went away, didn't she?" James said. And when Emma asked how he knew that, he explained, "I was at my friend Paul's house for lunch, and I heard his mother say so."

Emma sat stiffly as if every muscle were tense. Never would she rid herself of that picture, of that vile woman with Adam, of the lace dress slipping down. And of him . . . And of her . . .

Day after day, she sat there proper and erect and cheerful before the children, but never acknowledging either by word or look that Adam was present, too.

"It's been more than a month," he said as they passed each other on the stairs. "How long can we go on like this? Is there no such thing as forgiveness? Am I to be doomed and punished forever because of one wrong act?"

"You're not punished. You're not doomed. You're well taken care of. The house is peaceful. Your meals are on time, your clothes are pressed, your children have a caring mother—you have nothing to complain about except that I will not, I cannot, share your bed."

Back in the room where Simon's photograph still stood on a chest, she sat on the bed and stared at his weary old face. Possibly he had gotten Adam's mother "in trouble" and had abandoned her because he had found somebody else. These days, her mind was full of such ugly thoughts. It was unlike her to have suspicions and ugly thoughts. These thoughts do not belong with the love of music. Yet many composers of the world's most exalted music had often done very ugly things. If it had been that one time, then perhaps, no matter how awful it was or how it hurt, it would be possible perhaps to say that the wine had done it.

Yesterday Adam had asked her what they should say about Uncle Leo. They had been speaking over the phone, which Emma found easier than speaking in person. "The kids are asking more questions," she said, "so our answers must be consistent. Jon wonders where Uncle Leo is. I told him again that he had gone back east.

"It didn't satisfy him. He said he knows

there's something wrong, and what is it? It's almost impossible to fool Jon."

"Then let's not fool him. Tell him that there's been an argument, but it's your personal business and that's that."

"He also sees that you're not talking to me. They all know that you don't sleep in our room."

"I'm not comfortable anymore in my old bed."

"That's nonsense, and they know better. Boys of their age think about sex seven days a week. I remember my own thoughts about my father and mother. There are odd moments even now when that old story, the sad truth or the sad untruth of it, rushes into my head."

"I'm sorry you have that memory, but I can't help you."

"I'm not asking you to help me. But think of the children."

"So you believe they're going to be ruined for life because I don't sleep with you?"

"What kind of question is that? Emma, please . . . I want you back. I'm so sorry that I hurt you."

"I have to call for Eileen. I have to hang up."

When the telephone clicked, a wave of silence swept through the house. One could drown in such lonely silence. She went into the kitchen to say something unimportant to Rea, if only to hear the sound of a voice.

"I hope you're feeling better this morning," Rea said.

"A little, Rea. Thank you."

She knows. Of course she does, although she can't ever guess why.

Soon the whole community that is our world, our friends, the parents of our children's friends, and everybody at Cace Arnring, will know that all is not well in our house. Well, let them. I have no shame, she told herself. I have my pride. It's not my fault, anyway.

It was almost devilish, though, how in the most innocent conversations the subject came up. At a school concert one night, a neighbor described the dress she was to wear at a wedding.

"Seven years old if it's a day. But it's a Madame Blanche, the most beautiful flowered chiffon, and I plan to wear it forever. Her work was art."

People were joking one evening at George Cace's house. An invitation from one of the

Caces was not to be turned down, short of a medical emergency. There, one of the guests, a woman with a poor sense of humor, brought Blanche into the conversation.

"One of the dressmakers—Mrs. McQueen, I think—was a very good friend of hers. She always said that Blanche had a crush on your husband, Emma, and all of them knew it. Well, why not? A good-looking guy like him? I'll bet she did."

"What rot!" Adam exclaimed. "I hardly spoke ten words a month to that woman."

In silence they rode home together. There Emma went directly to a closet where her best clothes hung in dust-proof bags. She drew them out: embroidered white silk, blue velvet, flowered summer linens—the needy would have them all. If no adult had use for such as these, let their children parade in them on Halloween.

And for the next three evenings, reporting a bad contagious cold, Emma did not come to dinner.

Her head ached. She wished she could go to sleep earlier and sleep longer, although even that did not always bring relief because of her dreams. There was in particular a repeated dream of frustration: She was in the car on the way to the dock, where, as so often before in her life, she was about to board a ship going to Europe. She could see it, a huge, dark whale nosed alongside the pier with smoke coming out of its funnels. It was about to sail. But the car was stuck in traffic, so that she had to jump out of it and start to run. Now she was running as fast as she could, yet she couldn't seem to move ahead. Her legs moved up and down in the same place. And the ship glided slowly away without her, while she was still running.

In the evening they had always taken a walk together. It had been a private time while the boys were doing their homework or already asleep. Mostly, they used to talk, but sometimes they would stop to hear the cricket chorus, or an owl's hoot, or merely the rustle of trees in the wind.

Adam called it "listening to the world, the *real* world." She understood. The town, the store, the money—all these would rise and fall again, as they always had done, but crickets, birds, and wind would stay. They always had.

Watching at the door to the rear terrace and seeing him climb back up the hill, she knew the familiar route he had been walking. The tall black poodle lay down beside him as he turned to look out again at the view. He was holding the little white dog and stroking its back.

She read his mind. He was thinking now how short life is, the life of this loving, gentle little animal, and every other life. Such moments were almost religious. He had not had them very often, as well she knew. But he had them, and she was the only person who knew that about him. To others he was the smart man who "got things done."

But no one else could know. Not even his own mother, if she had lived, might have known that in a public place he could not bear to see a child being struck in anger and had to be held back from interfering; that he would not wear any tie except striped ones; that he wanted his breakfast coffee to be lukewarm; that he slept without a pillow, and naked in the summer; that he hated having to be well dressed and starched at work; that he overtipped wherever he went because "There, but for the grace of God, go I."

When she began to cry, she backed away from the door and ran upstairs to the room that she had taken for her own. There, at the window, she looked down again. He was still there, stroking the dog and looking out toward the quiet fields. And she was still crying.

Time came rushing back: that day in the dining car on the train, the lover on the river-bank, the bed on the wedding night, the baby Jon and all the other babies, and then time again, rushing away, never to come back.

We are two halves of a whole, he says.

After a while when it was dark, she heard him coming up the stairs. He would be carrying the old white poodle, who could no longer climb. By the small sounds he made, she could tell that he was walking to all the children's doors to listen and check that lights were out. Then he would lay the dog beds on the floor of the hall. After that, she heard him go to the bedroom and close the door.

From her head to her feet, fear shivered and trembled. A person looks for some precious thing that has been dropped in the darkness, and prays to find it.

She knocked on the door. "Adam? It's your Emma. Please, I want to come in."

Ten months later, the family stood for the second time around a bassinet festooned with pink ribbon and looked down at a small object wrapped in a pink receiving blanket.

"It's nice that she's a girl," Andy said. "She can play with Eileen and keep them both out of our way."

The older boys laughed. Adam wondered what they were actually thinking; most boys in their middle and late teens did not suddenly find themselves presented with still another baby sister. Yet everyone seemed pleased and very interested.

"I think she's going to have red hair like yours and mine, Mom," Andy said. "See that little fuzz on her head?"

"The main question," Emma said, "is her name. Dad and I had the idea of letting all of you come up with some suggestions."

"Her name can't be Susie," Eileen said, "because Susie is my doll and belongs to me."

"Of course," Adam assured her. "The name cannot be Susie. How about Emily?"

The boys agreed that that sounded too much like Emma.

"How about Virginia, after Jon's girl-friend?" James suggested, which naturally brought a furious denial from Jon.

"I don't like her anymore, and you know it. Never did like her much, anyway."

Andy giggled. "What about Kate, like Kate Smith? You like fat girls."

So it went with laughter and argument until Jon made a serious suggestion.

"How about your mother's name, Mom? Eileen's named after Dad's mom, so this should be your turn."

Adam said quickly, "Louise. That's the name we both like, and if none of you can come up with something nicer, that'll be her name. Louise. So now you boys have two little sisters to watch over, and I know you will."

"These two girls may well grow up to watch over their brothers," Emma said, laughing. "We women are pretty tough."

Adam would not have guessed that this brave little boast of hers, made with her children surrounding the bassinet, could have disturbed him. But, like an arrow, it had gone straight to his heart, or his brain, or wherever it is that memories are stowed away but never lost. Ten months ago she had knocked on the door, and now this baby was here. Twelve months ago, he had lain in bed and pleaded: *Please, God, don't let him come back. Please.* That is what Leo had done to him. Leo, to whom he had never been anything but kind.

You're rotten, you're hideous, you poison the air with your stench. May God damn you.

Leo had brought out a side of Adam that he hadn't known existed, a corrosive hatred he hadn't known himself capable of.

He looked at his two elder sons. Thirteen and fifteen, they were, still a good way from manhood. Yet somehow they brought a young man to his mind: his own brother Jonathan, who had been old when he was still a child. *Truthful* and *trustworthy* were the words. *Decent, humane.*

That evening he called these sons aside to ask them for something. "It is very important that you will give me your word and keep it. It is about my brother Leo. Will you give your promise that you will never speak of him, never even mention his name at all, to anyone? It is a very serious, grown-up thing that I am asking of you. As far as I am concerned, he does not exist, and he should not exist for you, even when you marry someday, and for as long as you live. Will you do this?"

Two pairs of startled eyes met his. Very serious, they were. He saw the men they would become in only a few more years: decent, responsible, and strong. He saw, too, that they understood his plea, that they knew, as they had known from the start, that something important had happened within this family, probably some man-woman thing. Yes, boys their age know everything about it, except for the pain that can come with it.

He saw that they knew he was treating them like men, and they responded like men. Each shook his hand. "Solemn promise," said Jon. "Scout's honor," said James. Then Adam kissed his sons, thanked them, and went back upstairs to Emma.

Chapter 22

Time hurries by. New green leaves sprout; a season has passed when they brown and fall; all of a sudden, it is another year.

This was a good town, and it had been especially good to Adam Arnring. He felt sometimes as if he were sailing once more over smooth seas, with hardly a ripple to disturb his balance. His business, in spite of the Great Depression, was surviving. His children were healthy, and if sometimes they caused any worries, the worries were very minor ones.

It would be easy, he thought, to take those blessings for granted. But peace and plenty are not given to everyone, and those who have them must make willing repayment. And so it was that Emma gave free lessons to talented children who could not afford to pay, that Adam added acreage and play-grounds to the park he had already given to the town, that he and Emma made a concert hall out of the aged movie theater and brought orchestras to play there, and made small gifts to people like Archer's son, who wanted to go to a famous chef's school in New York.

So the years slipped away. Then suddenly it was Sunday, December 7, in the year 1941, and life took a sharp turn with the bombing of Pearl Harbor.

The following May, one day after graduat-ing from college, without waiting even to discuss the matter with his parents or wait-ing to be drafted, Jonathan went directly to be recruited into the air force. Then he and Elizabeth Daniels went down to City Hall and were married. Having done that, they rang the doorbells at their respective homes and made their joint announcement.

What is a parent to do or say? There is nothing at all to *do*; this man of twenty-two has not waited to be urged or forced; he has rushed to fulfill his obligations to his country. What can a parent say, but show good cheer and pride while gamely stifling his fears?

"Married!" cried Emma, embracing the bride. "You could knock us both over with a feather. But at least we can be so happy that it's you, Lizzie. You've heard a hundred times, I'm sure, how your mother and I used to wheel your carriages side by side. Now tell us: What are your plans? When are you going?"

"Flight school," Jon said. "I want to pilot a bomber. So we'll be heading south next week. Lizzie'll be with me till I go overseas. She can get some sort of job while I train."

He looked proud, and so young, and so vulnerable. Adam swallowed hard before speaking.

"We must get together with your parents, Lizzie, and have a gala send-off."

"That's what my mom and dad said."

"Then we'll have two send-offs," Emma declared stoutly. "We can eat two big dinners within one week, can't we?"

At the front door they stood watching Elizabeth's car disappear down the road. When they looked at each other's faces, they could see that neither had any words with which to express his feelings, and each turned back to the task at hand.

My hand is trembling, and I am ashamed.

Who am I to be any different from all the other hundreds of thousands whose sons are going into the line of fire? But perhaps their hands are trembling, too? Adam asked himself. But it is only that I have the first Jonathan on my mind. Surely one loss like that is more than enough from any family. I am ashamed, I who have always been proud of my optimism, my certainty that if you keep your head and keep calm, everything will work out. Now, when I should have confidence, I have none. I know as I sit here in my safe little room that my son will crash from the sky in flames.

And if this war lasts, then James will go. . . .

He got up from the chair and went outdoors into springtime, where birds crowded the feeder and naturalized daffodils sprinkled the grass. At the movies lately, they had been showing the same spring scenery ripped and blown apart, houses crumbled, and young men dead. If I could do something about it, I would, he thought angrily, but there is nothing I can do.

Andy was pushing Eileen on the swing. He was a very nice kid, a very nice one, but no student like Jon and James, not driven to excel, yet he did. Sometimes it seemed as if everybody in town must know Andy Arnring, or that he, so friendly, enthusiastic, and even a little bit nosy, too, must know everyone.

Fourteen, he was. God willing, the war would be over before he would follow his brothers overseas. . . .

So he stood there watching his children, wondering what life would do to them, and what they would do with life if they should be lucky. Certain skills were inborn. Long ago, that first Jonathan had known what he wanted to be, and now young James seemed to be following in those footsteps. Jonathan would follow his father into the business. The girls, of course, would get married. They were both pretty and would be even prettier in a few years. Neither one of them would look like their mother, but then, how many women were there who had Emma's beauty and her talent?

Music, it seemed, had died out in this generation. Eileen, at eleven, had been having piano lessons for three years now and was already starting to rebel. Eileen was a rebel, anyway. Her shrieks of delight were loud and her skirts flew as she soared on the swing, while Louise below was waiting for her turn. Three years younger than her sister, it seemed that she was always waiting for her turn and having to wait too long. She was far too shy for her own good.

It was easy enough to bring them into the world, wasn't it? But what to do with them, and for them afterward was another matter. It seemed there was so much more for parents to worry about than there used to be. Simon certainly had never stood watching his children and trying to plan their future. Now the choices were limitless. Anybody could be anything. The worry now involved the psyche; Freud had done that.

He called out to Andy. "Look at those weeping willows. They need water. Take the hose, please, Andy, and I'll take care of the swing. Now get off, Eileen, and let Louise have her turn."

"It's not time yet. I haven't finished my turn, Daddy."

"Yes, you have. I've been watching you for ten minutes. Now get off."

"Louise is such a crybaby. She wants everything just because she's younger."

"That isn't true. She hasn't said a word. Now climb on, Louise."

Sometimes Eileen annoyed him. She wasn't girlish enough. She didn't play very much with dolls anymore, but liked to hang around her brothers, who didn't want her in the middle of their football practice. But he tried hard not to show his annoyance. And he thought again of his father, who had never hidden the fact that Leo annoyed him—not that there could be any comparison between Leo and any children of his.

It had been a long time since he had thought about Leo. As far as Adam was concerned, Leo might as well have evaporated. What point was there in thinking about a person who didn't exist anymore? And anyway, who can worry about the past while the world, or a large part of it, is burning?

"At least," Emma said as they were listening to the news that night, "Jon is starting his life with a fine, dependable girl from a solid family. It will be nice to share our grandchildren with them. Think of that, Adam."

She was trying her best with her usual optimism to console him. But lying beside her that night, he had his dreams, and he could not prevent them: First Jonathan's face was smiling under his Air Force cap, and then he was crashing to earth in flames. Then came the face of the first Jonathan, complete to the faint worry lines on the forehead, then Leo... *I said some awful things to him and maybe I shouldn't have, even though he deserved them* ... and Pa telling me that sometimes people just hate each other ... Faces. Faces.

Chapter 23

Outside, the November dusk is falling, while inside, for the first time in many years, all the chairs around the table are occupied, Emma at one end where the pies are being cut, and Adam at the other, where the remains of the turkey lie on a platter. They smile at each other without words. There is no need for any words. The boys are home.

All is what it used to be. A small fire flickers under the mantel, the candles flicker over the table, while memories flicker through Adam's head: waiting with heart in mouth for the mail, the weekly films of wreckage, the times when they stood in line to give blood, the little girls learning to knit socks for the soldiers, and Andy's constant misery over his rejection by the military because of his eyesight.

Even now, James has just finished assuring him that "without people like you working in defense plants, Andy, an army has no weapons."

James has a way with people. It is no surprise that he wants to be a doctor; he has always wanted only to be a doctor.

They are having their second pieces of pumpkin pie, when Adam asks Jon when he is going to take off his uniform.

"Well, not for a long while, Dad."

"What do you mean? That you're so spruce in it, Major Arnring, with your gold leaf that you can't bear to part with?"

Adam jokes, but the truth is that Jon, with his major's gold oak leaves and a ribbon on his chest, is really remarkably well turned out.

"No. I've made a final decision. I'm staying in the service."

"Staying in? Staying in?"

"Yes, I love the life. And Elizabeth's willing."

Jon looks around at the silent faces, all turned, as if commanded by a single thought, toward Adam.

"We always had an understanding that you'd go into the business," Adam says.

"I know, and I was very interested in it. I appreciated the chance, and I always will appreciate it. But my heart's in the Air Force now. I've had four years of it, and they've changed me."

Talk about sinking hearts, Adam thinks. Mine has sunk to my shoes. He was going to take my place. He was going to carry on what I've built out of next to nothing. True, I have no right to plan my son's life for him, but a father can hope.

It is a few minutes before he is able to re-ply. "I am more disappointed than I can say, Jon. Of course I have no right to be so dis-appointed, but I have to be truthful. Selfish, but truthful."

"I'm sorry, Dad. I'm truly sorry. You wanted to hand this over to one of us, I know."

"Tell everybody more about what you did on the home front, Andy," says Emma, inter-rupting the uncomfortable silence.

So Andrew does. The wineglasses are re-filled. Emma scoops ice cream and brings in a bowl of fruit. The painful subject is dropped.

The boys' letters during these last hard years have naturally told almost nothing. Only now could one know that Jon had piloted one of the bombers that crossed the channel on D day, or that James had spent two weeks in an abandoned German farm shed during that final, desperate Battle of the Bulge.

Yes, they had done their part. Any disappointment on his part was unimportant and ungrateful. He was thinking so when the following evening there was a polite knock on the door, and Andy came up to the desk where Adam was working.

"I was wondering," he began, "whether I could be the one to work in the store. What do you think, Dad?"

The father was embarrassed in front of his boy. But he wasn't a boy; he was eighteen going on thirty! There was something about him, though, that made one think of him as a boy. What the deuce could he do in Cace Arnring, that citadel of perfection? He didn't even dress neatly enough to be a salesman in the men's department, which was very small and already had enough salesmen.

"You wouldn't like it," Adam said. "After working in a gun factory, you wouldn't like being a clothing salesman, and that's what a department store is all about."

"Well, if I don't try it, how can I know whether I'd like it or not?"

One couldn't very well argue with such a reasonable statement.

"Give me a chance. If I don't satisfy you, just throw me out."

Jon would have been a presence in the store. He would have risen to department manager and up. And up.

"I'll work for nothing. Try me, Dad."

Suddenly Adam remembered another time and another young man whom he had not wanted to work at the store. But Leo hadn't wanted the job. Had he?

"Okay," Adam said finally. "Come to work with me on Monday, and I'll find someplace for you."

In the stockroom late Monday afternoon, Adam went looking for his son.

"How are you doing, Andy?" he inquired.

"Not badly, I guess. I've been counting things and putting them where I'm told they belong." Andy looked around and lowered his voice. "It's not especially stimulating work, to tell the truth."

Somewhat stiffly, Adam retorted, "It has to be done, though."

"I know, I know. But I was thinking of

something as I went along. These thick cotton sweaters here—they've been around a long time, I hear, so they'll have to be going on sale, which is too bad because they're really nice, and they could bring in money, you know," Andy said, looking so wise that Adam was amused.

"They could? How?"

"Simple. Have the alterations ladies make a felt outline of the words 'Chattahoochee High,' stitch it on every sweater—takes a few seconds with a machine—and these would fly out of the store. The guys would love them."

"You think so?"

"Sure. And if you wanted to go a little further, you could have some with the words *soccer, baseball,* et cetera, if anybody wanted that, too."

The markdown on a few heaps of sweaters was hardly the end of the world. Yet Andy's face was alight with his proposal, and his eyes were so eagerly searching his father's eyes that Adam couldn't bear to disappoint him. "It's something to think about, Andy."

At dinner that night, Andy wanted to know

whether Adam had made up his mind about the sweaters.

"To tell you the truth, I haven't had time to think, but I will."

"I have a lot of other ideas, you know."

In Emma's smile, Adam read her thought: *Cute. Isn't he the cutest?*

"Tell us," she said.

"Well, I was thinking about that glass-roofed space you have. You could get a lot more publicity out of it instead of just using it for big affairs. For instance, last year when Eileen and Louise had their artwork on exhibit in that store the school rented, you could have donated the space. The light from the glass roof would be perfect, all the parents and grandparents would have to walk through the store to get to the stuff—it would be great! Don't you think so?"

"You could put my picture in the center," Eileen said, "with my name in larger letters because I'm a daughter of the store."

"I don't know," Louise said, "that wouldn't look quite fair, would it?"

Eileen admonished her. "You're always afraid of what people will think. Will you ever learn to stand on your own two feet?"

Emma's impatient sigh was audible. *Oh,*

those two sisters again. When will they ever—

"I hear," Andy said, "that Jon is being transferred to a base in California. James told me yesterday."

He was truly, truly kind, Andy was. Somehow, whenever in his presence the two girls started a battle of words, he managed to head it off by changing the subject.

"Let's leave the store till the weekend," Adam told him. "You and I will sit down together and talk."

On Friday evening, Jeff Horace's weekly column bore the heading:

ARNRING'S SECOND GENERATION PRESENTS HIS IDEAS.

Stunned beyond words, Adam read on about Andy's ideas, to which more had been added: *The glass-roofed room could be used for chamber music, such as his mother's quartet; serious new artists from other parts of America could have their first exhibits at the Cace Arnring store . . .*

Flinging the paper down, he demanded of

Andy, "What the devil is this? Have you gone crazy? Do you realize what you've done? You called Jeff Horace?"

"Dad! I didn't. I didn't ask him to put this in the paper. I did cross over when I saw him on the other side of the street, that's true. I know he's a good friend of yours, and I just wanted to say hello. We just talked, that's all."

"You wanted publicity, don't fool me, Andy."

"Well, maybe I did have a little thought about something, but never all this."

"You shot your mouth off. You made a fool of yourself, and of me. How am I going to explain this to the people, to the board, to the staff? I could wring Jeff's neck. He knew better than to do this. And friend or no friend, I'm going to give him a piece of my mind."

"Dad, I'm genuinely sorry. It was innocent, believe me—"

So it went in the Arnring house all Friday evening until exhaustion came at midnight and the lights were turned out.

But unexpected events occurred on Saturday. The men's department was crowded with high school boys who wanted a decorated sweater, who put down their deposits and were promised one within ten days. The main floor was crowded with young men and women, all friends of Andy's, who were surprised to learn that he'd started to work there. They all made quite a stir of enthusiasm on the ground floor, adding so much to the pre-Christmas enthusiasm that Adam came down from his office to see what the bustle was all about.

"I read in the paper that you might have an exhibit of children's artwork here, Mr. Arnring. Do you remember me? Miss Bratton? I taught Louise in fifth grade. Such a darling, sweet child. I missed her when she went on to sixth. Are you really going to do it? I hope you do. It would be marvelous, Mr. Arnring."

Adam did not remember her, but naturally he said he did. Nor did he know what he wanted to do, or what the board would want to do, about these exhibits, concerts, and all the rest of the stuff. But he was certainly being forced to think hard about them. What on earth had gotten into Andy's head?

Six months later, June roses flamed in pots on tall new iron stands throughout the Cace

Arnring store. Business, during the past half year, had increased by two percent. Andy Arnring, now in charge of Customer Relations, was as visible and as welcome as the roses.

"He told her she needed a bag to match her new shoes," one of the saleswomen reported to Adam. "He actually brought her over to me, and she bought two bags. He's so friendly with that smile of his, and of course, that red hair. People don't forget him."

Reilly also had something to say. "The kid's a natural. He's a whole lot like you, Adam. The energy, the drive . . . just like you."

"Strange," Emma said when Adam repeated Reilly's words. "Of all our three boys, I'd have said he was the very least like you. Isn't it odd how you think you know a person, even your own child, when you really don't at all?"

Chapter 24

The years went by, the boys all married and had children of their own, and every year the family gathered on Thanksgiving day to celebrate in the same way. Nothing ever changed, and nobody ever wanted any substitutions for the blue-and-white china, or the silver candlesticks, or the chrysanthemums on the center of the table.

Andy and his lovely wife Bernice came with their boys Tim and Doug. Elizabeth and Jon were there with their twin boys and two more younger ones, all of them very proper—unlike Andy's jolly, noisy fellows. Jon was now Colonel Arnring with an eagle on his shoulder, and he was the most proper of all. Next to them sat Dr. and Mrs. James Arnring, with Raymond and Susan. Eileen's customary tailored suit contrasted with Louise's customary pretty dress. Adam was thinking that the dress looked like one they had just had in the store's window last week, when Louise's voice cut through the general hum of adults and squeals of children.

"I suppose now is as good a time as any to make my announcement to you all. I am going to get married."

After a second of silence came a babble of voices. "What? When? Who is he? You never said—"

No, she never had. There had been a succession of boyfriends, mostly solemn, not very attractive, fellow students in the Classics Department. Glancing down at the other end of the table, Adam read Emma's mind. Louise had used her own savings to go with a group of young women on a tour of Europe last summer. So how, and where—

"We met on the ship going over, and we fell in love. I know it sounds crazy."

Yes, coming from careful, prudent Louise, it did.

"We spent every day in Paris and Rome together. Carlo changed his plans so we could go home on the same ship. He's very responsible, so you don't need to worry. He plans to come here next month, and you can meet him."

Adam's thoughts were racing. Louise was such an innocent! He'd hardly trust her to get safely through traffic in any major city. What did she know about people who cheat, lie, and fool an innocent like her? She'd hardly ever been out of Chattahoochee.

"Where does he live?" asked Emma.

"In Brazil. Rio de Janeiro."

"You're out of your mind," said Jonathan very sternly.

"I don't think so. You will like him when you meet him."

Bernice, in her usual calm way, asked Louise to tell them more about Carlo, how old he was and what kind of work he did.

"He's twenty-five. He works in his father's business, some kind of banking that I don't know the first thing about." Louise's smile was enough to break Adam's heart. "They have a ranch, too, about five thousand acres, he said. And Mom, you'll be happy to hear that he knows a lot about music. He doesn't play any instrument very well, but he goes to all the concerts. So now I guess

I've told you everything I can, until you meet him."

Jonathan rebuked her. "You haven't told us anything at all."

"Let's get down to brass tacks," said James in his best bedside manner. "You said he was coming to see Mom and Dad. So until that happens, it makes no sense for any of us to have an opinion. I suggest that we finish our dinner and go outdoors. It's a wonderful day."

But it had not been a wonderful day; there were too many unanswered questions in it.

"What do you make of it all?" Adam asked Emma when they were alone that night. "She walks in and calmly announces that she is going to be married and move a couple of thousand miles away. Just like that."

"You haven't heard anything. Eileen told me confidentially that she's going to have artificial insemination. She went to a medical school and described the kind of father she wanted for her child. She says she's too busy with her editorial work on that women's liberation magazine to think of getting tied up in marriage. Can you believe it?"

Emma was brushing her hair with her back to him. But he caught her tearful face in the mirror, and for an instant he seemed to see what she would look like in old age. It made him terribly, terribly angry. It filled him with fury.

These stupid daughters! Wrecking their lives while we can only stand and watch. It's as if they had taken the years, the care, and the example we gave them, and tossed it all into the trash heap. My God, how it hurts! It's an amputation. It's a wreckers' ball—

"But at least," he said, as if he were grasping something steady to hold to, "the boys are all fine, with their good wives, their good kids, and their common sense. They're a blessing to count on. They're family, our full old-fashioned family."

"Not quite full," Emma said.

"What do you mean?"

"You have a brother."

"Emma, please. Every couple of months, especially on Thanksgiving, on this special day, he seems to pop into your head and bother me. Why?"

"Just because it is a special day. Don't you ever wonder where he is having his dinner, or whether he's having any dinner?"

"I don't very often get angry with you, Emma, do I?"

"No."

"Well, I don't want to. But leave me alone about Leo. I gave him money, and if he's lost it the way he lost all Pa's, that's his lookout. If you need somebody to worry about, think of Louise and Eileen. Aren't they enough?"

Restless, and as his thoughts churned, Adam walked down the hall to his little office, stared out into the night, and suddenly remembered something. He opened the bottom drawer of the desk; there lay a set of leather diaries, volumes thick enough to hold a lifetime of jotting. It had been one of those gifts that are too nice to discard, and yet are not used. Now that so much was happening and there were so many new children and grandchildren to think and worry about, he would use it.

So we have finally met Carlo. I have to admit that he really is an extraordinary young man. He has what the French call "savoir faire." Knowing exactly what, in the circumstances, a young woman's parents would want to know about him, he presented us with a portfolio of pa-

pers and photographs, showing his parents, grandparents, city house, country house, bank accounts, and letters from various important people, including a bishop. He is Catholic, and expects Louise to become one, too, which she is going to do. We see no reason to disapprove, except that our girl will be so far away from us. But then I think of my father, and millions more like him, who left home knowing that they would never see it again. At least now we have airplanes, and will see Louise very often, I hope. We have to look at it that way.

The wedding was beautiful. Louise looked, not pretty as always, but absolutely beautiful. We can only pray that she will be happy. But how will we know when and if she is not? She is so tender, and so easily hurt. I still wish she had a little of her sister's spunk. It was hard to keep back tears when she left with Carlo, covered in rice, in a car that was covered in flowers, on the road to the airport.

Emma whispered, "This is the kind of wedding Sabine wanted for us."

Actually, there were many people there who had been at our wedding. Jeff Horace is retired, but now and then he writes a feature article, and there is no doubt that he will be impressed enough by Carlo's elegant, aristocratic-looking family to write one. Reilly, retired with the nice pension that Andy and I insisted on, looked old and rather bent, but he has the same jolly face. Archer, who has the same pension, looks happier since his wife died. (An awful thing to say, but true; she must have been a hellion.) Mr. Lawrence is dead, but Mrs. came, dressed soberly although not in black since, of course, nobody wears black at a wedding. Rudy and Rea have moved to the country, also with a nice pension, so there are new faces in our house.

Eileen brought pictures of her Danny. You can often tell whether a baby is handsome, even at the age of three months, and this one is. I should think it would be hard for a woman not to know who her baby's father is, but obviously it *doesn't bother her. Modern times! Somebody asked her whether her wedding will be coming next, and she laughed.*

"Not on your life," she said. "I've got everything I want now without having to keep a man happy and pleased with me."

No, I don't admire her spunk after all. I can't imagine how, after living in our house, she could have such a thought about marriage. But, as long as she's satisfied, I guess we must be, too.

Carlo's best man was his brother, Leo, which bothered me. I can never feel comfortable when I hear that name. I keep thinking, in spite of what I say to Emma, that I should probably try to find out where he is. Then I remember that he could have ruined my life and Emma's, and have put the thought away.

Adam wrote:

It is well known that the older one grows, the faster time speeds. We had not seen Louise in a year and a half, and all we can think is that we have seen a transformation. She lives in a grand house on a street of grand stone houses that make our house look like a cottage. There she is, pregnant with twins, which may well run in our family because Jonathan has them, too. There is no trace of shyness in her behavior. She presided over a beautiful dinner party in our honor, and Carlo is proud of her for providing the entertainments that are part of his business. With all of this, she is active and hopes one day to be director of a school where blind children can obtain a first-rate education.

These people have an enormous family, so many aunts, uncles, and cousins that Emma and I felt almost envious. They all live close by, and Louise is the only one who wasn't born in the neighborhood. Carlo's brother Leo is especially close to him. I had to admit to Emma that I feel ridiculous being uncomfortable about the man's name. But she said, and has said again, that it is not ridiculous. It is something that nags inside my head, she thinks. It is tel-

ling me to "do something" about my brother.

But what should I do? I suppose I could hire detectives to find him, although it would probably not work, or at least it would take years; look at all the criminal cases that are unsolved. Besides, he doesn't want to be found. He said so in no uncertain terms. So let us leave well enough alone. We are calm and happy with children and grandchildren, and ask for nothing more.

Chapter 25

One day there was a message from Jon on the answering machine. He left no number. He would call again. Goodness knew where he had been transferred now. They hardly ever stayed longer than eight months to a year in the same place. In some ways, it was an inconvenient way to live, Adam thought. But in most ways, there were great advantages in being able to see the world and enjoy a nice house wherever you went, along with continuing paid education for your children. Since Germany a few years ago, Jon and Lizzie had been living on bases in Saudi Arabia, India, Italy, and finally, back home now in North Carolina. It was just about time, Jon had explained, for a desk job, and possibly, in not too many years, a promotion to lieutenant general.

Well, he had earned it. He had seen some mighty big changes, this man had, from peace through war to precarious peace, and from propeller to jet.

The phone rang, and Jon spoke. "How are you, Dad?"

"Fine. And you? On base or off, this time?"

"Well, it's not quite settled. Dad, Lizzie's left me."

The words did not register. One can hear some foreign expressions that, because of the wars, have become fairly familiar so that they are recognized when heard, yet it takes a few seconds before the brain accepts and translates. So "left me" was not immediately clear to Adam.

" 'Left you,' " he repeated.

"Yes. She is in love with another man."

"That makes no sense" was all he could stammer out.

"No, it doesn't, does it?"

"Who is he? Where is he?"

"It doesn't matter who he is. He's in Europe, and she's gone back to him."

Jon. Lizzie and Jon. What could he say? What does one say to a person who has just had or is about to have an amputation?

Then he thought of something. "Your children. What about them?"

"Dad, you're forgetting. They aren't babies

anymore. They're in the world. They have their own lives." Jon's voice broke. "Thank God they have."

"Where are you now?"

"On the base."

"Shall Mom and I fly down, or would you rather come here? We need to talk and straighten this out."

"It can't be straightened out. I've been try-ing for months, for a year, almost."

"Maybe if we did the talking? Or do her parents know?"

"They know. But she's in love. She says she's loved this man for three years. We hadn't been getting along so well, you see, but I didn't know . . . I mean, I thought she was just tired of all those moves, and I told her there'd be no more of them, that I was getting a desk job, permanent, along with a permanent house . . . I didn't know there was another reason."

"I can't think of anything to say except that we need to see you. If your mother could talk to Lizzie—they were so fond of each other. Your mother won't believe this."

"Nobody can. People always thought we were . . . we were perfect together."

"Jon, we've got to see you."

"All right. Soon, Dad. Soon. I'm hanging up now."

In total shock, Adam sat with one picture in his mind: the newlyweds, each twenty-two years old, triumphant, delighted, and innocent, at the front door. After a while he got up and went to deliver the news.

"I'll call Lizzie's parents," Emma said promptly. "We really haven't been all that close since they moved so far away, and that's too bad, but we always got along so well, and I'll call right now."

Adam opened the door and sat down on the terrace. There was nothing wrong with his heart, the doctors said; it was purely emotion that hurried its beat. He knew that as well as he knew that only the sight of the natural world—sky, sea, and space—would slow its beat.

Far above him a swirl, a cascade of small birds sped toward the south, skimmed the distant trees, and disappeared beyond the horizon. Their life was so simple! Why then did human beings not keep theirs simple, too? Love, marry, beget, stay "till death do us part"?

Always, always these conflicts! Lizzie and Jon, so perfect together! But also—and now he became aware that his fists were clenched—also his Emma's unknown parents, his own discarded mother, and always, always, Leo's taunts across the kitchen table: *Bastard! Bastard!* And his own cruel words in return.

"I spoke to Lizzie's mother," Emma reported now. "She was not rude, but she was very, very cool. 'There are two sides to every story,' she kept saying."

Adam sighed. "Yes, we know. His and hers. But then there's a third side; the truth. And who is to discover it?"

"Every day at my work in a big-city hospital," James writes, *"I see illness, death, and grief. It seems to me that the best medicine for disappointment and grief is work. Each of you has plenty of it, music for one, and the store for the other. Work all day, and if you get tired enough by the time night comes, you will sleep better."*

So every day Adam went to the office and read reports, of which there was surely never any shortage. Then he would wait for Andy to come and ask for the advice and opinions that he did not need at all; he was only being kind to his father.

Leaving the store one afternoon many months later, Adam discovered Reilly standing on the sidewalk looking at a display of resort fashions.

"Coming to work, Reilly? You're late again," he joked.

"I wish I was. I was a kid when I went to work for old man Rothirsch. This place is all I ever knew."

"Let's have lunch," Adam said, although he had planned to go straight home.

"Okay, but nothing fancy."

"No, fancy. What are you doing, saving my money again?"

"No, saving Andy's money."

It was the same old banter, and it felt good. "We'll eat where the lawyers eat. It's still the best place in town."

At the restaurant they sat down and studied the menu. "Have lobster," Adam said.

"Costs a fortune."

"Don't argue. Lobster for two," he told the waiter, and then asked Reilly whether he remembered the time he had urged Adam not to be seen in this place with Miss Emma Rothirsch.

"Sure do. It was on account of Mr. Lawrence. Dead now. Everybody's dead, or on the way there. Even Archer, that darn stiff-upper-lip Englishman. Used to make me so darn mad. Best friend I ever had, along with you, Adam."

Reilly was an old man now, how old Adam could only guess. The jolly, innocent face was lost in a mass of wrinkles; the sparse hair was gray, and only the brown, friendly eyes were the same.

"How's the family, Reilly?"

"Good, thanks be. And thanks to you, I was able to help them along. The grandkids are all married and have kids of their own. You remember Tom, used to wait at the door for me on his roller skates? He's got a store, his own store, hardware, in Milltown. Doing well, too. You wouldn't recognize him. Guess I wouldn't recognize your James, either."

"Well, James is the same. Busy, busy. In a couple of years, his son will be starting his own practice. Neurosurgery, he wants. Sometimes I think of my brother Jonathan.

He would have gone out to India, or Africa, and worked in the jungle."

"You think he would. But you never know how people will turn out."

"Yes, I guess you're right. Louise, that shy little thing—remember how she was? Used to come into the store and never say a word? Well, she couldn't be more different now. And our Eileen, the tomboy, the feminist who didn't believe in marriage—have I told you the latest?"

"I don't think so."

"It's actually funny. Her Danny—and he's really a nice kid who loves Eileen and bosses her around—well, he knows a girl in his class who is the total opposite of anything that Eileen stands for. But she has a father, a widower who wants to marry Eileen. And it looks as though he will. So it only goes to show that you really never know, do you?"

"I wonder whether you've heard anything about Theo Brown."

"Not in years. Didn't he move out of town and open an office someplace else?"

"Yeah, but things didn't go too well. I was having a couple of drinks last night with some guys who used to drive for him. Said he was in a nursing home, running out of money. Knowing him, you know it's a high-class, expensive place, and they're about to put him out of it."

"Pretty sick, is he?"

"He's got a couple of months to go, they said."

He tried to get ahead, Adam thought. He tried desperately, even tried a deception of which, being the decent man I once knew him to be, he must have been ashamed. Lying there now, alone and waiting for death, he must think of many, many things. . . .

Adam shuddered. And then he asked a question. "How much does it cost?"

"Why, I don't know. A lot, I'm sure."

"Ask your guys where he is and I'll call the place. They can send the bill to me."

"You're going to do that for him after what he did to you, or tried to do?"

"Ah, why not? But just keep it to yourself, Reilly, will you?"

Reilly nodded, hesitated, and spoke. "There was another guy at the bar who said something about a guy he used to see in his neighborhood, in the apartment house. Name was Arnring, he said. He wondered what had happened to him. I said I didn't know, but if it was the same Arnring, he had moved away, out of town, about a hundred years ago."

How much Reilly knew, Adam had no idea. But he must know that something drastic had happened. He might even have heard something from the dressmaker gossips. Reilly enjoyed gossip as long as it was not cruel. He had brought up the subject because he was merely curious by nature, that was all. But this curiosity was not going to be satisfied, and Adam deftly changed the subject.

Still, it lingered in his mind. Walking back to the store, he came to the bank and the corner where he had had his last sight of Leo, scurrying away while some young girls, tittering as Leo passed them, had brought an instant of compassion into Adam's fury.

That evening, he questioned Emma. "If by some chance Leo had slipped back into town, we'd know about it, don't you think so?"

"I imagine we would, sooner or later. But after all these years, you should try to find him anyway, Adam. You really should."

She had no idea . . . no idea . . .

"If you can forget what Brown tried to do,

why can't you forget what Leo did? Life is so short. Haven't we found that out? And you've seen how quickly things can happen. In an instant, everything changes. Think of your brother Jonathan."

"Jon was no Leo."

"But if he had been 'difficult,' shall we say, to put it mildly, and you had been angry at him for some reason, for any reason, and had not yet gotten over it when he died, how would you be feeling now?"

"I repeat: 'Jon was no Leo!' You're not making sense, Emma. Let's drop the subject."

People, and life in general, were contrary and unpredictable. Leo, the solemn loner, had triumphed over Adam. Brother Jonathan, analytical and wise, had given up his life because of an unworthy woman.

Adam looked around the beautiful living room, with the fire bright in the grate and autumn flowers everywhere. Here was the peaceful family home, here were the far-flung people come together as always for Thanksgiving.

Here sat Louise, the shy and docile

daughter who, having married the man she was determined to marry no matter how uncertain her parents had been about him, had become the competent mistress of a household and family in South America. Now in his mind's eye Adam saw the house that still astonished Emma and himself whenever they went there to visit. Never could anyone who had known Louise as a child have imagined her as the mistress of that house and mother of four splendid children she now was. Nor could they have imagined her as the director of a charity school for the blind, which she was.

Next to her sat Eileen, the sister who had never gotten along with her. Looking unmistakably contented, she who had once disdained the role of wife was accompanied by her husband, a large, rather masterly gentleman who raised horses far from the New York City that she had vowed she would never leave. With them was her Danny, a young man with the charm, wit, and blond hair that must derive from his anonymous father.

Then there were Bernice and Andy with their sons; James and Sally with their girls;

and their son Ray, now a finished neurosurgeon, who was holding his little Emma.

Peaceful home, Adam thought again. In spite of sorrows, there was always so much for which to be grateful. And wouldn't Pa have loved all this?

The tall, attractive young man who sat across from him caught his eye and smiled. "A wonderful day," he said in accented English. "I thank you for inviting me. It's my first visit to the States."

He was Louise's brother-in-law, but Adam had forgotten his name. "I'm not good at remembering names. I'm sorry."

"You don't see me often enough to remember. My name is Leo."

Of course it was. How could he have forgotten?

Or was the better question: Would he ever be able to forget?

Chapter 26

He wrote:

Emma did a lovely thing. She bought a dog for us. Our poodles have long been dead, and there has been so much happening in our lives that we never replaced them. And yet, with everyone gone, the house felt empty. Yesterday she passed some people taking a large puppy into the pound, and, being Emma, she stopped to ask about him. He's a mix of Irish setter and something else, red as a setter, but smaller. His owners died, and nobody wanted him. So she bought him and brought him home, complete with veterinarian's instructions, a warm coat, new bowls, and a handsome basket. His name is Rusty. She could not have known, and I did not say, that his huge, clumsy paws

*and his mild gaze reminded me of
Arthur.*

*I don't think I've ever been so pleased
and touched by a present.*

The dog, and the fact that Adam no longer
had the same responsibilities in the store,
made a difference. Emma no longer had as
many pupils, either. In the afternoons, they
were able to take long walks with Rusty and
sometimes drive with him to that remote
place on the riverbank that now felt like their
private property.

"Do you remember our first time here?"
Emma asked one day as they unpacked the
lunch basket. "We had Rea's doughnuts.
There simply are no doughnuts anywhere
like the ones she used to make."

Indeed he remembered. He remembered
the coots that were still sailing down the
river exactly as if the world hadn't changed,
which for them, it had not. He remembered
that Emma had wanted him to make love to
her, and that he had been afraid to try any
foolery with Sabine Rothirsch's niece. He
looked at her now. There were a few strands
of gray in her hair, as in his own. The years

had been kind to them. He leaned over and kissed her.

They ate their sandwiches. Rusty paddled in the water, shook himself, and lay down to gnaw on the bone that had been brought for his entertainment.

"I heard something interesting this week," Emma said. "Somebody who had recently been in Paris found out what happened to Blanche. Apparently she had been living the high life in a beautiful apartment on the Isle St. Louis, but then the Nazis came and got her."

"They got a lot of people."

He did not want to hear about Blanche, and yet he could not keep from asking who Emma's informant was.

"A woman at the music school. I hardly know her. She had heard it from an old lady who used to work in Blanche's department. And the old lady heard it from the man in Paris who thought a friend of Blanche's might want to know what had happened."

"Do these people have nothing better to do than rake over every little piece of ancient history that they can dig up?"

"Why not? No harm was meant. Why are you so angry?"

"I'm not really angry, just annoyed. Do I need to explain that the subject is—shall I say 'unpleasant'?"

"Not to me, Adam. Not anymore. That's long past. As you said, it's ancient history."

Mollified by her voice, he said quietly, "Okay. Maybe I don't like ancient history."

She was not finished. "I know you don't. You also don't like to tie up loose ends."

"What do you mean?"

"I'm talking about your brother Leo."

Would no one ever leave the subject alone? If it wasn't Reilly who brought it up, then it was Emma.

"You've come to terms with other things in your life. So why can't you do it with Leo before it's too late? Who knows how long any of us is going to live?"

"I wish you would stop bringing this up, Emma. You mean well, but of course you can't read my mind, so you can't understand. Then why do you bring it up again?"

"I don't know exactly. It's just that there's such a thing as forgiveness."

"Exactly what does 'forgiveness' mean? It's not that I wish him any harm. I truly don't. But I don't want to be bothered with him. I don't want him to appear at our door."

"Because of me? I wouldn't care what he might say. Truly I wouldn't."

God only knows what he might invent . . .

"I don't mean to preach or sound holy, Adam, but it seems to be so—so narrow-minded that you can't accept the fact that, yes, he did something awful to you, but it's over with. Let's put it behind us."

"Narrow-minded? How can you say such a thing to me of all people? With all my faults, you have to admit that my mind is open to everybody. Why, right here in our own family, we—I—have loved and accepted everyone. My grandson Raymond is Jewish, my son Andy's wife is a Methodist, my daughter Louise married a Catholic, and in my business we have both whites and blacks. So what are you talking about?"

"I didn't mean that kind of narrow-mindedness, although God knows there's enough of it in this world. I just said 'forgiveness.' Opening your heart is what I meant. You'll feel better if you do. Leo will stop haunting you. You've done this for other people. I've seen it. Theo Brown and—"

"They weren't my brothers."

"He hurt you dreadfully, poor man."

" 'Poor man'? Who? Leo, or me?"
"Both," said Emma.

That night Emma went to bed with a chill
and fever. In the morning when she was
feeling no better, Adam called their old
friend Dr. Bassett, who prescribed an antibi-
otic. On the third day, she was neither better
nor worse. On the fifth day, she died.

As if from a vast distance, Adam heard
words that meant nothing to him. What
difference did they make, these explana-
tions, these neutered, gentle voices, these
terms like "endocarditis," "bacterial," "heart
valves"?

He became aware that, at the other end of
the room, Andy was talking on the telephone.

"Mom left us an hour ago," he heard, so
Andy must have been talking to James. "Endocarditis and stroke. Yes, our old friend
Dr. Bassett came. Yes. Very quiet. Probably
hasn't accepted it yet. Bernice and I will stay
here all night, or a couple of nights. Yes. Oh,
a girl? Six pounds two? About the same

time Mom died. I'll tell him now. Tomorrow? What time? Let me know so I can send a car to the airport for everyone."

So one dies, and another is born. When Adam got up from the chair and went outside, the dog went along. It seemed to him that the dog understood his grief. Or was this really grief? It seemed to him that he was feeling nothing. The world had simply stopped, and it was of no importance because the black sky was studded with stars and this little earth was as nothing among them.

After a while, he went back inside where Bernice and Andy were sitting in the living room. He sensed by the way they looked at him that they were asking whether they could help. But he walked on past them, went to the desk in his little den, and pulled out the diary.

What could he write? He felt as if he must mark this night with a poem, something memorable, or a profound prayer. But he could think of nothing like that, so he simply wrote the date and three words: *Emma died tonight.*

Then he put his head down on the book and closed his dry eyes. He was sitting there with his heart shuddering in his chest, when Andy came and led him up the stairs.

"I'm living too long," Adam said one day in the second month of mourning. "I dread the coming of spring without Emma. Did you know that every year when the tree frogs sang, she always said how glad she was to have lived to see another spring? Yes, I'm living too long."

In her soft way, Bernice rebuked him. "She wouldn't want you to say that, or feel that way, Dad. She accepted what has to be accepted."

"I know. But this house is unbearable. Everywhere I walk in it, I see her. The silence is unbearable. I need to get out of here."

"Where would you go?" asked Andy.

"I don't know. Somewhere in town, I guess. Find an apartment, two rooms near the store, the way I began."

Andy smiled. "You wouldn't be able to take Rusty, so you'd better stay here."

"You're joking, but I'm serious. I'll give you this house. Sell your place and move in here. It's much nicer here than where you are now. You know it is. I'll make a present of the house and everything in it."

"Rusty, too?"

"I'm not joking, I tell you. Will you take it or won't you?"

Bernice spoke promptly. "If Andy agrees, I would answer yes. But there'd be one condition. Only if you will stay here, Dad."

"With all our crew?" Andy wondered. "Two girls, two fellows with girlfriends? Their noise can shatter your eardrums."

"It's the silence that's hard for Dad to hear, Andy. I rather think he would welcome some happy noise."

So it was that Adam Arnring's life entered a new phase, a phase he never could have imagined.

Chapter 27

One day when Adam opened the bottom drawer in his desk, he caught sight of the diary, concealed by a pile of papers. It had been years, four or five, since he had put a word in it. Opening it now, he discovered the last ones he had written: *Emma died tonight.* He sat there staring at them. Then suddenly, feeling an irresistible compulsion, he picked up the pen and began to write. There ought to be some record, some notice taken, of the kind of human being Emma had been and the life she had lived.

So he wrote every day, and sometimes more often, as the long past unraveled in his memory. After a while it began to seem as though he were talking to Emma.

You would be happy to see how Andy and his family take care of the house. Bernice sprays the rosebushes that you always worried about. She has a piano tuner come once a year so the tone is still perfect. Tim is taking lessons, but even though he keeps them up, I can tell he hasn't got the touch. Still, he likes to play popular melodies, so he'll entertain his friends and himself when he goes to law school. And most likely he'll entertain himself for the rest of his life. Your piano won't go to waste.

Louise's son Giorgio is a different story. You were the first to notice his promise when he took his first violin lessons. Louise writes that he is becoming something of a prodigy at the age of fifteen. He has already been invited to play with a fine little orchestra at home, and who knows but that someday we shall be hearing him in the United States, too?

The sorry thoughts I have when I look around at all the faces is that we almost never hear anything from Jon's children, except for a rather formal Christmas card from various scattered places, here and abroad. I regret to say that their mother must have poisoned their

"Well! Eleven years old, and you know how to read minds!"

He was laughing inside, but with her, not at her. He looked quite nice when he laughed, too. You would never think that he was so old; you'd expect him to be all shriveled up and bent over and bald, but he wasn't. He must have been a very handsome man when he was young, because he looked so handsome in pictures. It gave Emma a soft, funny feeling to be here with him, first because he was her great-grandfather, and she didn't know anybody who had a great-grandfather. Even a lot of her friends' grandparents were already dead. The second reason for that soft feeling was that she knew he was not going to forever.

silence was sad, and somehow she break it. "I suppose you always had a ce you like them so much. Did you when you were little?"

He used to sleep near my bed. as Arthur."

ncy name for a dog."

My father found him. He had he and a lot more puppies. g on the side of the road

minds in some way. I ask again: Is it possible that Jon was at fault, so that she left him for another man? We'll never know. And perhaps it is just as well.

All of us here get loving letters and phone calls from the family in New York. Ray is becoming a name in neurosurgery, James says. He is teaching now at one of the city's great medical schools. Almost more important is the fact that he has wonderful children, especially the little girl, Emma. She does not look like you, but in a way that is hard to describe, she reminds me of you: very bright, gentle, sure of herself, and quick to get the point.

Adam wrote furiously, driven by what force he could not explain, to get everything down and omit nothing. Nothing? Well, he knew what he was leaving out. And sometimes he toyed with the idea of doing something about Leo, but then he did not do it.

In pain, he wrote about James's sudden death of heart failure at the age of fifty. One of his sons was gone now, yet he lived on, still strong, unbent, with a full head of thick white hair and a few gray hairs in it. In pleasure he wrote about a visit with Andy and Bernice to the Cace Arnring in New York and a happy side trip to Eileen on the horse farm. He wrote about looking forward to yet another Thanksgiving, and to the summer visits of Ray with his family, when he would see young Emma; although of course he would never say so or in any way let it be known, she was Number One. She was his darling.

✳

"So you didn't want to go with your dad and mother to see the hospital this afternoon?" Adam asked one summer day.

"I'm not interested in hospitals," Emma said.

"No? Why not?"

"I don't know. I just wanted to be outside here. It's so different from New York. I like looking around at everything, all the flowers and trees, and the dog. We don't have a dog because Mom doesn't want one, which is selfish, don't you think so? Otherwise, she isn't selfish at all, but I would love to have a dog like Rusty."

"Rusty wouldn't be happy in the city, you

know that. He needs a lot of space to run around in."

Space enough there was; a steep meadow climbed the hill at the back of the house; another meadow slid down a hill at the front of the house. And around the house lay level acres where a soft breeze blew through the cottonwood trees, the oaks, and the spruce.

Adam was in his big chair with Rusty on the ground beside him, while Emma was sprawled on the grass with her chin between her hands.

"Oh, I would love to live here,"

"That's why I like to come every

"Well, your dad's a doctor, a New York, so you have to li

"I know, but wherever see the hospitals."

"That's natural."

"He says he d didn't have th one here fro ter you g derstand w

"You do?"

"Yes, it's becau off and be stuck up.

with nothing to eat or drink, so Pa brought them home and took care of them as best he could. Arthur lived to be very old, and I loved him."

"Your father had a kind heart, didn't he? And I guess your mother had, too."

"She did."

"You look like your father in those pictures where he's standing on the lawn, just about where we are now. I only saw one of your mother, though."

"My father had plenty of them, but when he moved here to be with us, he lost them somewhere, all but the one that you've seen."

"I know. She looks pretty in that big old-fashioned hat. What was she like?"

"Oh, Emma, that's a hard question. I was very young when she died, so how much can I remember?"

"I remember things from when I was very young. I remember Dad smoked a pipe while he watched television, and he let me knock out the ashes."

"How did you enjoy your trip to Yosemite? We took all our grandchildren there, and before that, we took our children."

It was plain that he had changed the subject on purpose. He didn't want to talk about his mother, though he talked enough about the horse called Whitey and about the grocery store. She had noticed that before today.

"It was great," she said. "I want to go back out west again to see the Grand Canyon and the Hopi reservation. We had some movies about all that in school, so I'm very interested in Native Americans."

"Indians?"

"You're not supposed to call them that anymore."

"Sorry. I do remember reading something about it. Have you read *The Oregon Trail*?"

"Nobody reads Parkman very much, my teacher says. But I found it in a library, and I thought it was great."

"Well, you're the second Emma who thought so. The first day I got to talk to my first Emma, she was reading it. It seems like yesterday."

"I know what you mean. It seems like yesterday that I was in first grade."

The old man smiled. "Ah, you're a lovely person, Emma. I wish my Emma could see you."

"You were really in love with her, weren't you?"

"I was. I still am."

"And you never got a divorce?"

"Whatever makes you ask that? Your father and mother never got one, either. Everybody doesn't get one."

"No, but lots of people do. I'll bet you half the people in my class have two sets of parents."

The old man shook his head. "I'm sure some of it couldn't be helped, but not all of it. Not even nearly all of it. You have to—to overlook things, to be patient, forgiving, and not let anger—"

He stopped and looked so *serious*, she thought, almost the way people do when tears are starting.

She sat up, feeling suddenly uncomfortable and hoping he wasn't going to cry, which would be awful. But no, he was smiling again.

"Look around, Emma. Just look at this beautiful world. You're a bookworm, so you'll surely come across this someday: 'Summer afternoon—summer afternoon; to me those have always been the two most beautiful words in the English language.'

And then you'll think of us two—no, three—
you and me and Rusty. I love you, Emma.
Remember that, too."

It was sort of embarrassing, but it was also
nice for a person's great-grandfather to say
that. In a funny way, it sort of belonged with
all kinds of other things here today, things
like Rusty's friendly wagging tail, or the
white clouds floating.

"Do you hear voices, Emma? They've
come back. Let's go see."

The house was asleep, but Adam roamed
the rooms. It was as if he were restlessly
looking for something and was unable to remember what it was.

Then he went outside. It was a white night,
when the moon leaks its brightness all over
the sky and outshines the stars. Far off in
the distance once occupied by level fields,
all green and gold with grass and grain and
scarce dots that each signified a ranch
house, now loomed a circle of high-rise
buildings with a cluster of suburban devel-
opments around them.

Life moved. It changed in myriad ways.
Young people lived together without mar-

riage, and married people, with or without children, moved from one marriage to a new one, or to no marriage at all, without any trouble. Yes, life had changed and was still changing, no matter how an old man close to a century in age might feel about it.

He wondered about that little girl today, eleven years old and so wise. If she were to live as long as he has lived, how would her world look then?

Far off a dog's bark carried through the stillness, and Rusty replied.

"Hush," Adam said. "You'll wake the whole house."

The windows on the second floor were dark. In the main bedroom, Andy slept beside Bernice. Good people, they were, steadfast parents and citizens and friends. He felt glad that they were living in this house. Once he would never have believed that a person could love a mere house as he loved this one. Stepping back on the lawn, he gained a better view of it as it lay, long and gleaming, like some live creature resting in its nest of trees. Strange, he thought: We had wanted something very simple, and it is simple, yet it is known as one of the finest houses in the area. If Emma had ever thought about that, she would have been amused.

Then he went back inside to the music room, and stood looking at the concert grand for quite a while. After that he went into his home office, where he opened the deep drawer on the side of the desk. There lay a pile of his diaries, and he stood there, too, looking at them for quite a while.

What good were they? They contained nothing of importance. Mere jottings of intensely intimate emotions, some thoughtful, some even humorous, some painful, they were of no use to anyone except to satisfy curiosity or to encourage troubling speculations. And with sudden resolve, he lifted the heavy pile of books, lugged it to the kitchen, and there began to destroy it.

From the cabinets he took a few bottles of dark vinegar to stain the pages, after which he soaked them under the faucet until they were totally illegible. Into the garbage cans beyond the back door he threw them, and after that, returning to the kitchen, cleaned up every trace of the mess.

After that, in the hallway that led to the stairs, he stopped to look at the collection of photographs that hung on the wall. They had been there so long that he never noticed them anymore. He had never seen any reason to display them, but Emma had liked them, so there they were.

There was his father standing next to Whitey and the wagon. There he was again, the young father with Adam and Leo. Adam was smiling up at him, while Leo wore his supper-table face. There was Leo in a class picture, the only one with his head turned away from the camera.

Now, suddenly, Adam realized that he was seeing something he had never *truly* seen before. He had seen it, but not *truly*. Why that had been, he was not able to say. He knew only that at this moment he was overwhelmed by it. For a long time he stood there looking at the faded photographs. And in accordance with his lifelong habit of collecting, quite without willing to, small scraps of quotations and of poetry, some words of Housman's came to mind.

And how am I to face the odds
Of man's bedevilment and God's?

Then he turned the light off, and summoning Rusty, went upstairs to bed. His exertions with the diaries had tired him more than he could have expected if he had thought about it beforehand. Yet he was relieved that he had done what he did.

It seemed to him that the air outdoors was filled with the twitter of birds. Often a solitary bird will awaken at night and call, but this music was something one heard at dawn, so perhaps it was near dawn? I can't tell, he thought, but anyway, it doesn't matter. I could look at the clock, but I'm too dizzy, and the bed is so comfortable.

His thoughts wandered. Simon had died in this bed. Poor Simon, he had not had an easy life. But he had had Rachel. Perhaps he had had Rachel before he had my mother? Perhaps he had hidden my mother away on a farm until she had me? I have no birth certificate. I never had one. So do I therefore not exist? If you don't have a certificate, you don't exist. Even Emma existed; the authorities had given her a certificate, and then Sabine had come to take care of her. And wasn't Sabine a funny one?

Light and dark are spinning across the ceiling. All the faces are spinning. They flash by and they recede. Children. Grandchildren. The living and the dead. Emma. Pa.

Leo sits with Pa. No, across the table. Poor, frightened, ugly little boy. Ah, Leo, I'm not angry. Not anymore.

I'm going to find you . . . Write a letter . . . My brother . . . Tomorrow . . .

When they came looking for Adam in the morning, he was dead. He had died peacefully in his sleep without thrashing or struggling, the doctor said. "His heart simply stopped. It was time."

This was the first death Emma had known. Common sense told her that indeed it was time for Great-Grandpa Adam to die, because he was so very old. So she could not feel too sad, nor apparently did anyone else, except to say that Adam would be long remembered.

Before and after the funeral, people sat around in the library that was filled with his books, and talked about him. They read aloud the newspaper that spoke of what was called *philanthropy,* and there were many letters to the editor.

He was a quiet man, one wrote, and very unassuming. You would never know that he had any more than a couple of dollar bills to rub together in his pocket.

He seemed to be somebody who would live, and ought to live, forever, another said. I keep thinking that he'll turn up on a bench in the park tomorrow.

Even the governor of the state had praise for him, for his important gifts and his small, private acts of kindness to people of every religion, race, and walk of life. He spoke of the splendid parks on either side of the river, the wilderness acres throughout the state, the hospitals, and the university in the city, the music program that he and his wife had instituted in its schools, the volunteer ambulance service that he supported, and half a dozen free nursery schools. Few citizens, the governor repeated, had ever done as much for the state as Adam Arnring had done.

"Dad was a strong, calm man," Uncle Andy said. "He never let anything get the better of him, and never was ruled by his emotions. There was never any mystery about him. You always knew where you stood with him, and he concealed nothing. He was completely honest, and had no secrets."

I don't know about that, Emma was thinking. He must have had secrets, because everybody has some. And *emotions,* don't they mean what people feel? I think he felt a lot. The way he looked when he talked about the other Emma, the way he said *summer afternoon,* the way he looked at me, and even the way he loved his dog. I think you're all wrong, Uncle Andy.

Those were her thoughts. But when a girl is only going on twelve and is well brought up, she does not contradict the grown-ups.

Epilogue

A gentle darkness fell over the New Hamp-
shire mountains as Emma and her husband,
Charles, sat among the party guests in the
pink and white garden.

"This house was the cottage on the Snow
estate, that huge stone place up there," the
hostess was explaining. "Oh, it's different
here, now that the Snows are dead. They
were such friendly neighbors, a lovely couple, and we miss them. She was blind and
he took wonderful care of her."

"He was a remarkable man," the host
added. "He spoke five languages—German,
Russian, Japanese, and I forget what else.
During the Second World War he worked for
Army Intelligence, deciphering codes. He
came from an old, distinguished New England family and knew enough about American history to write a book. In fact, he did

write some books, very successful ones, translations."

"Snow really was a 'character,'" he continued. "Lovable in a way and also a bit of a snob. He liked to be with prominent people, old-money types. And still, he had a big soft heart for the underdog. A lot of you must remember, don't you, the time on Main Street when some boys were teasing a girl about her acne, and he got furious? I sometimes thought such rage didn't seem to fit with the rest of him."

"Perhaps it did fit," someone said. "He was a tiny, terribly ugly little man and he must have suffered plenty in his time."

"Well, maybe. But I don't know." The hostess mused, "He did have an easier life in some ways than most people ever have. Remember the story of the sulky?"

Emma asked her what a sulky was.

"It's a one-horse cart that holds one person. It was a fashionable luxury way back in those days when he was a boy. Once when he was driving out in the country—I have an idea he must have been a loser in school and terribly spoiled at home—he saw a litter of puppies abandoned beside the road. So he took them home and called the favorite

'Arthur' after President Chester Arthur. We loved that story."

"The strangest, saddest story of all is his death," the host said soberly. "He was writing a letter when he had a heart attack and fell to the floor. There were only a few words, something like these: *Dear Brother, I am old and it is very late to talk about things that were so awfully, terribly wrong. I have been looking back at my life and seeing myself very differently. Now I want to tell you how sorry I am about what I said and how I hurt you on that day so long ago—*

"That's all there was. The crazy thing is that he had no brother and had never had one."

"You can't be sure of that," somebody else said quietly. "What do we ever really know about one another?"

There was a silence. He's right, Emma thought, looking up as the first stars gleamed through the thickening night. How can one human being see into another's mind or feel his heart and judge him? In the end, we have only compassion to give.

Once, in a book by Joseph Conrad, she had read some lines and promised herself to remember them:

It is when we try to grapple with other men's intimate needs that we perceive how incomprehensible are the beings that share with us the sight of the stars and the warmth of the sun.

ABOUT THE AUTHOR

BELVA PLAIN lives in northern New Jersey. She is the author of the *New York Times* best-selling novels *Evergreen, Random Winds, Eden Burning, Crescent City, The Golden Cup, Tapestry, Blessings, Harvest, Treasures, Whispers, Daybreak, The Carousel, Promises, Secrecy, Homecoming, Legacy of Silence, Fortune's Hand, After the Fire, Looking Back,* and *Her Father's House.*